THE

LIBERTY LAUNCH

THE STUPID SHALL BE PUNISHED

A NOVEL BY GEORGE PALMER

Copyright © 2014 by George Palmer
Cover Design by Rob Kudej
Interior Design by JT Formatting
The Bay of Naples Map courtesy of Pictorialgems.com

First Print Edition: December 2014
Library of Congress Cataloging-in-Publication Data

Palmer, George
    The Liberty Launch/George Palmer – 1st ed
        ISBN – 13: 978-1505385991
        ISBN – 10: 1505385997

    1.The Liberty Launch—Literature & Fiction
    2. Literature & Fiction—Sea Adventures

10 9 8 7 6 5 4 3 2 1

For all the lost sailors.

For Pauline   Fair Winds!

George

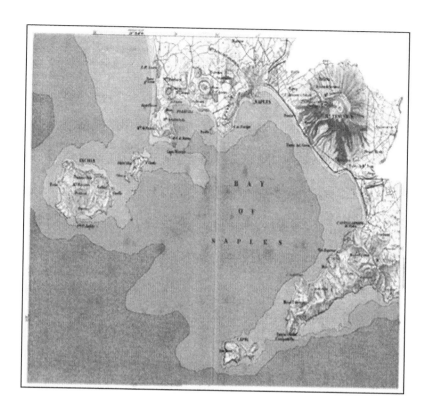

"No meritorious act of a subordinate should escape his attention or be left to pass without its reward, if even the reward be only one word of approval. Conversely he should not be blind to a single fault in any subordinate, though at the same time he should be quick and unfailing to distinguish error from malice, thoughtlessness from incompetency, and well-meant shortcoming from heedless and stupid blunder..."

John Paul Jones

"The stupid shall be punished."

R.R. Zarn MMCM (SS) USN (Ret)

CONTENTS

FORWARD

SOMETIMES THE CAREFULLY LAID OUT and time-tested procedures and processes that have made our navy the objective-driven, well-oiled, perfectly functioning machine that it is just break down. No one can predict when or how but when the breakdown happens it can't be missed. No one ever starts their day thinking, "Gee I guess I'll do something half-assed today." But Cassandra herself couldn't have predicted these debacles. They go by many names but sailors usually call them what they are, "fuck ups".

Some of these are small and don't create a tidal wave of pain. They only result in inconvenience and embarrassment. That's when someone else has to step in and do the job the transgressor fouled up.

Others though are awful and result in ships or sailors getting hurt or killed ... and people fired. Those are the kind everyone dreads, they are the ones the Safety Center and the warfare schools use as examples. Classes in every technical school in the navy stress being wary of the same conditions. Company Officers at the Naval Academy spend hours teaching Midshipmen to recognize signs of them. But still they happen.

There is a third kind however, that no one thinks about until they read about it in the newspaper or one of the navy publications weeks or months after it happens. These are the "there-isn't-a-rule-for-it-so-I-think-I'll-just-wing-it" kind and when Pandora peeks out of her box things tend to snowball. This tale is one like that. It's a fictional account but it's partially based on an actual event. Of course the names of the sailors and the ships involved have been changed to protect the innocent … and the stupid.

CHAPTER 1

SEAMAN WILSON

YEOMAN SEAMAN SAMANTHA WILSON WAS frustrated and angry. She had been working for the past four days transcribing the Captain's notes on the incident when her magnetic card typewriter started spitting out gibberish. When the last page stopped printing she pulled the magnetic card from its slot and reseated it. She turned it off and started it again and it was just the same. She cycled the power switch once more but it didn't help. Twenty five pages of detailed data, scrambled and unrecoverable. She wanted to cry it was so demoralizing. She couldn't even redo the work, the stupid typewriter's memory wasn't working right and nothing she tried seemed to help. She even reread the manual that had come with the new IBM 660. Nothing helped, there was no "if it does this just do that" that seemed anywhere near the realm of "the stupid black piece of junk just lost its mind!" She hadn't been this mad since that little bitch Ruthie Evans beat her out for Homecoming Queen… by one vote.

"Guess I'd better go see if the Chief can help", she thought and started down the passageway to the Admin office. She found him mediating an argument that was going on between the three rated yeomen in the office and he didn't look happy. She began, "Excuse me, Chief could you give me some advice on the mag card typewriter? The damn thing is spitting out gibberish and I can't make sense out of what it's doing."

"Give me a minute, Wilson I'll come take a look after I get the

1

plan of the day cranked out for the XO."

"Thank you, Chief, I'll wait for you in the Captain's Yeoman's office."

Five minutes later he came in. "Let's see what's goin' on with this thing, Wilson this is the newest model we have aboard and it isn't compatible with our older units." He hit the switch to turn it on and fumbled with the card reader feeding in a blank card and beginning to type. After three lines of type he hit the PRINT PAGE command and watched as the three lines of type were printed out as commas and semicolons. Not one character was correct. "Looks like you're screwed, Wilson. You'd better grab one of the old Royals and burn some midnight oil. What's the Captain got you working on anyway?"

"It's his detailed statement of the incident that happened two weeks ago when that Russian plane buzzed us during the UNREP and the *Porter* scraped against our starboard side. It has to be ready for the Court of Inquiry later next week and I already made a 40 page appendix that has all the chart data and the input from the Ops Officer and the Navigator and excerpts of the ship's logs. I had about 25 pages of the Captain's notes already put in when the thing went crazy. Chief I don't know what to do; altogether it's like 65 pages of detailed data, I'll never be able to redo everything by the time the Captain needs it!"

"I've got an idea, Wilson let me check it out before you start hitting the panic button. I'll let you know after chow."

"Thank you, Chief I'll work on something else in the meantime."

She was just binding the copies of the charts and figures addendum package the Captain wanted when the phone rang. "Wilson I've got you covered. They have an IBM 660 at the document center in Naples we'll anchor at 0800 tomorrow and you can grab a ride in to the harbor. The supervisor of the document center is an old buddy of mine. He'll let you use his 660 all day Saturday if you need it. You should be able to finish everything with time to spare. I'll give you directions to the center at the Naval Support Activity, just ask for Chief Warrant Officer Martinez and he'll set you up."

"Oh gosh thank you, Chief! You've saved me five days' worth of work. The stuff the Captain gave me is so cryptic it took me hours and hours just to figure out what he wanted. I guess the one thing I've learned out of all this is that you should never trust some fancy new machine just because it seems like the coolest thing on the block!"

"No problem, Wilson just make sure to catch the first boat in and get a ride over to the NSA. Be sure to say hi to my old friend Juan Martinez. He and I went to boot camp and 'A' school together and he's done very well in the navy. He'll make sure you get your project done with no problem whatsoever.

In the meantime check with the Supply Department and see if we carry any spare parts for the damned thing. You know I was against giving you the 660 until we had put it to the test and had a degree of confidence in it. The Admin Office is the place to break in new equipment, not the Captain's Yeoman's Office, but the Admin Officer decided otherwise so there we are. If we had done it my way you would be finished by now using one of our old machines."

"I guess it would have been better that way, Chief I hate not being able to do my job. Well, I'll check with the supply people and see if they can help but I doubt it. I don't think it came to us via the supply system I think it was an open purchase item that the Admin Officer pushed through just before we got underway from Norfolk. I remember because it came the day after I relieved Petty Officer Mason as Captain's Yeoman. Remember he got picked up for drugs ashore and the Captain made sure someone took over before he got processed off the ship. The Chief Master at Arms stood over him as he showed me all the open projects and the Captain only let him leave when I said I understood everything. The very next day the 660 showed up and the IBM man showed me how to run it."

"Okay, Wilson I've got the picture. Supply probably can't help. Just get on the first launch tomorrow and you'll have all morning and afternoon to work on the Captain's project. I'll make arrangements for the local IBM rep to come out to the ship on Monday and he can get your 660 squared away for you. You aren't in the duty section are you?"

"No, Chief I'm not. I'm in section four and we'll have the duty on Sunday. I should crank out the appendix and the 25 pages I've already finished in like 15 minutes; then I have at most 5 or 6 pages to build from the Captain's handwritten notes. It should only take me an hour or so to do that. I should be back on the liberty launch headed for the ship by noon with any luck. Maybe after that I can hit the beach again and see something of Naples."

The Chief hung up and the young Yeoman put the mag cards and the Captain's notes in her briefcase. They would be safe inside when she took the launch in the morning. She knew the weather was predicted to be good and there wouldn't be any danger of her work getting wet. There would be plenty of liberty launches too. She had overheard the First Lieutenant telling the Captain he would have all their boats in service and they would make liberty runs every half hour from their anchorage to the Fleet Landing in the Naples harbor. She would make sure she had a seat on the first one though, it was good to be friends with someone who could help her. Her pal BMSN Terri Holden would help she was sure. Terri lived in the same berthing compartment and she would see her that evening before chow. Now all she had to do was see the Captain and report her status on his project.

Captain Christensen was in his stateroom when she knocked on the door. He was enjoying the first few minutes of relaxation since his day began. The last of his Department Heads had left only moments before. The Captain was a busy man. It took a lot of work to run a ship and his needed more than most, his was special; *USS Dwight D Eisenhower CVN-69.* He was the leader of a ship that held almost six thousand men and women. Almost four thousand in the ship's company and two thousand more in the embarked Air Group. That wasn't even counting the Battle Group's Admiral and his Flag

4

Staff. She knocked and announced herself, "Captain it's Yeoman Wilson, Sir."

"C'mon in, Yeo."

She opened the door, stepped inside and closed it behind her coming to attention as her eyes grew accustomed to the lighting in the big room. She always marveled at how much more space the Captain had in his living quarters compared to the tiny space she had in the Deck and Admin women's berthing. Just one bunk in a tier of three; she shared her space with eight other women sailors. The Captain even had his own head right behind the door by his desk. She had to share a head with seventeen other women. She got her thoughts in order. "Good afternoon, Captain I just wanted to stop by and report where I am on finishing the Court of Inquiry package, Sir".

"Excellent, Yeo I'd like to review the whole thing Sunday afternoon. It'll be a load off my mind when it's all over with!"

"Yes, Sir. I've finished binding all the copies of the charts and figures package. Here's one for you to look over when you have a moment. I had the Quartermasters help me with the charts so I know everything is accurate."

He took the pamphlet from her and flipped to a page. There was the whole incident in a nutshell. *Ike's* track for the 30 minute period before and after *Porter* had brushed her while transferring the Admiral back aboard by high line. There were other chart pages too that showed the radar picture and the tracks of all the other ships in the Battle Group as well as the path of the Russian jet and the track of the AGI. It was clear and concise and the Yeoman had done an excellent job adding the typed information and annotations. "This is wonderful, Yeo! An excellent job, thanks for working it all out from my cryptic notes and hen scratches."

"No problem, Captain," she smiled. "I think I finally figured out your handwriting. I had a problem with the narrative though, the IBM stopped working this afternoon when I was about 90 percent done with it. The Chief set me up at the document center in Naples though, I should be able to finish it there tomorrow after we anchor. He has a friend who runs the center. It should be a piece of cake, Sir."

A look of concern came over his face. "Do you need any help on it, Yeo? I'll put the whole Admin Department on it if you say the word. That package has my whole career riding on it."

That information caromed around her brain and consumed her conscious thought with shivering effect and she felt like the flight deck had just fallen on her. If she couldn't do her job how could the Captain make the Court of Inquiry understand all the things that caused the incident? How could they understand all the things that he had done to prevent it? She had to do her job and do it well ... for him.

"Captain, I won't need any help, Sir. It's my assignment and the Admin Department shouldn't have to shoulder my responsibilities. I won't let you down, Sir."

"Seaman, you're a good sailor. I'll have my gig ready for you as soon as we anchor. The Cox'n will deliver you to Fleet Landing and when you finish call back to the ship and he'll come pick you up. We'll make arrangements for a navy car to take you to the support activity."

She was aghast, "Oh no, Captain! I'll be on the first liberty launch in the morning. I have a friend who can get me a seat aboard. I don't want special treatment, Sir. I can do it; please, Captain I don't want to appear to be getting special favors."

He smiled, "Alright, Wilson. Have it your way. I'll be ashore tomorrow for the reception at the AFSOUTH O-club. The Fleet Commander is throwing it to celebrate finishing the National Week exercises. I won't be back till late. Just leave a copy of the whole package here on my desk. I'll get to it Sunday morning. Now get along to chow, and thank you. You're a great Captain's Yeoman."

"Aye, aye, Sir. Have a nice time at the reception tomorrow." She closed his cabin door behind her, walked to her office and locked the door for the day. She had a smile on her face all the way back to her berthing compartment. The Captain had a way about him, he always made her feel like an important crewmember and she strove to do her best to please him.

She found that a few of the other women she shared berthing space with had finished their work for the day and they went down to the Crew's Mess together. Wilson looked around. "Hey has anybody seen Terri this afternoon? I have a favor I need to ask of her."

Boatswain's Mate Third Class Joy Martin shook her head, "No, Sam she was working on getting the anchor windlass greased for tomorrow morning. She may have some other work left to do too. She's in tomorrow's duty section so she'll probably be involved with the liberty launches. Is it something that I can help with?"

"Joy it has to do with going ashore in the morning. I have a project I'm working on for the Captain and I have to go to the Naval Support Activity to finish it. I want to make sure I board the first liberty launch. It's very important. I was hoping Terri would be able to save me a seat. I know the first launches will be full of senior sailors going ashore and I don't want to be bumped for somebody senior."

"Don't worry, Sam I'll talk to the Duty Cox'ns and make sure they all know it's you and that it's something important for the Captain. In fact, I think my Division Officer is on the watch bill to be the Officer of the Deck after we anchor. He'll make sure you get off in the first launch. C'mon let's get in the chow line I'm hungry."

Wilson took her food tray and sat down next to Joy and a few other sailors she knew at a table where spirits were running high, the morale aboard was always very good. *Ike's* 'fleet reputation' was widely known as being a 'can-do' and a 'happy ship'. She knew that because the Captain frequently made comments to those effects in the letters he had her type to families of their sailors. He liked to use phrases like: "You should be very proud of Jack, Mr. and Mrs. Smith, his promotion to Petty Officer Second Class was well deserved and his contributions to his shipmates is part of the reason we are a 'happy ship'". She would type the letters and he would add a few words afterward in his longhand and she would type the envelopes and mail them. It was part of her normal routine to handle his outgoing letters and she counted on doing 40 or 50 for him every week.

Tonight though there was even a jollier mood at the tables. She overheard two of the guys in the Air Department talking about going on liberty and the fun they were expecting to have in Naples. At the next table some of the members of their embarked Helicopter Squadron were boasting that they would probably drink so much beer ashore they would make *Ike* ride a couple feet deeper in the water when they got back aboard with their full bladders. One of them even challenged the other to a 'pissing contest' afterwards.

Wilson thought that sounded both ridiculous and disgusting but she pretended not to hear the exchange. In the end the 'contest' wouldn't take place. The people in the Helicopter Squadron would be much too busy to do anything that stupid.

CHAPTER 2
THE PORT VISIT

THE PORT VISIT HAD BEEN scheduled for months. The Task Group would be divided up so that all the ships could enjoy a few days liberty. *Ike* and some of her consorts would descend upon Naples while other ships would visit Livorno, Gaeta and Brindisi in Italy and some would visit ports along the Cotes de Sol. It was coordinated so that ships could support each other but not overwhelm any one particular port with half the sailors in the Sixth Fleet all at once. It allowed for sailors to experience many different cultures during their deployments. It also prevented a single port disaster from impacting all the ships in the Task Group.

The nuclear powered ships weren't as lucky as their fossil fueled cousins, only a handful of ports were approved for their use and special arrangements were always necessary well in advance for them. *Ike* would anchor at the standard approved anchorage in the Bay of Naples and her liberty party would be ferried ashore in 50 foot launches. The trip would take 15 minutes and in good weather the panorama of Naples Bay and the surrounding city was a beautiful sight.

USS Porter DDG-78 was one of the lucky, she would be able to moor stern-to-the-pier (old hands call it a "Med moor") in the Naples harbor. Her sailors would be able to come down the brow and walk directly up the pier to catch a taxi anywhere in the city, anytime they chose. A ten minute walk would take them to the USO and the

"Bluebird", the Enlisted Men's Club.

USS Montpelier SSN-765 had a pretty sweet deal too. She would moor at the "molo" at the Italian Naval Base across the harbor from Fleet Landing. Special facilities were available for her use there and the Italian sailors provided an additional layer of security to protect her from violence in the event of a terrorism incident.

These ships had been working together since they deployed to the Mediterranean months before and there was a certain amount of comradery between them, notwithstanding the fact that each was from a totally different part of the navy. Their sailors labeled each other as, "airedales", "skimmers" and "bubbleheads" but it was all in fun. They all had common goals: to finish the deployment professionally, to have a good time on liberty and not to get caught doing anything stupid.

Montpelier glided noiselessly into the harbor and stood by for the tug which would push her gently against the pier as the Italian sailors caught her mooring lines and made her fast to the ancient stone molo. She would be able to shut down her reactor plant and take on well-regulated shore power afforded by the big generators the navy had purchased and installed at the Italian navy base. It had cost the taxpayers millions but it was necessary in order to convert the 50 hertz European current into the 60 hertz current Americans and their ships use. It would allow *Montpelier's* Captain to let the "nukes" in his Engineering Department enjoy some liberty too.

This was the first long port visit for the Battle Group. They had deployed from their individual homeports three months previously and joined in mid-Atlantic. The real workup began then. Seven destroyers, an attack submarine, *Eisenhower* and her air group and a fast support ship that carried the fuel, food and munitions they would consume They were augmented by maritime patrol aircraft operating from Rota, Spain and of course they were shadowed by their ever-attentive Soviet AGI – an intelligence-gathering auxiliary ship. Its task was to stick as close to the Battle Group as possible and record everything of note with its bristling array of antennae.

They had departed from their east coast homeports in the early spring and wouldn't go home again until Thanksgiving, an 8-month cruise of the Mediterranean. They would make up half of the combatants in the US Sixth Fleet and would relieve another Battle Group which would be headed home as soon as the handover of documents and responsibility was complete. The power represented by the combined Battle Groups and the Amphibious Group with its embarked Marines was enough to make the Soviets and their allies think twice before trying to expand their influence in the Mediterranean. They were the show of force that US foreign policy displayed to aid in keeping the peace. The politicians call it the "balance of power". Sailors call it boring holes in the ocean.

The planning and scheduling that preceded the Naples port visit involved the staffs of every echelon of the navy. Staffs at the Task Group, Task Force, Fleet Commander and C in C levels had coordinated to ensure the ships would actually be there when they were supposed to be. Naval Support Activities in the Mediterranean, in Europe and back in the States provided tangible and intangible support to the ships and the 10,000 or so sailors who would be enjoying their first time ashore in three months.

The State Department had contributed effort too. Ambassadors had met over coffee to nod sagely as the navy's plan was laid out for them. Thousands of sailors would be acting as de facto ambassadors of their country. Liberty for sailors is an important component of US foreign policy. After all if the ships stayed at sea all the time, how would our allies ashore and the world at large (courtesy of the news media) know that all that power and might was even there, much less committed to their security? On each of the ships careful preparations were made to ensure that every sailor was reminded of his or her responsibilities. Each ship provided a contingent of Shore Patrolmen, specially trained men who patrolled publically to help ensure good order and discipline within the liberty party. Briefing officers visited each of the ships to point out areas where the sailors should observe caution, establishments which were "out of bounds" to navy men as well as advising them where a good time could be enjoyed. All the right precautions would be taken before the first liberty call was sounded.

Ashore all was in readiness too. Shopkeepers, pizza makers, waiters, bartenders, taxi drivers, sellers of twenty dollar fake-Rolexes and "ladies" who would sell a good time for twice that price and half that in time eagerly awaited their chances to interact with the men and women in navy blue.

IKE WAS HALF A DEGREE from her "letting go" bearing with barely any headway. The Captain, the OOD and the rest of the Bridge team were intent on carefully bringing her massive bulk to a halt right on their selected spot. The Navigator called "mark" and the Captain smiled and nodded.

"Let go the anchor, veer chain to one two zero fathoms and set the windlass brake!" Lt Ackman annunciated it clearly, just as she had been taught at the Naval Academy and she'd practiced the evening before in her stateroom. "All back one third! Navigator I'm killing ship's way and setting the anchor. All stop! Anchor Detail put on the stopper and station the Anchor Watch. Captain, request permission to secure the underway watch and shift the watch to the Quarterdeck."

"Make sure the anchor is holding first, Lieutenant. Have the Navigator take fixes at five minute intervals. When we have six showing us in the same spot, call me in my stateroom. Go ahead and have the liberty launches put in the water."

"Aye, aye, Sir."

The First Lieutenant reported the stopper was in place and the Anchor Watch reported he was stationed. She gave permission to secure the Anchor Detail. "First Lieutenant go ahead and get your liberty boats in the water. We'll rig the boom at the port gangway."

He responded via the phone from the fo'cs'l. "Get the liberty boats in the water and rig the boom at the port gangway First Lieutenant aye, Bridge." He turned to the Master Chief Boatswains Mate. "Master Chief get your party to the davits and lower the barge the gig and four of our 50 footers. We'll keep one at the boom on standby, the other three can make the scheduled runs. The XO told me we'll make runs on the hour and the half hour but the initial liberty party is gonna be huge. It'll take all three boats to handle it."

"Aye, aye, Sir. Chief Penniman is in today's duty section. He's had the barge and the gig swinging in the davits since we slowed down to anchor. Everything is in good hands, Sir."

"Good, make sure that our Duty Cox'ns have a good brief on the rules here and what to expect in the harbor. I don't want one of them to embarrass us with the other ships around."

"Aye, aye, Sir I'll take care of it personally."

WILSON BRUSHED HER HAIR AND put on her lipstick in front of the mirror in the women's head. Her blues were pressed and her Havelock was sitting on her bunk with her briefcase and her purse. She had passed the Division Officer's personnel inspection after breakfast and she was ready to catch the first liberty launch as soon as it was called away. Her friend stopped by their berthing compartment to get her hat.

"Hey, Terri are you working the liberty launches today?"

"Hi, Sam yes in fact I get to be Cox'n under instruction this morning. The Chief has me paired up with 'Bad Billy' Bates. Billy will show me the right way to run a liberty launch. Maybe I can finish my Cox'n qualification during this port visit. Hey I see you're all ready to go, come along with me and we'll meet Billy he's just putting our launch in the water."

The two women sailors made their way to the Quarterdeck where Ensign Evans was just getting his watch team squared away. He had instructions from the XO to announce liberty by Department at 0900 and to load the first liberty launch as soon as it was ready at the boom. Seaman Holden saluted him. "Good morning, Mr. Evans.

I heard you would have the first watch. I'm going to be Cox'n under instruction today with BM-2 Bates. I just wanted you to know I'm working on my quals for it. Oh this is my friend Sam Wilson, she has a request for you, Sir."

"What is it, Wilson?"

"Sir I'm the Captain's Yeoman and I have a job to finish at the Naval Support Activity for him. Would it be possible for me to be in the first launch going ashore? I'm supposed to meet a Warrant Officer there so I can use his equipment to finish my project for the Captain. If I can get ashore right away I can have it finished by noon."

"Well I suppose that's reason enough for a Seaman to have a seat in the first launch. I'm betting you have to sit between two E-9s on your way to the landing. Stand by here out of the way and I'll have Holden and the Cox'n save a seat for you." As he finished speaking he heard the first boat's engine as it arrived at the boom alongside to make up and commence boarding the liberty party. He turned and nodded to one of his men, "Pass the word."

The Petty Officer keyed the 1MC and speakers all over the ship bleated out, "Liberty call, liberty call! Liberty is granted by Department for sections one, two and four to expire onboard tomorrow at 0800."

The sound of hundreds of feet in leather shoes slapping on the gray steel decks and ladders told the whole story. *Ike's* crew and her embarked Air Wing were anxious to get ashore and the liberty launches would be the most used pieces of equipment in her inventory for the next few hours. Ensign Evans held up his hand and cautioned the oncoming horde to wait until the first boat was ready. He looked down to the boom and saw the Cox'n salute him and call out, "Fueled and ready to go, Sir is Seaman Holden ready to be my understudy?"

"She's on her way down and I've got a passenger for you, take care of the CO's Yeoman, she's going ashore on business for him."

"Aye, aye, Sir!"

14

The two women sailors saluted and made their way down the ladder. Wilson found a seat in the launch and clutched her briefcase on her lap. With any luck at all she would catch the same boat back at noon and then she could do some sightseeing. Seaman Holden took her post by the helm with BM-2 Bates. He spoke softly to her as he explained how the controls for the engine worked and gave her advice on the amount of rudder to use as they got underway from the boom. He was an old hand at it. This was his second Med Cruise and Naples harbor was an old friend.

The boat filled rapidly as 140 eager sailors clamored down the gangway and found seats in the craft. Enlisted men and officers alike were anxious to be off the ship in search of a good time. Bates was satisfied with the loading and gave a hand signal to the young Bowhook. He took the turns of his line off the cleat and Bates backed clear of the boom shifting the rudder and clutching the transmission to go ahead. He smoothly pulled away from *Ike* and crossed ahead of the ship as it swung at anchor. "Holden, take the wheel and bring her to the right easy, point at that church spire over past the landing. Keep her speed where it is, we're hardly rolling at all."

As the boat made for the landing they saw a gray destroyer lining up to approach the pier ahead of them. Wilson heard Bates tell her friend it was *Porter* getting ready to moor. "She has her whole deck gang aft to handle the med-moor what a hassle, they'll be the rest of the morning and that part of the pier will be tied up until they finish. Throttle back when we get near them, we don't want to get in the way of the tugs. Here we go, come left and slow down, get ready to back down as we make the landing."

She shifted to reverse and the engine revved as distance between the gunwale and the pier closed to a few feet. One last burst of power and Bates gave the signal for the Bowhook to jump down onto the pier and take turns on the cleat with the bow line. "Keep her idling ahead as we start to disembark. Where's your friend? We'll get her off before everyone else. She can check in with the Duty Chief in the office at the head of the pier. They'll get her a lift over to the Naval

Support Activity."

Wilson gathered her things as Bates motioned for her to disembark. The Seaman finished his turns on the cleat and came back down the pier to help the crew off as the liberty party stood and began to disembark. He helped Wilson over the gunwale and onto the pier. She stood aside as the other passengers in the launch clamored ashore.

Holden said, "Sam the Duty Chief in the Senior Officer Present Afloat's office up the pier can probably get you a ride to the NSA. Do you have any money for a cab afterward?"

"Gosh I didn't think of that, all my money is back on the ship."

Bates heard her and reached in his pocket. "Here take this it'll see you through the morning." She reached out and took the bills he held out to her.

"Gosh thanks, Boats. I'll pay you back when I get back aboard." She put the money in her pocket and squared her Havelock. It was 30 yards from the boat to the SOPA office and she was the only customer for the Duty Chief as she opened the door and walked in. "Good morning Chief, I'm trying to get to the NSA so I can do some work at the document facility there. Is there a shuttle or something that I could catch a ride over on?"

The Duty Chief looked her up and down. She appeared squared away and she seemed businesslike and friendly. He had just assumed the watch and was in a good mood. He made the instant decision to help her. "Yeah hang on for a second, Seaman the van should be back in 5 minutes or so. I'll have my Duty Driver run you over. Do you want to use my phone to call anyone?"

"Thank you, Chief but I don't know the phone number. I have to meet Warrant Officer Martinez at the document center. Is there a phone book I could use to look it up?"

"Here you go, Seaman." He handed her the booklet and she found the right page and dialed the number.

"Document Center Chief Warrant Officer Martinez speaking, Sir."

"Good morning, Sir. This is Yeoman Seaman Wilson. I'm the Captain's Yeoman on *Eisenhower*. Chief Thomas contacted you yesterday I believe and made arrangements for me to meet you so I can finish a project using your IBM 660. I just caught the liberty launch ashore and I'm at the SOPA Pier Office. The Chief is arranging a ride for me to come to the NSA. I was wondering where to go to find you when I get there? I've never been to Naples before, Sir."

"When you come in the gate you'll see the tall office building to the left of the parking lot. Come to the third deck and my office is the fourth door on the right when you get off the elevator. I'll be here for the whole morning, Wilson."

"Thank you, Sir. I think the van just got here." She could see the gray navy van just pulling up at the head of the pier. Two sailors climbed out and sauntered across the parking area and into the office. The taller one said, "Hey, Chief okay if me and Johnson go get something to eat now? We were on that working party this morning and missed breakfast."

"You can go just as soon as you take Seaman Wilson here over to the NSA and you gas up the van. It shouldn't take you more than half an hour. I'll see that you have a long lunch and there's nothing important this afternoon that I know of. Oh wait, the Admiral is flying out of Capodichino this evening to go up to London. I'll need one of you to go along with his driver and show him the way."

"Oh Hell, I was hoping to get off early this afternoon, Chief. Why can't the Admiral pick out a driver who knows what the fuck he's doing on his own?"

"When you have the horsepower to tell Admirals their business, Saunders then open your mouth; in the meantime get yourself back in that van and give this Seaman a ride to NSA. You can eat when you get back. Johnson, get down to where *Porter* is mooring and see if you can help the line handlers on the pier. Come back here when she's moored."

Both sailors left to do as the Chief ordered and Wilson gathered her things to go with Saunders and get her ride to the NSA. "Thank

17

you, Chief," she smiled as she went out the door.

Saunders showed his attitude immediately. He was a Third Class Petty Officer and being ordered to take a Seaman to her destination caused his ego to take a pounding. Hell he hadn't even had breakfast and that damned Chief had messed up his evening too! He had planned to shove off as soon as he could con one of the others in the NSA duty section to cover his 20-2400 watch as Duty Driver. It just didn't seem fair. "What's so important with you and your shit there, Seaman?"

Wilson could tell she'd have to do something to change his attitude to make the ride even the least bit pleasant. "I'm the Captain's Yeoman on the *Ike* and our IBM 660 went out of commission before I could finish an important package for him. I'm going to the NSA document center to use theirs. I'm sorry you got roped into taking me but I asked the Chief if he could help and he said you would be right back with the van so here I am. I hope the rest of your duty day is better."

He grunted and narrowly missed hitting a blue Alfa Romeo darting out from a double parked space on the Viale San Gennaro. "Better keep your mind on the traffic, Petty Officer Saunders. We both want to get there in one piece."

He shrugged but didn't speak and he paid better attention to his driving for the rest of the way to the NSA gate. Wilson got out and thanked him. She showed her ID to the sentry and he let her through the gate where she found the parking lot and the tall office building on the left as she had been instructed.

The Petty Officer stationed at the Quarterdeck on the first deck logged her in as a visitor and directed her to the bank of elevators just down the passageway. She took the first one to the third deck and knocked on Warrant Officer Martinez's door before entering. It was a small office with three metal desks crammed together, a row of tall gray file cabinets and stacks of paper in file baskets. Her office aboard *Ike* was bigger than this and much more squared away too. The only thing this had that was better than hers, was a pair of dusty windows letting in the morning Neapolitan sun.

"Hello Sir, I'm Seaman Wilson thank you for agreeing to let me use your IBM. Ours just went snaky and no matter what mag card I put in the reader it just spit out gibberish. I sure hope yours can help me, it should only take me a moment to find out."

"Good morning, Wilson my unit is just in the next room. You picked the right day to have a problem, all my local labor has the weekend off and I usually come in with my Chief and our YN1 and we do all the classified work when they aren't around. None of them has a security clearance you see. I should have had Chief Thomas send me a message with your security clearance data but he vouched for you and that's good enough for me." He showed her into the adjoining room where she put her things down on the empty desk that held the IMB 660's familiar black bulk.

A moment later she had it powered up and fished out the first of the mag cards from her briefcase. She slid it into the card reader, pressed PRINT and the musical electro-mechanical sounds began at once. Even better, a sheet of paper began inching out with neat blue-black letters that formed complete sentences. Sentences that Captain Christensen had sweated over and Wilson had been frantic about when her villainous machine had turned them into an unintelligible hodgepodge of carats, pound signs and ampersands. She felt a wave of relief course through her as the pile of completed pages grew. She put in one mag card after another until she had the thick package stacked neatly on the desk. Only six more pages of the Captain's cryptic notes and she would be finished.

"Mr. Martinez, I don't know how to thank you! I can finish the rest in an hour or so. Thank goodness!"

"Hey don't mention it, Wilson just tell 'Terrible Tommy' Thomas that he owes me one." He laughed as he shared with her the times when he and his friend had hit the beach together at YN "A" school, back in the day.

Wilson was inspired as she read the Captain's notes and recognized what he intended as his short cryptic markups slashed away at the Ops Officer's original write-up. There were the OOD's thoughts in black and the Navigator's in pencil, even the XO's in green; but the Captain's in his flowing bold fountain pen ink were the real lodestone for her final typing. "It's strange;" she thought, "How can he keep so cool and focused about the whole thing? Everyone seems to have a different recollection of events. They all seemed to blame everything on *Porter* when things went wrong and they scraped against us."

But the Captain pointed out that the Russian *Backfire* bomber was the real culprit. It had screamed overhead at 150 feet during the hi-line transfer and almost everyone's attention had been riveted on it. Surely the *Porter's* OOD's had been. She knew it too. She had the radar track of the bandit's path over *Ike* and *Porter* tucked in the figure package that would accompany the Captain's presentation. She could see what the Captain was doing. He wasn't trying to save his own career, he was trying to save the CO of the *Porter's*.

Wilson worked steadily for the next hour, her attention riveted to the scene the Captain was painting with his words. She didn't even hear Chief Berg ask her if she wanted a cup of coffee before he unplugged the pot for the weekend. She didn't hear Warrant Officer Martinez when he told the Chief to lock up after she was finished and to make sure she had a ride back to Fleet Landing.

She proofread her final sheets on the screen and hit PRINT. Then she went into the text of the final two pages and made a deletion and an addition of her own, an alternate input for the Captain to consider. She hit PRINT one final time and the last two sheets slid down the paper path into the tray in order, the final sheet ending with the Captain's typed name and the space so he could sign it above that.

She could finally relax and looked around the office, "Oh hello, Chief I'm finally finished. I'm sorry I don't even know who you are. I must have been concentrating on the work and didn't see you. Where is Mr. Martinez?"

"He shoved off about half an hour ago. He had to take his family shopping. His daughter is going to the Prom next weekend. I'm Chief Berg, Mr. Martinez asked me to make sure you get safely back to Fleet Landing.

CHAPTER 3

CHIEF BERG

WILSON SCOOPED UP THE PAPER package and the Chief showed her to the big Xerox machine. She made an insurance copy of the package and stuffed it, the original and the mag cards safely in her briefcase. He checked that the safe drawers were all locked and shut off the lights, locking the door behind them. "C'mon, Seaman let's get a burger downstairs and then I'll run you back to Fleet Landing. I have to drive by there to get to my apartment anyway."

They took the elevator to the first deck where a Petty Officer at the Quarterdeck logged her departure. They walked downstairs to the Navy Exchange Cafeteria. The clock on the wall behind the counter showed it was 1120. She had managed to finish with plenty of time for the Captain to review the whole package. "What are you havin', Seaman? They make a good burger here and they have a lot of other good things too. I'll get us a booth."

She reached in her pocket and pulled out the money the Boatswain's Mate had given her and counted the bills, a twenty, a ten, two fives and a few ones. "I'll have a cheeseburger and a small green salad with Italian dressing please."

The counterman passed her order to the cook and she walked to the register where the cashier took her money and made change as the Chief came up behind her.

"I put my hat on the table in the second booth over there. If you need to hit the head I'll bring our food over when it's ready."

She thanked him and went to the women's head. It had been a long morning and she was glad to use it and to wash her hands. She hadn't realized how dirty they were. The ink and dust from the office washed off her hands and left her feeling clean again. When she reentered the cafeteria the Chief had already put their orders on the table and he was sitting there waiting for her.

"How did you get to be the Captain's Yeoman on an aircraft carrier, Wilson? That's a job for a very senior First Class and normally it's a Chief. You must be pretty special to have that billet."

She knew what he was thinking because she'd had to put up with it from some of the other Yeomen shipboard. "Chief I got the job because the First Class who had it before me was an idiot and got himself in trouble over drugs. I had just reported aboard and hadn't been assigned a job yet and I had 12 hours to learn everything and accept responsibility for all the Captain's ongoing projects. He had over a hundred fitness reports to finish before we got underway and I did them all and without even one mistake. I've been his Yeoman ever since and before you even say it, no I'm not sleeping with him. He's a fine man with a nice family, I even met his wife and he's the best officer I ever met."

"It's okay, Wilson hey it happens all the time. You're a good lookin' woman and I ... I'm sorry I didn't mean anything disrespectful towards you or him. Can we start over?"

She was worked up and red-faced and had some tears welling up in her eyes but she nodded. "I'm sorry too, Chief I shouldn't have flown off the handle at you like that but I've had accusations before and I don't like it. It's just so unprofessional when someone ... you know what I mean."

"I know Wilson. Hey I don't even know what it's like on a carrier. I spent my sea time on a tin can and then on a tender. Then I met a local girl and we got married. I put in for duty here in Naples so she could be close to her family. I speak Italian because we use it every day in our home so I get called on a lot here for work with the locals. I'm a Yeoman but more often than not I end up helping in writing contracts for local labor and projects around the support activity."

She had regained her composure by then. "How long is your tour here, Chief and what's it like living on the economy in Italy?"

He smiled, "Well it's different, I found that out in a hurry. My original tour was three years but I asked for an extension and I'm hoping I finish out my career here. I know some people who have done it. There's a 'mustang' Lieutenant Commander who has been here for over 15 years. He's the guy they count on to break up strikes and restore order when there are riots, like the one a few years ago when that Marine killed a taxi driver. That was a bad one. Hey my wife and I have two little girls, both in the armed forces school system here. Oh, one thing you should know is that you never want to buy anything here for the asking price. The locals all bargain and they see it as a sign of weakness if some sailor whips out his wallet and pays right away. Always counter with 'mezzo'—half what they're asking."

He laughed remembering how his wife had carefully schooled him before sending him out on his first solo trip to the market. Wilson giggled as he told her the story, complete with hand gestures and facial expressions. "Gosh, Chief I thought it was hard just learning the language of the navy! You had to learn that and Italian too. You must really love it to want to spend the rest of your career here!"

"Yeah I do. The people are friendly in a carefree sort of way and the food is fabulous. If you get a chance to try it you should go to one of the nice restaurants over by the Opera House and order seafood. Nobody serves seafood like the Neapolitans do. Oh and try the local wine. My father-in-law bottles his own and you have to taste it to believe it."

She laughed, "That sounds like a lot of fun, Chief. Hey while we're talking, what things should I go see while we're here in Naples? I don't have a lot of money but I would love to see some of the sights."

"See if you can catch one of the tours that go over to Pompeii or

Herculaneum. Pretty fascinating stuff and you can get to see what it was like living during the time of the Roman Empire before Christ was born. I think the USO has some tours like that. Their headquarters is only a couple of blocks from Fleet Landing. Anybody can show you the way. Hey speaking of way, let's finish and I'll run you back to Fleet Landing. Then I suppose my wife has a list of things she wants me to do before dinner tomorrow. We always have her family over for a big spread Sunday afternoon. Her sisters and cousins and God knows who else. It'll probably be 30 or so this week."

"Thanks, Chief I'll check at the USO this afternoon. I have the duty tomorrow but maybe I can tour on Monday."

They finished their meals and took their paper plates to the trash. She got her case and looped her purse strap over her shoulder. They put on their hats as they climbed the stairs and exited to the parking lot. He led the way to a battered tiny blue Fiat. "Gas is expensive over here so we use the cars with the smallest engines. This one is only 500 CCs but I get over 50 kilometers to the gallon. No seat belts required over here either so hold on tight!"

She laughed as he started the engine, clutched and moved the gearshift to begin the trip to downtown Naples. Along the way he pointed out the various landmarks he thought she should see. "There's the soccer stadium. You don't want to be anywhere near it when there's a game, the traffic is murder. There's 'Edenlandia', it's the local version of Disneyland. Up the side of the mountain there is the Vomero district, really expensive shopping but a great place for pizza. That's Posillipo up there, that's where the Admiral's villas are."

They continued along down the busy streets approaching the waterfront. "There's the San Carlo Opera House, it's one of the finest opera houses in the world, they say the acoustics there are perfect. Ah here we are, the head of the pier as promised." He downshifted and brought the tiny "cinquecento" to a halt at the waterfront.

She opened the door and turned to him before she got out, "Chief I'm really sorry I was hyper with you. Please accept my apology and let me say that you have been very kind to me this morning. Not many people would have taken the morning on a weekend to help another sailor. By the way, it's Samantha Wilson but my friends call me Sam, I hope you'll be one of them and if there is ever anything you need that I can help with, please let me know."

"Sam I'm Lowell Berg but my friends all call me 'Ice'. I do consider you a friend and a damn fine sailor. If you ever need anything I can help with, you just let *me* know. I have a local phone and the number is just like my name laid out on the phone dial. Call if you need me."

She shook his hand and got out taking her briefcase and shutting the door. "Thank you, Chief," she smiled. "You're my 'Iceman' that's for sure!" He laughed and waved as she turned to walk to the landing.

She could see the wake of *Ike's* departing launch and one of the Shore Patrolmen told her the next one would leave the ship at 1200. It would take ten minutes or so to make the run to Fleet Landing and it would depart again at 1230. Wilson knew she would have to wait at least that long before she could complete her task. It didn't matter though, she remembered the Captain saying he would be at the reception. He wouldn't be able to look over her work until Sunday anyway. She took a seat on the bench at the head of the pier to wait. The noise of the nearby city traffic and the sounds of the harbor relaxed her and made her mind drift. This was the first time she could feel calm in two days.

THE VOICE HAD A VERY familiar ring to it, "Hey don't I know you? Aren't you Samantha Wilson from Corning Iowa? Didn't you used to date my brother Greg?"

Her eyelids fluttered open to reveal Ron Carter, the older and taller of the two Carter boys, standing before her dressed in navy blue and wearing the crow of a Second Class Petty Officer with crossed cannons above his chevrons. He was a Gunner's Mate and the patch on his shoulder bore the name of his ship, *USS Porter DDG-78*. Her face showed the degree of amazement she felt.

"My goodness, Ron how are you! I haven't seen anyone from Corning since I joined the navy. How is it possible to run into the older brother of my old high school boyfriend on the pier in Naples Italy?"

"I don't know, Sam! I heard from Greg that you broke up after you both graduated but I didn't know you joined the navy. Where are you stationed? What have you been doing since you left Southwest Valley High? I remember you were one of the cheerleaders for the Timberwolves."

She laughed, "Go 'Wolves'! Well as you can see I went to Yeoman 'A' School and I was meritoriously advanced to Seaman early. Then I was sent to *Eisenhower*. Just as I reported aboard there was a bad problem with the guy who was the Captain's Yeoman and I got picked to take over the job. I've been aboard for three months now and the last two I guess I've shared with you here in the Med with the Battle Group. I can't believe it's such a small world!"

"Hey that's really something isn't it? Wanna hear something even weirder? Remember Ted Manckowicz he was on the football team with me, we were seniors when you and Greg were sophomores? He's on the *Montpelier*, he's a Third Class Machinist's Mate! I was just on my way to visit him on his boat, it's over at the Italian navy base. So what are you doing here at Fleet Landing do you have to go back early?"

"I had to come ashore to finish a project for my Captain. I had to go to the NSA and use a machine at the document center there. It only took me a couple hours and now I'm going back aboard to leave the package on his desk. Then I thought I might hit the beach and take one of those USO tours. Maybe I'll go to Pompeii or someplace."

"That must have been a real important job. Doesn't *Eisenhower* have the equipment aboard that you needed?"

"My IBM went nuts and I had about 60 pages of work that were lost. I had to use the one at NSA. My Chief made arrangements with an old friend of his so they were waiting for me and their IBM worked perfectly. I was lucky, you know it's funny how sometimes old friends can make it easier to get things done in the navy."

"Don't I know it, Sam! Once I had trouble finding a part for our gun mount in the normal supply channels and I went to the Gun Boss and let him know there was a problem. He had a friend in the world of supply who got it shipped to us overnight. Hey some of us on *Porter* are thinking of going over to Ischia and seeing the sights, having a picnic and going for a swim. Wanna go along with us? I'm inviting Ted along, we've got food from the galley and permission to use one of the ship's boats for the afternoon. I'm not sure what time we're going but if you come over to the ship after you finish with your Captain's task it would be fun."

"It does sound like fun but I'll be outnumbered by *Porter* sailors." She laughed, "And probably the only girl too. If I go you have to promise to bring me back safe and sound and no monkey business. Are you wearing civvies or uniforms?"

"We'll probably just have T-shirts or dungarees and our bathing suits on but you could wear civvies over your suit. Hey what about this? When we get ready we'll stop by the *Ike* with the boat and call you from the Quarterdeck. That way you can wear anything you want and not have to worry about the Shore Patrol. Don't worry Sam you'll be among friends."

"Okay, Ron I'd love to go and the price is sure right. I don't have a lot of money to spend on liberty fun. Besides I have to return some money to someone who helped me out this morning. I'll shift to dungarees when I get back to the ship and I'll have my suit on under them. What do you think? An hour or so?"

"Probably more like a couple of hours, I was hoping Ted would show me around his sub before we come back to *Porter* and get the boat and the food and everything. I'd say look for us about 1330. That should still give us plenty of time for fun and sun on the beach."

"Oh that's great, Ron. I'll be ready to go then and I'll leave word with the Quarterdeck Watch that I'm expecting you. Oh here comes the launch now, I'll see you later on."

She gathered her purse and briefcase and walked to the side of the pier as the liberty launch's engine roared in reverse bringing it to a stop and the Bowhook leapt down and put his turns on the dock cleat. Forty or fifty sailors eagerly scrambled out of the launch and passed her as she stood waiting for her chance to board. Finally the Cox'n gestured to her to come aboard. "Damn, Seaman you sure are heading back early. I haven't picked up anyone heading back to the ship at all. This is my third run today and you are the first person I've seen coming back off the beach.'

"Well I wasn't really on liberty, I had a job to do ashore. Now I'm finished and I'll go on liberty after I get back aboard and change my clothes. Where are BM2 Bates and Terri Holden? Aren't they still making the runs?"

"I was their relief, they come back on at 1600."

"Excellent, I'll be able to find them then. Bates lent me some money this morning and I have to pay him back."

"He's my section leader and you can probably find him on the Fo'cs'l this afternoon until he comes back to relieve me."

"Thanks, Boats."

"You all set there, Seaman?"

She smiled and nodded and he ordered, "Okay take in forward and shove off Henry. We won't have any other passengers heading back so we might as well not wait here. Let's go."

The Bowhook took off his turns and leapt aboard as the Cox'n backed away from the pier and began the turn that would head them out of the harbor and take them back to *Ike's* anchorage.

Wilson rose from her seat on the center thwart slightly so she could see over the gunwale. To the left was the ancient castle that Chief Berg had called the "New Castle" during their ride to Fleet Landing. He had laughed when he said "New" because it was over 500 years old. But it was newer than the "Old" castle which was twice as old. To the left of the castle she made out the molo with its row of Italian ships alongside. And there was *Montpelier* tied among them. "She's pretty small compared to the Italian corvettes. Even the patrol boats look bigger," she thought. "It would be fun to visit a sub though, maybe I could even get them to give me a ride! I wonder if women will ever be able to serve on one. Well, no matter, I love it on *Ike.*"

The Cox'n brought them to the boom and helped her out onto the accommodation ladder. She climbed it and saluted the Quarterdeck Watch. "Request permission to rejoin the ship, Sir."

The OOD saluted her and granted permission.

"Sir, I'm Yeoman Wilson, the Captain's Yeoman. I just finished some work ashore but I'll be going on liberty later this afternoon. One of *Porter's* boats should be coming by to get me. Can they have permission to make up at the boom until I can join them, Sir?"

"Yes, Wilson where will you be in the meantime? I'll have the Watch call you when they get here. Who do you know on *Porter*?"

"A Gunner's Mate, Sir. He's from my home town and I used to date his little brother. I'll be in the Captain's Yeoman's office, Sir."

"That's fine, Wilson." He turned to the Petty Officer on watch, "Put it on the status board to call Wilson in the CO's Yeoman's office when *Porter's* boat arrives."

"Thank you, Sir." Wilson saluted him and left the Quarterdeck. She went to her office and locked the copy of the package in her desk and stowed the Captain's notes, the mag cards and her briefcase in a locker. She went down the passageway and found the Captain's Mess Supervisor.

"Petty Officer Sims I have this package for the Captain, he told me to leave it for him on the desk in his stateroom. Please make sure he sees it when he gets back aboard. I may not be here because I'm going on liberty in a little while but I'll be back this evening." She handed him the package.

"Okay, Wilson I'll make sure he sees it."

"Thank you." She left headed toward the ladder and her berthing compartment where BMSN Terri Holden was just changing her uniform.

"Hi, Terri how did you do with Bad Billy? Is he ready to sign off on your quals?"

She laughed, "He says I need to make a few more landings and underways to get the feel for how the boat handles and he wants me to practice doing it in the dark too. He says distances appear differently in the dark. But, he said I did really well this morning."

"That's great, Terri! Is he around? I have his money for him and then I have to change clothes. I'm going on liberty with some of the guys from *Porter*. They have one of their ship's boats for the afternoon and we're going to Ischia to have a picnic and go swimming. Funny, I met my old boyfriend's brother at Fleet landing. He's a Gunner's Mate on *Porter* and another guy from my home town is on *Montpelier,* he's coming too."

Holden smiled, "He told me to meet him at 1530 so we can relieve the Cox'n that's making the runs now. I think he's up on the Fo'cs'l now. Have you ever been up there?"

"Once I had to take the Captain something while he was holding Mast and it's quite a walk from the office. I'll go find him now. It was nice of him to lend me the money. I only spent a few dollars for lunch at the NSA. Thanks, Terri I'll be back to change after I find him."

Wilson started for the Fo'cs'l and found that most of the sailors she met were headed in the other direction. They were headed toward the Quarterdeck to get in at least some time ashore. It wasn't just *Ike's* sailors, more and more of the people she met along the way were from the embarked air squadrons, officers and men hurrying ashore to share the glories of Naples and a few 'birras' before shifting over to the local vinos.

She found Bates on the Fo'cs'l just getting ready to put some polish on his shoes. "Hello, Boats I wanted to thank you for the loan this morning. I didn't really need much but here you go. I thought it was very nice of you to make the gesture and thank you for taking my friend Terri under your wing and helping her in her Cox'n training."

He took the money and slipped it into his pocket without even counting it. "Hey, Wilson thanks. It's okay, Holden's gonna be real good with a little practice. So did you finish your hot project for the Captain? She told me you were really sweating it."

"Yes I did, thank goodness they had a system like ours and that my mag cards weren't messed up. It only took me a couple of hours to finish. Hey, how come they call you 'Bad Billy' anyway? You don't seem so bad to me," she laughed.

"It's because before I came in the navy I used to box "Golden Gloves". I boxed for the Police Athletic League in Pittsburgh. That's the name I fought under, 'Bad Billy'. It came along with me when I enlisted," he grinned.

"I'm from a tiny town in Iowa and the closest thing we had to a Police Athletic League was some guys on our high school wrestling team. I've never seen real boxing except on TV. You seem to have done pretty well though, I don't see any cauliflower ears or anything."

He chuckled, "There used to be a Fleet-wide boxing competition every year but I guess that's over. Maybe someday there'll be another one and you can come watch me box. I work out in the gym a lot but there aren't many others aboard that like to box. Maybe something will come up who knows."

"I'd like that, Boats I hope something does come up. Hey thank you again for the loan, I have to get going now though; I have to go change for going ashore. I hope I see you running the launches again soon."

"Thanks, Sam that's what they call you isn't it?"

"Yes, it is," she laughed. "Have a great day, Bad Billy I'll see you around." And she headed aft again on the long trek to her berthing compartment.

She put her dress blues away, donned her swimsuit and pulled on a set of dungarees over it. She tucked her ID card and ten dollars in her pocket and put on her sneakers and her *Ike* ball cap. She was halfway out of the compartment door when she remembered they would be going swimming. She rolled two towels up into a cylinder and stuck them under her arm. She was as ready for a picnic as she would ever be. It was a few minute walk to her office but she had time on her hands until they came for her in *Porter's* boat so she didn't hurry.

She did some busy work when she got there, sorting reports for filing later and updating the officer's social roster with the names of the new Ensign and the Lieutenant Junior Grade who had joined the ship's company a few days before their Naples port visit. Then she opened the shipment of new Captain's stationery and note cards. She put the stationery in her desk drawer. She used it to type his correspondence for his signature, but she would take the note cards to his stateroom. She knew he was almost out of them. He liked to hand-write those for her to stamp and mail. She kept a log of all his correspondence coming in and going out. She turned on her music player and was just beginning to hum along with the melody when the office phone rang.

"Captain's Yeoman's Office, Seaman Wilson speaking, Sir."

"Wilson this is Chief O'Connor at the Quarterdeck. There's a boat alongside from the *Porter*. Your friends are waiting for you."

"Thank you, Chief, I'll be right there."

She took the ladder two steps at a time. When she got to the Quarterdeck the OOD, Chief O'Connor and two other sailors were waiting for her. The tall one turned around and she saw that it was Ron wearing dungarees and a t-shirt. He smiled and came to attention. "Here she comes, Sir. Thanks for calling her. Thanks Chief, I'll bring her back safe and sound. We're going out to Ischia for a picnic on the beach."

She saluted the OOD. "Request permission to go ashore, Sir."

He returned her salute, "Permission granted, Seaman. Have a good time with your friends."

"Thank you, Sir." And she followed Ron down the steep ladder to the boom. *Porter's* motor whaleboat was there with five sailors inside. Four men and a diminutive woman with a strikingly beautiful smile that reminded her of her china doll. Wilson smiled to herself. The odds were better with another woman along.

CHAPTER 4
THE MAINTENANCE RUN

BMC GROVES MADE IT VERY clear to the men that their first priority was to get the damaged motor whaleboat turned over to the NSA's boat rework facility. Then they would pick up the replacement boat and bring it safely back to the ship. The damage had occurred when *Porter's* port quarter had struck *Eisenhower* a glancing blow during the personnel transfer that had been interrupted by the Russian aircraft screeching in on them that foggy morning in the Adriatic two weeks ago. "The side is partially crushed just below the gunwale but it will ride high in the water with just you and the Engineer aboard Gleason. Make sure the rework facility signs for the boat and you'll probably have to sign for the replacement one. Make sure the replacement has all its equipment and safety gear with it before you sign."

"I got it, Chief let me get Fettes. He's my boat Engineer, we sure won't need a Bowhook on this run. How far is it to the rework facility anyway?"

"It's about ten miles Gleason, it's just past the point over there on the right. It's at the NATO base called 'AFSOUTH', the town there is Bagnoli. You can't miss it. Check with one of the Quartermasters and they'll show you on the chart. Make sure you have enough fuel to get there safely."

"Okay, Chief I'll get Fettes and we'll check with the Duty QM before we get underway. I think I have a handle on it. Have a good time ashore. I'm off tomorrow so I guess I'll see you on Monday." Gleason climbed the brow and stopped to talk with the Quarterdeck Watch. "Can you track down the duty Boat Engineer and have him meet me up on the Bridge? I gotta go find the duty QM."

"Sure Artie, I'll page him and have him meet you there. What's goin' on?"

"We have to take that damaged whaleboat over to the rework facility and trade it in for a new model. The Chief told me to get it done this morning and we already have permission from the CDO and everything. I just wanna make sure I know where to go, this whole bay is full of docks and wharves and I don't want to screw it up and turn the boat over to the wrong people."

The watch paged FN Fettes as BM3 Artie Gleason made his way to the Bridge. He found the duty QM who took him into CIC where they pulled out the chart and the port guide and took them out onto the Bridge. "See here we are right across from Fleet Landing." QM2 Spencer pointed with his pencil, "Now here is the point over on the left. That's that high sheer cliff over there. You'll round that point and come right. There's a causeway there and this little island 'Nisida'. You'll go to the west of that right up here to AFSOUTH." He traced the coastline for Gleason as he explained the route he would have to take.

"Hey, Spencer can you make me a tracing of that part of the chart and label a few landmarks for me? This bay is pretty damn wide and I want to do this right. It's the first time the Chief has trusted me for something important and I don't want to foul it up."

"Sure let me grab some tracing paper."

Spencer drew the coast outline and penciled in their current location and the boat's destination. Then he circled and labeled the landmarks they had used when they piloted their way into the harbor. "Let's measure this out for you Gleason. It looks like if you take a straight heading of about 230 when you clear the end of the pier and hold that until you pass the point it's about seven miles. Then you'll come right and it's about two miles to clear Nisida then it's about two more to AFSOUTH."

FN Jimmy Fettes joined them just as Spencer finished showing Gleason the route. "Hey, Artie I checked the engine over this morning before we put it in the water and I just checked the fuel. It's topped off and I'm ready to go."

"Good, let's get in our blues then; I'm going to stop by the mess and get a couple of bottles of water and maybe a sandwich if they have any out. I figure it's gonna take us an hour to get there and that means we won't get back 'till after noon. Chow will probably be over. You know what? I'm gonna ask the CDO if he can have the cooks keep some chow warm for us before we go."

"Okay, Artie I'll meet you at the boat after I change into my blues."

Gleason changed out of his dungarees and stopped by the mess. He filled two water bottles and got some apples. There were no sandwiches that morning. Back on the Quarterdeck he paused to talk with the OOD. "Mr. Tate I'm ready to shove off, Sir. Fettes and I are swapping out the damaged whaleboat this morning but we probably won't be back 'till after chow. Is it possible to have the cooks save rations for us?"

"Who's going with you, Gleason?"

"Just Fireman Fettes, Sir. We have to keep the boat light so we don't ship water though the damaged strakes."

"Okay, Gleason there isn't a ripple out there in the bay so it should be smooth sailing for you. You're bringing the new boat back with you?"

"Yes, Sir. The Chief told me I'd probably have to sign for it." He had a thought as he was speaking. "Sir, what's the phone number here on the ship? In case there's a problem I'll give you a call."

"Hang on, Gleason I'll get it for you." He turned to the Watch who copied the number onto a 3x5 card and handed it to him.

"Take this, Gleason. Be careful now and we'll see you later. I'll have the cooks keep something warm for you."

"Aye, aye, Sir." Gleason saluted and made his way down the

brow. He found Fettes waiting for him in the whaleboat. "Here you go, Jimmy have an apple and a bottle of water. They didn't have any sandwiches but Ensign Tate said he would have the cooks save some chow for us. Let me get my little chart set so it won't blow away and let's go."

Gleason started the engine and let it idle as Fettes handled the bow line then he put the transmission in reverse and smoothly backed clear. Fettes joined him at the wheel as he swung the bow out and headed to pass the head of the molo and the ships med-moored to it. He was well clear when he turned to the southwest. He had the sheer cliff on the point in sight and could use it as his guide on the long track across Naples bay. He and Fettes had the best spot of all to take in the panorama of the beautiful scenery. "Hey, Jimmy you know what they say about Naples don't you?"

"You mean see Naples and die?"

"Yeah, I'm not sure where that saying comes from but I hope it's bullshit. I've got no death wish motivation. I just wanna get us safely there and back."

"You and me both, Artie."

They motored along in silence enjoying the sights and sounds of the busy bay. Fishing boats came and went and the sleek hull of a Costa Guarda patrol boat passed them on its way northwest in search of cigarette boats smuggling in the product their name implied. Gleason eyed the promontory as he drew abreast of it and he turned to the left to keep a thousand yards away. He could see the causeway connecting tiny Nisida with the hilly bump of land north of the point. "As we round that little island to starboard there Jimmy keep your eyes peeled for something that looks kinda' navy, or at least kinda' military. AFSOUTH should be over there on the right, a couple miles from the little island."

"Got it, Artie hey is this going to be a brand new boat or some piece of junk that some other ship cast off and these rework guys repainted and fixed the leaks with chewing gum?"

"You've got me, Jimmy. The Chief told me to look it over and make sure all the equipment and the safety gear was aboard before I sign for it but other than that I have no idea what to expect. I hope it's a good boat though, the one we're turning in is top notch except for the staved strake where somethin' on *Eisenhower's* starboard quarter crunched into it. You know I was on the Bridge when that whole thing went down. We were damn lucky we didn't lose the Admiral over the side when that fuckin' plane came blasting right for the Bridge. I almost crapped my trou when that happened."

"Hey, I heard all about it from Don Olsen, he was up on the Signal Bridge and he told me the noise from that damn plane was so bad it hurt his ears and he had trouble hearing for a week afterward. Hey, I think I've got that AFSOUTH in sight. There's a couple of docks and some sheds there on the right. Sure looks like a little industrial facility to me."

"Let's get in a little closer and I'll call on the portable radio and see if it's them. I know the Chief set this up so there must be somebody there to expect us this morning."

Gleason pointed the bow at the distant pier and it grew larger as they neared it. He was 500 yards out when two figures emerged from the long low building nearest the pier. One was in dungarees and the other work khakis. "Guess this is the right place, Jimmy at least they have the right clothes on. Get ready to tie us up right where they are standing on that rightmost pier. I'll come in slow and you can jump right out near that cleat there."

"Okay, Artie but I want you to know that I'm putting in for a fuckin' pay raise as soon as we get back to the ship. I'm doin' the job of a 'snipe' and a 'deck ape' this mornin'."

"Go right the fuck ahead, Jimmy. I'll support you on it."

"In the boat, you the guys from *Porter*?" The man on the pier wearing khakis didn't even need a bullhorn.

"Yes, Sir! My Chief said it was all set for us to swap boats here today. Request permission to make fast, Sir."

"Bring it on in, Cox'n. Tie 'er off there behind the Mike boat."

Gleason slid the throttle back to the stop and the boat glided forward in a smooth line until just feet from the pier then he put the rudder hard over to swing the bow out and the stern toward the dock. He shifted the rudder and the knuckle effect stopped their forward motion a foot out from the pier. Fettes jumped over from his stance at the bow. Two quick turns on the cleat held the injured boat in place. The Chief Warrant Officer walked to the edge of the pier to look at the boat. "Is it just that damage there on the port bow or is there something I can't see, Cox'n?"

"No, Sir that's all I know about. It happened when we kissed the side of *Eisenhower* a couple of weeks ago. It was punched in by something under her elevator."

"Okay, my people will check it out. Come up to the office and we'll go over the paperwork together."

"Aye, aye, Sir. My Chief told me to turn it over to you and you would have another one for us to take back. He told me to check over the replacement boat carefully and ensure it had all its equipment and safety gear. Can I sign for it or does one of our Ship's Officers have to do that?"

"You can do it, Cox'n don't worry we'll get to that. I just want to make sure we do this right. Now here's the straight skinny. All the navy's boats are in what we call the 'Boat Pool' just like all the navy's clocks are a part of the 'Chronometer Pool'. Each ship is assigned some based on her size, complement and function. When one needs work that's beyond the ship's force's capability to handle it they trade it in and draw a like boat. The one that needs work is then put back in serviceable condition and reissued. No ship actually 'owns' any boat, they just have the use of them. C'mon in the office and we'll get this taken care of."

Warrant Officer Mason was the coolly efficient expert in everything there was to do with navy small boats. He had been a Chief Boatswain's Mate on battleships and had seen every type of problem a boat could undergo and had personal knowledge of every seam and every fitting on any boat anyone could imagine. If he said it was 'good to go' it was gospel. He was in charge of the rework facility and the navy couldn't have found a better man. He would take good care of the sailors from *Porter*.

Gleason shuffled through the papers that went with the new boat. There was an hours log for the engine and the registry papers showing which ships had used the boat throughout its lifetime. He saw that it had been built by the manufacturer two years before he was born and had been used by seven different ships over the years. Most recently it had been a part of the *USS Prairie AD-15*'s boat equipage. There was also the boat's compass book showing that it too had seen a long service. He and Fettes followed the Duty Petty Officer to the shed were the boat they were getting was stored. It was in davits ready to be lowered alongside the pier. There were several other boats in the shed, each at a different stage of reconditioning. Two had their engines removed, one was in a cradle rolled on its side so that workers could remove rotted or broken strakes and replace them with new ones from the large bundles of hardwood lengths stacked along the bulkhead.

The building smelled of pitch, fiberglass epoxy, paint and fuel. Gleason could see the level of work that went into getting a boat ready for reissue. It was real sailor's work. They climbed into the boat and counted the life jackets stowed in it and made sure there were as many as they had turned in with their damaged boat. The boat anchor and the lines seemed fine and the fire extinguisher had been recently charged. Gleason was satisfied, everything looked good swinging there in the davits. The proof of the pudding though would be getting it in the water and finding out how the engine was after they were waterborne. "If you're satisfied there, Cox'n I'll lower her in. I just have to slide the davits out to the edge of the pier."

Gleason and Fettes stepped out and climbed down. The Petty Officer opened the sliding door on the shed and began cranking the handle that made the davits move along the cogged steel tracks to the stop at the side of the pier and the davit arms held the boat out over the water. They had never seen a movable davit before and its operation was fascinating. When the boat was out over the water the Petty

Officer motioned them to stand clear and he disengaged the pawl and started the falls downward. When the boat was even with the edge of the pier he said, "Here's where things get interesting."

The boat's keel was in the water but it had to be lowered another foot or so to wet the hull to its normal riding depth. Gleason climbed in and rode down the remaining way until he felt the motion of the boat on the water and the falls went slack. He carefully searched the sides and the seams for any water running down to the bottom as Fettes took a battle lantern and aimed it down into the engine compartment looking for any leakage from the shaft gland. None was apparent. Fettes checked the oil in the sump and the water hoses to the cooling pump. Nothing was amiss. He checked their fuel and found the tank a third full, enough to test the engine. "Artie we should ask them for fuel and top off before we head back, we're only a third full."

Gleason checked the rudder for smooth operation over the whole throw and saw that the cables were new, not frayed, and well lubricated. "Okay, Jimmy let's start 'er up and see how she runs before we back away and check her for all speeds away from the pier. I want to make sure of everything before we take her back to the ship. We may find something when we run up her speed."

The Petty Officer from the rework shop heard the exchange, "Hey, Cox'n check her engine here next to the pier. Run it up to any speed you want, just don't put it in gear."

"That's no test! If the shaft and prop aren't turning, how can I tell how much real vibration there is?"

"Listen, Mac I can't go on liberty until after you take the boat and get the Hell out of here. I don't want to be screwing around here for the rest of the day just because you want to dick the dog checking out the shaft. Check it out on your way back to Fleet Landing."

"No, I'm doing it the right way. I'm responsible for this thing and I guess I'll just have to talk with Warrant Officer Mason if you think differently."

"It'll be hard talking to him now, he left twenty minutes ago and he told me to handle the situation here. You're a Third Class and I'm a Second Class so I'm not taking any of your bullshit. Now get the Hell going and get out of here before I write your ass up!"

Gleason was pissed now but he kept his head, "Alright, fine. Just let me use your telephone there to make a call back to the ship. I need to report this situation to my First Lieutenant and then let him fight with the Naval Support Activity. I think the key word there is **SUPPORT**! I'm betting my First Lieutenant will not be happy and I know him, he takes names and kicks ass. I'm betting he raises enough Hell with the NSA Duty Officer that you get direction right away and I get to test this boat out for the rest of the damned day!"

He paused while the officious Second Class blinked and re-thought his position.

Gleason went on, "Look I'll keep it to a minimum out there. I just want to check for vibration. Go ahead, Jimmy let's get her running and see how she is."

Fettes opened the fuel cock and they turned over the engine. It caught right away and Gleason idled it while they had the engine cowling open. There was only smooth turning of the flywheel and normal engine noise. "Jimmy, hop up and pull the pin on the clevis in the forward hoisting pad, I'll get the after one."

When they were waterborne and free of restraint Gleason put the rudder over and threw it into reverse. The stern began to walk away from the pier as the familiar prop motion forces moved them to the left, like the effect of a gyroscope. He revved the engine as they backed away. "Keep watching the shaft at the gland there, Jimmy. Let me know if you see any leakage."

When he was comfortably clear of the pier Gleason shifted the transmission to go ahead and it clutched normally. The engine ran smoothly as he increased speed and kept the boat on a straight course away from the pier. Fettes signaled the "okay' sign with his thumb and forefinger. "Alright I'm gonna slow down now and then go astern, if it's gonna vibrate it'll do it then. Keep watching the shaft gland Jimmy."

The engine slowed and when Gleason judged they were slow enough he hit the shift lever and threw the transmission into reverse. The boat began to wallow as the remaining forward way was lost and the engine appeared to lug as the increased torque on the prop loaded it down. He sped the engine up and held it at power as they gained sternway. He put the rudder amidships and then fishtailed it, moving it back and forth for maximum stress effect. Fettes stood and ran his handkerchief over his forehead. "No vibration I can see and the shaft gland is only weeping. It's looking good, Artie. I felt the gland with my hand and it must be well packed, no heat or anything. There's no leakage from the cooling water hoses either. Hey as far as I'm concerned it's the best boat engine I've ever seen. It's painted nice too."

Gleason nodded, "Thanks, Jimmy let's go back in then and tell Petty Officer Dipshit there that we're taking her as is. I wouldn't want to be accused of holding up the asshole's liberty. I'll go up and sign for the whole thing while you go to our old boat and get the bridge to bridge radio, the chart tracing and our apples. I'll be back as soon as I make it all legal."

The stop alongside the pier lasted only 3 minutes; the time it took BM3 Arthur Gleason to walk to the shed, sign the requisite papers and make his way back to the spanking clean, gleaming boat that would soon become the object of worry, concern and wrath at all levels of the navy.

CHAPTER 5
MM3 MANCKOWICZ

"HEY, MANK THERE'S A SKIMMER 'cannon cocker' topside, says he's looking for you. You know a guy named Carter? Says he's from the *Porter*. Says he's an old friend of yours." TM1 Bellows found Manckowicz bent over with his face buried in the tech manual for the Oxygen Generator looking for the part number for the tiniest, most important O-ring on the entire ship, it was the one which kept the oxygen and the hydrogen separated as the big Treadwell machine made the oxygen they breathed when *Montpelier* was submerged doing her job. One hundred and thirty sailors breathed 130 standard cubic feet of oxygen per hour and the "O2 generator" made just enough to keep them all supplied ... when the thing wasn't broken down.

MM3 Theodore Manckowicz was the ship's expert on the machine. He had a feel for it and had shown time and time again that he could make the scary gray tower with the flashing multi-colored lights crank out its essential product and not let it become a hydrogen/oxygen bomb, as it had on many other submarines. He was the guy who kept them from gasping. He was a vital part of *Monty's* manning plan and the crew felt he was a good luck charm as well. He was the guy who could drink two cans of Budweiser at once ... without spilling a drop. He could still stand after drinking a dozen of the double-barreled brews and walk to the door of the bar by himself, stepping over the prone bodies of his other quaffing competitors on the way. Most of the crew had made money on their "Mank" bets.

"Shit yeah I know the fucker! He's the best damn quarterback in the state of Iowa! He can throw a football 80 yards through a hoop the size of your whitehat! He's a skimmer?"

"Bet your livin' ass he is and he's standin' topside right this minute jawin' with the Duty Officer. Better get up there and get the fuckin' situation under control before somebody figures out that you are indispensable, then you'll give up all hope for liberty while we're here."

"Thanks, 'Windy' I'll be there as soon as I get this crap off my hands." He hurried to the sink where he found the squeeze bottle of concentrated non-ionic soap and shot a dot of it on his hands. A few moments of operation of the ultrasonic element and his hands were pristine. He climbed the steps out of the Auxiliary Machinery Room headed for the ladder to Operations Upper Level.

"Up ladder! Gangway, regular navy comin' through!" Manckowicz grabbed the handhold and pulled his shoulders up level with the deck hatch. His barrel chest, thick biceps and shoulders filled the cylindrical space to the point that hardly any sunlight made its way past him down the hatch. "I hear there's a skimmer up here lookin' for a real ass kickin'."

"Hey, Ted it's great to see you!" Carter hailed him from his leisurely stance leaning against the sail. "Hey don't you guys have any level decks on this thing? How can anyone walk on this boat? The whole thing is curved, it's like standing on top of a whale! Your Duty Officer just said it would be okay for you to take me on a tour of your sub, I've never been on one before; how 'bout showin' me around?"

Manckowicz had him in a bear hug by then, "Sure, Ron but how the Hell did you find me?"

"Your Mom talked with mine and I just got a letter last week from home. Man I was really surprised when I found out your sub was in our Battle Group with us. I hope you aren't in the Duty Section because I made arrangements for you and me to go out to that island we passed coming in. It's called Ischia or something. I got one of our ship's boats for the afternoon and I've got a Cox'n and some chow from our galley. A couple of others are goin' along too, we'll have a swim and a picnic. Hey, remember that girl that used to date my brother? She was a cheerleader when we were seniors, Samantha Wilson, she lived out on the county highway not far from your place. She's a Seaman on *Eisenhower!* I ran into her at Fleet Landing earlier and she's comin' on the trip with us. I told her I was on my way over here to find you."

"Nah, I'm not in the Duty Section but I should check with the Auxiliary Division Leading Petty Officer before I shove off. I want him to know where I stand in fixin' my favorite friend Mr. Tread-well." He led the way below through the Ops Compartment Hatch and toured his friend through the Control Room. When they reached the Crew's Mess they found the A-Division LPO sitting at a table speaking with the Chief of the Boat.

"Hey, Mank who's your friend?"

"This here's Ron Carter, we played football together in high school, and he's off the *Porter*. Ron this is Master Chief Tomkins our Chief of the Boat and MM1 Stevens my LPO."

Carter shook hands with them as Manckowicz made his request, "Steve, can I go on liberty now? I can't do anything more on the generator until the parts get here. That should be tomorrow, then it's an easy fix. I should be in the middle of the pressure drop test by 1600 tomorrow. Ron's takin' me on a picnic."

"Yeah, go ahead. I guess everything's under control. The Captain, XO and the Engineer are all off at that big reception with the brass and the NATO people at the O-club. I'll let the Eng know where you stand on the generator when he gets back this evening."

"Thanks, Steve." Manckowicz turned to his friend. "Sit down and have a coffee, Ron. I'll drop down to berthing and shower. What are we wearing on this excursion? All I've got is uniforms and a pair of jeans here on the boat. We don't really have much locker stowage on here."

47

"You can wear your jeans and a t-shirt but bring a swim suit if you have one. We'll pull in at some little bay over there where it's sandy and have a good swim."

Carter went to the beverage cooler, filled a cup with "bug juice" and sat down with the Master Chief and Stevens to wait for his friend.

"So you're a *Porter* sailor, Carter? Heard you guys are in a heap of shit after that collision a couple weeks ago."

"Nothin' we can't handle, Master Chief. Hey we still got this port visit, if we were in really deep shit we would probably still be at sea making race track patterns in the water while the rest of the Battle Group was in port havin' decent liberty. How did you know we were involved in a collision with *Eisenhower* anyway? I thought no one was supposed to know about that 'til the big fact finding is over with."

"We saw it happen, Carter. We were at periscope depth right behind you and *Ike* communicating with the Admiral's staff when it happened. I was Diving Officer of the Watch and Stevens here was standing Chief of the Watch. Our Captain was on the radio telephone just checking in on the net when the OOD let out a yell and the skipper grabbed the periscope from him. Then he ordered a course change so we wouldn't run right up your ass. He and Lieutenant Sweeney saw every bit of it between them."

Stevens added his assessment. "Yeah, Carter and if you think about it the ships that had anything to do with it are all right here in Naples. Maybe that's a coincidence but I doubt it. I'll bet the investigation into the incident is driving all of our port visits this weekend. If you ask me, something is about to happen."

"'Damn, I never thought about it like that. Now that you mention it we had heard we were getting a port visit in some other Italian port, Livorno or something, but it was changed to Naples. Could be you're right, Stevens."

"Well no matter, Carter what's done is done, so you and Mank played football together eh?"

"Yes, Master Chief I was quarterback and he was the best pullin' guard in the state of Iowa for three years runnin'. Made 'All-State' as a sophomore. I can't figure why he didn't go to Iowa on scholarship. I was surprised as hell to find out from my mom that he went into the navy, let alone that he was on this sub!"

"He's been aboard for 10 months now and he's the best damn A-ganger we've got 'cept for Stevens here, of course. He qualified fast and he's an excellent technician. He's our expert on the O2 generator, we couldn't get along without him. So make sure he gets back to us safe and sound."

"I got ya, Master Chief. It's just gonna be a few of the *Porter* crew and a Seaman off *Eisenhower* we went to high school with, Sam Wilson."

Manckowicz stepped around the corner into the Crew's Mess and Carter rose from the bench seat at the COB's table to go with his friend. "See ya later, COB", Manckowicz quipped. "Don't worry, I'll play nice with the skimmers."

"Liberty is up at 0800, Mank. Make sure you're here and ready to work."

"Got it Steve. See ya in the AM."

They left the boat and walked up the molo together. The molo itself teemed with children from families who lived on the sleek looking cigarette boats tied to the quay by the Italian Costa Guardia. "Cigarette" both literally and figuratively. The men who piloted them were in prison for smuggling but their families still lived aboard the impounded vessels. Manckowicz explained to Carter that their briefing officer had warned them that the children were mostly thieves and pickpockets who stole anything they could just to support their families.

They made it to the street gate where an Italian Marine dressed in his blues and armed with a submachine gun dismissively waved them through. When they were on the sidewalk alongside the crowded thoroughfare Carter spoke to his friend, "Seems like they think a lot of you, Ted. That Master Chief said they couldn't get along without you. How do you like it on there?"

"It's good, Ron. A good crew and some top-notch officers. Our Captain just got selected for "real" Captain and he'll probably leave us after we get back to the states but our XO and my boss the Eng are really good too. If we get a new CO that's an asshole it won't really matter, they'll make sure the crew isn't badly treated. How is it on that ship of yours? How big is the crew on one of those tin cans?"

"Well we have about 300 in the crew and I think we have 24 officers. We have an ASW Helicopter so that's extra people in our Air Department. The crew is good, we're pretty tight. Hey we've got our share of no-loads just like any ship does but I don't think we've had a Captain's Mast since we've been in the Med."

"Ron, on *Montpelier* I don't think we've ever had a Captain's Mast." He thought again, "Well since I've been aboard we haven't anyway. We have 118 crew and 14 officers so that means you have more than twice what we have."

They walked along together dodging families and mothers parading along the waterfront with baby buggies and strollers. The traffic noise and the sound of the trolley cars mixed with the calls of the street hawkers who offered every kind of souvenir they could imagine. They dodged a gang of kids offering packs of Marlboros. "Watch out, Ted the briefing officer said that these kids are nothing more than a gang of pickpockets. Better keep your hand on your wallet until we get over to Fleet Landing. Only a couple of blocks to go."

"Yeah, our briefing officer told us that this guy 'Napoli Joe' whoever he is, has thirty fake Rolexes, fifteen on each arm. I guess if you don't want a Rolex he'll sell you his little sister and she's supposed to be a virgin. Can you imagine that? A 70 year old virgin right here in the center of Naples!"

"Hey our briefing officer said we should watch out for the 'campfire girls'. They're supposed to be out along the street by the stadium. They're hookers and at night their pimps throw old tires down by the curb and douse them in gasoline. They burn for hours and the hookers use them to keep warm and as advertising for their business."

"Yeah, Ron we heard all about those campfire chicks too, but the word is that they aren't even women. They're supposed to be 'twinks' and some of 'em are trans ... whatever they are." Manckowicz shuddered as he thought about it.

Carter laughed, "Hey, Ted I don't know but I guess it only costs about fifteen bucks to find out!"

"Get serious Ron, I'm not forkin' over fifteen bucks for any damn hooker no matter what she looks like."

They passed the door of a restaurant and the smells coming from the kitchen reminded them that it was close to lunchtime. Manckowicz stopped to peer in through the big windows. "Maybe we should have stayed and had lunch before we left, Ron. My stomach is rumblin' somethin' awful."

"Don't worry, Ted we'll snag some chow aboard before we set out, I need to get the group together when we get to the ship anyway. One of the guys we're going with is a cook so we should be in good shape. Hey, we're right down over there."

They threaded their way through the jam of cars, scooters and taxi's double and triple parked along the seawall waiting for sailors to hire them. Four or five of the drivers were engaged in a vehement, very emotional discussion waving their hands, wildly gesturing and pointing fingers at each other. The sailors changed their course and made for the break in the stonework that served as a gate to the ancient pier. Carter pointed at the stone pillar they were rounding, "See that, Ted? It's a mark left by a misaimed cannon shot. It's been there since 1798. One of Admiral Nelson's ships laid a shot there when they were rescuing the King and Queen of Naples from the revolutionary mobs. There's a lot of history that happened in this old port."

Manckowicz looked at the broken stonework, "Makes you glad the English were on our side since back then. Well for most of the time anyway. Hey, where are we goin' on this boat trip, I've never heard of this 'Ischia' place? Is it nearby or what?"

"Ted it's the island your boat passed when it came into the Bay of Naples. I don't know how far it is but you can see it right out there. See the big hills and the mountain right there over on the left?"

Carter pointed to the ancient island to the southeast of the Bay. "Supposedly the Roman emperors built palaces and resorts there back in the day. It was their version of Las Vegas. Now get a look over there on the right that's Capri. That crazy emperor Caligula, the one that married his sister and had people killed for the sport of it, his palace is there. There's supposed to be a bunch of thermal spas on those islands, the Romans built fancy baths there too. Lots of volcanic activity here you know."

Manckowicz stepped around a loose coil of hempen rope that lay at the foot of a plank which served as a gangway for a small red and yellow tugboat moored alongside the molo. Small children played a noisy version of blind man's bluff on her stern as the owner's wife casually hung her washing on lines strung between stanchions on her afterdeck. "Look at that, Ron I bet they have less space aboard that tub than I do on *Monty*."

"No kiddin', Ted. Probably the whole family lives aboard. I've heard of that in China and some other Asian places but I guess it's pretty widespread if the Italian boat people do it too. Hey we're there."

The *Porter's* tall stern was rigged with crossed lines holding it fast to bollards on the molo and the steep aluminum brow led up to the Quarterdeck where the watch was stationed. Carter started up the brow with Manckowicz a few steps behind. "Permission to come aboard, Sir?"

The CDO was there instructing the Quarterdeck watchstanders and returned his salute, "Permission granted Petty Officer Carter, who's your friend there?"

"Mr. Wheeler this is my friend Ted Manckowicz we went to high school together he's stationed on *Montpelier*, he's coming with us on the boat trip this afternoon. The XO approved the trip for anyone who wanted to go. I think there are a few others signed up. Did they get that new boat from the support activity yet, the one that the First Lieutenant was talking about?"

"Hello, Manckowicz welcome aboard. Yes, Gleason and Fettes just got back with the new boat it's tied up at the pier but they have to fuel it before the trip. I sent them to chow and if your friend is hungry the cooks can fix you both up before your little trip. We'll muster the liberty boat picnic detail here on the Quarterdeck at 1330. Hand me the sheet, Seaman Zerbel it's right there by the status board."

The Seaman passed him the list, "Let's see," he scanned it quickly; "Looks like you'll be senior man Carter. You'll have MS3 Barton and PN2 Stanfield, Gleason will be your Cox'n and Fettes will be your boat engineer. That's all that have signed up so far. I'll have an announcement made for anyone else not in the duty section that wants to go along to check with me here. Why don't you take Manckowicz and get some lunch? I'll check with Fettes and see how he's doing with the fuel."

"Aye, aye, Sir. C'mon Ted let's see what's for lunch."

They made it to the Crew's Mess a few minutes later, just in time to grab their trays and sit down with the few members of the duty section in the mess. Carter saw Gleason finishing his meal and waved him over to the table he and Manckowicz had claimed.

"Artie, this is my friend Ted Manckowicz, he's coming with us and I ran into someone else I know who's on *Eisenhower*. I told my buddy we'd bring the boat out to their anchorage and Sam could come along with us too. The CDO just told me there are only a few of us going so anytime you and Fettes are ready with the boat I guess we can shove off. He's gonna have an announcement made for any other takers but as far as I know it's just six people including you and Fettes."

Gleason held out his hand to greet Manckowicz." Nice to meet you, man. Yeah, Ron Jimmy finished topping off the fuel before we made it fast to the pier. Should be ready to go as soon as John Barton gets our chow for the picnic all together. I'm headin' up to the Quarterdeck now to report that the boat is all set to Mr. Wheeler. I'll meet you at the boat."

As Carter and Manckowicz finished their meals an MS3 approached their table. "Hey, Ron do you guys still have that big Thermos jug and that ice chest you had when we played the beer ball game in Norfolk last fall?"

"Yeah, John it's down in the Weapons shop. That's a good idea, I'll go get it and you can put our chow in it. Hey this is my friend Ted Manckowicz he's going along with us. Ted this is John Barton he's the best cook we have on board."

Manckowicz and Barton shook hands as Carter continued, "Oh and there's one more too, John we're stopping at the *Eisenhower* and picking Sam up on our way. Make sure we have enough for seven of us okay?"

Carter heard the announcement passed on the 1MC as he was returning from the Weapons shop with the cooler and jug. Barton filled the cooler with pre-pressed hamburgers, hot dogs, and potato salad. He added some ice and put the wrapped packages of buns, a steel grille, kitchen knife, long handled fork and a long spatula inside before closing the lid. Manckowicz filled the jug with water from the scuttlebutt and threw the heavy cooler up on his shoulder. Together they made their way to the Quarterdeck. Gleason and Fettes were there waiting for them and PN2 Stanfield arrived a moment later. Manckowicz thought she was the prettiest woman he had ever seen, she looked like a tiny doll to him. He had seen female sailors before but only ashore, as a submariner he served in a men-only environment, it was almost a shock but he finally remembered that some surface ships had women aboard.

The CDO looked over the group. "Alright troops here's the deal, liberty is up at 0800 tomorrow but the XO told me that he wants to make sure you get back here with the boat by evening colors. That's at 2035 in accordance with SOPA's guide for the day. It's 1340 now so that gives you a little under seven hours to get there, have your swim, picnic and get back here. Carter you're senior so you're in charge. Gleason you're sure the new boat is ready to go?"

"It is, Mr. Wheeler I made sure of that before I even signed for it. We took it for a little underway testing too. I know I pissed off the guy from the support activity because he wanted us gone and I wasn't going anywhere with a boat I wasn't sure was in tip top shape."

"Okay then, got all the safety equipment aboard and it's topped up with fuel right? And where again is this little expedition taking you?"

Carter chuckled, "Mr. Wheeler we're headin' out to Ischia. There's supposed to be some really nice beaches there. Oh, one more thing, Sir. We're stopping off at the *Ike* to pick up one more, a friend from my home town, I didn't even know was in the navy. I ran into Sam this morning up by the SOPA pier office. Don't worry, Sir we'll be back by colors."

"Go ahead then, have a good time and I'll see you all later."

The liberty party made its way off the brow in their dungarees and followed Gleason down the pier to the waiting boat. Fettes and Barton climbed in and Manckowicz passed them the cooler. They put it down forward of the engine compartment near the centerline at the bottom by the keel. Stanfield had brought along a pair of old navy blankets and tucked them under a thwart so they wouldn't blow away. Gleason told them all where to sit to balance the craft and asked Barton to act as Bowhook.

Fettes checked the engine as Gleason started it and it ran just as smoothly as it had on their trip across the bay from the support activity. Gleason shifted the transmission to reverse and nodded to Barton. He slipped the turns off the cleat and took in the line. Gleason backed them clear and steadied them on a course to clear the end of the molo. When he was in open water he cranked the throttle to a comfortable speed and headed toward *Eisenhower's* anchorage.

As the range to the huge ship decreased, Gleason could see the boom rigged to her port side and adjusted course to head for it. Three of her 50 footers were made fast there with the inboard one embarking some of *Ike's* liberty party. Gleason eased alongside the outboard boat and Barton quickly made them fast. Carter jumped out and dodged a few *Ike* sailors as he made his way up the ladder to the Quarterdeck. Gleason shut down the engine, it would probably be a while before Carter could get in touch with his friend and then make their way back to them. He marveled at *Eisenhower's* huge bulk and realized that if the boom had been rigged to her starboard side he would have been able to see where *Porter* had struck her during the glancing collision two weeks ago.

Ike's boat filled quickly as the afternoon liberty goers eagerly clamored in and took their seats amidst good natured banter and happy expectant faces. Gleason counted 42 men and women ready to hit the beach. The *Ike* boat's Cox'n gave Gleason a thumbs up and called out, "Backin' out in 3 minutes, Cox'n I'm on a strict schedule here."

Gleason gave him a nod and a quick hand wave of acknowledgement, before turning to address his own passengers, "Boat's pullin' out soon everyone; could be some wake so hold on. Wish Carter would hurry the fuck up and gather his buddy. We're wasting good beach time."

Ike's 50 footer backed smoothly from the boom and Gleason grudgingly recognized the other Cox'n's skill with a faux salute calling out, "Not bad, not bad at all, Boats."

Moments later Carter and his buddy were clamoring down the accommodation ladder. Gleason looked closely at the 'buddy' and thought, "Goddamn! Not bad, not bad *at all*!"

CHAPTER 6
RENDEZVOUS

"CAREFUL SAM, IT'S A LITTLE slippery along there, I'll have the boat move in alongside." Carter motioned to Gleason and they waited at the base of the ladder as the boat backed away and then edged in to pick them up. Gleason managed the move in moments and idled the engine while Carter stepped aboard, turned and extended his hand to help Wilson embark. She clutched her towels with one hand as she stepped aboard and shifted them to her lap as she sat down on the thwart.

Carter gave Gleason a hand gesture, "Let's go Artie, next stop Ischia. How long should it take us to get there?"

"I talked with the Quartermasters just before I saw you in the mess, it should be an hour to get there. Let me get clear of this big sonofabitch and I'll open her up a little."

He steered well clear of *Ike's* prodigious stern and swung the bow left lining up on the peak on the horizon. He moved the throttle ahead and in moments they were clipping along in the warm late spring air across the flat blue calm of the Bay of Naples. Moderate spray from the bow occasionally splashed up over the gunwale. Wilson pulled her *Eisenhower* ball cap down tightly as the breeze of their passage threatened to lift it off her head. She laughed as the others reached for the bills of their caps too, copying her move.

It was a perfect afternoon. Crystal blue sea, a cloudless sky and a warm wind in their faces. It was the kind of afternoon that friends could share having fun and would remember, for as long as they lived, as one of the best times of their lives. It was the kind of afternoon that caused Chambers of Commerce the world over to quickly call their photographers and capture it for their next brochures.

Carter thought it was time to introduce her to his shipmates, "Everyone this is Sam Wilson. She, Ted and I went to high school together. Sam was a sophomore when Ted and I graduated. She used to date my little brother. I didn't know she had even left Iowa and I ran into her this morning at Fleet Landing. It's pretty strange don't you think? Three people from a town no bigger than a pin prick on the map and we're all in the navy and making a port visit together!"

Stanfield was sitting on the next thwart and held out her hand, "Hello, Sam I'm Dorothy Stanfield a Personnelman, Second Class. I'm one of the six women sailors on *Porter*. It's nice to meet you; what do you do on *Eisenhower?*"

Wilson shook her hand and smiled, "Hi, Dorothy I'm a YNSN. I've been aboard for three months now. When I joined the ship's company there was a problem with a Yeoman who got in trouble and was being processed off the ship. I hadn't even gone into X Division yet, but I got chosen to replace the guy who was in trouble. I had only a few hours to get up to speed on what the Captain had going on, but they made me the Captain's Yeoman and I haven't been fired from the job yet!"

Stanfield laughed, "Ron asked me to go along on this little excursion because he thought you would be more comfortable if another woman was along so I guess you could say that I'm here for moral support. I've been the leading PN on *Porter* for a year now. My rotation date is when we get back from this Med run and I'm putting in for a billet in San Diego. I'll be able to go to college there in my spare time. I'm not sure if I want to make the navy a career but it has been good to me so far. Hey, let me introduce you to the others. I just met Ted here and you know him already but the rest of the *Porter* guys are still strangers to you. This is Jimmy Fettes he's our boat engineer, he's a Fireman."

Wilson leaned over and shook his hand, "Hi, Jimmy it's nice to meet you, where are you from?"

"Hi, Sam I'm from Cincinnati. I went to Engineman "A" school and I got detailed straight to the *Porter*, I've been aboard for a few months."

Stanfield gestured toward Gleason, "Our Cox'n is Artie Gleason. He's one of the old timers aboard he was here a year before me and he's due to make Second Class. If I remember the rating notice it's the end of next month. He'll be a BM2."

Wilson smiled up at Gleason and gave him a little hand wave. He nodded and smiled back. Stanfield gestured toward Barton, "He's John Barton, he's an MS3 and thank goodness he's along with us, he brought the food. We're supposed to have a little cook out later on the beach."

Wilson leaned toward Barton as he took her hand in a brief handshake. "Hi, John where are you from?"

"Hello, Sam I'm from Dallas. Nice to meetcha'."

Gleason grinned down and beckoned for her to come up with him on the Cox'n's flat and join him at the wheel. She climbed up in front of him and he had her grasp the spokes as he stood behind her looking over her shoulder and swaying easily with the motion of the boat as it plowed along, "Ron didn't say you were a girl, he just said 'an old high school friend' and he called you Sam so I assumed you'd be another guy. I sure wasn't expecting you!"

She laughed, "Well, Artie I hope you aren't disappointed. I'm just trying to get along in a navy that's pretty much a man's world, remember women have only been allowed on warships since 1978. I had no idea whatsoever that Ron would be here much less that Ted would be too! It's still pretty hard to wrap my mind around the chances of that happening. I met your other shipmates already but Dorothy didn't tell me much about you other than you are pinning on Second Class next month."

He caught the scent of flowers, either from her shampoo or something she had used on her skin, it disarmed him. "Well I joined the navy right out of high school. I was supposed to go into the army with a friend but my uncle convinced me the navy was a better deal. He was in during the big war and he used to tell me stories about the nights at sea in the Pacific and about hitting the beach with his ship-mates in Hawaii and in Australia. He got me interested in tin cans so I decided to strike for Boatswain's Mate. This is my first ship, I like it aboard. I have a good Chief and a good Division Officer. I'm getting more and more responsibility all the time. The Chief had me turn in our boat that got damaged in the collision and receipt for this one this morning. I come from a little town in Oregon and hey, maybe I'll stay in the navy I know there are lots worse things than this. So, what do you do on that big 'bird farm'?"

She liked the feeling of him behind her, his arms lightly touching hers keeping her steady as they swayed easily with the boat's motion. "I'm just a Yeoman Seaman but I try to do whatever I can for my ship. It's the only ship I've ever been on but I love her and I love my job. I guess I'm pretty lucky, I didn't have to do mess cooking or any of the 'new people' things. I caught a big break when I joined the ship's company, the First Class Yeoman I relieved got caught with drugs and they couldn't get rid of him until someone took over his duties and someone shined the spotlight on me. I only had a short time to learn all the things I would be taking over but I did it and I've kept the Captain happy ever since, he even had me do a big package about the collision two weeks ago."

She wanted to bite her tongue. What had made her say anything about the collision? The last thing in the world she wanted to do was spin up a *Porter* sailor about something as important as whether his Captain could lose his job or not!

He reacted like she would never have expected he might, "I was on the Bridge when that whole thing happened. It was the scariest thing I ever saw! That Russian bastard screamed in on us so fast and so loud I thought the damn thing was gonna come right through the windshield. The Captain was on his side of the Bridge and the OOD was keeping track of the personnel transfer. Maybe if he hadn't been, he would have been able to keep the idiot on the helm from flailing the rudder when the plane made him flinch and stumble backward."

"Well I think the Court of Inquiry is supposed to convene on Monday so it will all be over soon enough." She tried to change the subject, "How far is it to Ischia now Artie?"

"I guess we've been runnin' now about fifteen minutes and that's five miles. So it's about 15 miles to go. We should be there by 1530. We'll have to find a store or something and get some beer, it's gonna be a hot afternoon, I'm thirsty already."

He called to Barton, "Hey, John how 'bout handin' the water jug around I'm thirsty as a camel up here!"

They passed a ferry boat inbound for Naples crowded with cars and passengers. People along the railings looked down and waved to them and the pilot house door opened as the Captain came out to wave too. "How about that, Sam a friendly wave from another sailor! That's one thing I like about the navy and being on the water. Mariners are always friendly and helpful with one another."

She laughed and waved back at the ferry. "Artie what's that other island over there on the right?"

The wake from the ferry rocked them slightly, "I think that one is Capri. The Quartermasters showed me the Port Guide yesterday. It had the information about it. That's where the Roman Emperor's summer palace was."

She looked to the left and pointed to the imposing mountain on the mainland, "Is that Vesuvius?"

"Yeah, the Navigator used it as one of the features for fixes as we were coming up the coast to head in to Naples Bay. I guess it's been dormant since the 1940s but it sure is a beautiful sight."

Eisenhower was still visible but so far off it looked like a tiny gray bug on the surface of the blue water. The ferry wasn't even half a mile past them and she could see the name on its stern, '*ROSA-LINA MIA*' and underneath was her home port 'MARINA GRANDE'. "Isn't that sweet, I bet the owner named the ferry after his wife or his girlfriend."

Gleason looked over his shoulder, "Yeah, lots of the fishing boats are named after women too. And her homeport looks like a woman's name."

They made navy chatter for the next hour and Gleason let her steer the boat as he stood with her watching the island get larger and larger with each passing minute. He could make out buildings on the hillsides now and the tile roofs of the hotels and shops nestled in the cove beyond the point of land jutting out from the main part of the island. There were local fishermen too, bobbing along the shore and taking in their nets for the afternoon. A few had already finished their labors and were headed into the harbor. There were a few cars and the occasional small tour bus on the switchback roads that climbed from the water's edge up the steep verdant slopes. Gleason thought he could see terraced vineyards near some of the white-washed buildings on the sides of the slopes.

As the breakwater came in sight Gleason had her sit down, "Sam I'd better take it from here. There may be traffic in the harbor and I'll have to steer us over to the pier so we can check and find where to head for a good swimming beach and we'll go to a store and get some beer, our cold water thermos is getting pretty low too."

Wilson sat next to Carter again and he felt good about having her with him. He had tried to appear detached when she was standing on the flat with Gleason but the truth was, he was jealous.

They rounded the end of the stone breakwater and Gleason skillfully brought the boat up to the pier across from the ferry slip and right under the window of the little ticket office. Signs printed in Italian directed passenger and auto traffic to and from the ferry landing. The waterfront street was full of locals and tourists browsing the shops and a few people sat outside a restaurant sipping coffee.

Barton jumped to the pier and threw a pair of hitches around a cleat. Gleason shut down the engine and Fettes tilted the inspection cover up to check inside. Carter took over, "Okay everybody half an hour. Let's all use the head in one of the restaurants and I'll go buy us some beer at that little shop over there. Somebody take our Thermos and fill it. Dorothy you speak some Italian don't you? Can you ask a local where a good spot is for us to find a beach for swimming and where we can start a fire for our picnic dinner?"

She laughed, "I took Latin in high school and I think I remember enough so we can find a beach. Sister Mary Joseph would be disappointed if I couldn't."

"Okay then, and could you let the guy there in that little ticket office know that we'll be out of here and he can have his ferry boat dock clear again in half an hour?

She nodded and he turned to the rest of the party, "Everybody meet back here at 1530. Someone needs to stay with the boat so I'll relieve him after I hit the head and buy us some beer."

Wilson smiled, "Ron I have ten dollars I'll contribute it to the beer fund."

She handed him the money and he grinned, "Thanks, Sam. Anybody else wanna pitch in?" He collected forty four dollars and walked off to the shop with Manckowicz.

They returned fifteen minutes later with a case of Peroni, two bottles of local wine, two round loaves of Italian bread and a wheel of cheese. Stanfield came back with a brochure that had a colorful map of the island on its back cover. The helpful waiter at the restaurant had marked it to show a cove where they would find a 'spiaggia splendida'. The others rejoined them and they climbed back into the boat.

Gleason started the engine and signaled Barton to take in their bowline. "Here we go, everyone as soon as that boat gets by we'll head out."

The approaching boat was a gaily painted forty footer with a blue and white striped canopy over the seating area to protect the tourists from the sun. The group of tourists in it were just returning from an early afternoon excursion and talking excitedly in several different languages. Smiles were widespread. The operator waved to the sailors in their gray boat as he passed them close aboard headed to his normal landing spot at the head of the pier.

Gleason waited until the excursion boat was alongside the pier and then backed away. "Here we go for real, people. Hey, Dorothy which direction is that cove from here?"

She looked at the little map and leaned over to show it to Carter. The X the waiter had penciled on it was to the south of the town. "Artie it shows the cove is to the south of here, I guess you should turn left after we clear the harbor."

Carter looked at the little map and found the scale, it showed that the island was only a few kilometers wide. The distance to their 'splendid beach' wasn't far. "Artie it looks like it's only a couple miles south of the breakwater, it shouldn't take us long at all."

Gleason nodded and opened the throttle. They passed the mouth of the harbor and the crystal blue water sparkled invitingly as the boat turned to follow the coast. Their swimming party was only minutes away. This part of the island was sheer cliff overhanging the water. Jagged broken rocks rose from the sea like warning markers and Gleason slowed to pass them safely. It was the classical definition of a 'forbidding shore'.

Carter saw it first and pointed to the break in the cliff base that formed a cut, a narrow channel leading in to a wide strip of white-sand beach. The little opening was invisible from a quarter mile out and they would have the beach totally to themselves.

CHAPTER 7

THIS ISN'T ISCHIA?

GLEASON SLOWED AS HE EDGED the boat forward into the break in the granite wall of the cliff. His passengers could almost reach out and touch the rock sides as they made their way forward into the cove. When he was clear of the cut he gave the engine a quick burst and then shut it down, coasting forward the last few yards to the sand. The boat grounded gently in the shallows and Fettes shut off the fuel.

The crescent-shaped beach was a shelf projecting outward from the sheer wall for ten yards. It was fifty yards long and the fine white sand was the best any of them had ever seen. Polished driftwood lay at the base of the cliff, washed there by the action of the seas.

There was evidence that the beach had been used before and for purposes that were less than lawful. A pile of empty cardboard cartons lay discarded near the back of the sandy shelf. They weren't waterlogged at all, they appeared to be in the same condition as they had been when they were packed and sealed at the factory. There had to be over fifty of them, all with the big red letters spelling out the name of the American cigarette that was the favorite brand of Italy's smokers: 'MARLBORO'.

Smugglers had used this secret cove to break open the big shipping boxes and distribute the familiar red and white cartons to their confederates who took them into Naples and sold the untaxed packages individually. The distribution system was as simple and as ancient as the Neapolitan streets. A young boy or teenager stood at every intersection waving one or two of the distinctive packs and taking the money from drivers who paid two thousand lira rather than the five or six thousand lira which the taxed packs sold for in the Italian state-licensed tobacco stores. Smuggling cigarettes into Italy was big business and this secluded cove apparently played some part in it. Carter worked out the calculus of the situation and hoped the smugglers were long gone.

Stanfield grabbed her blankets, took off her sneakers and stepped out into the ankle deep blue water. She spread the blankets on the sand as the men unloaded the ice chest, the case of beer and the box of food Carter had bought in town. They stripped down to their swimsuits and put their dungarees in the boat where they would stay dry.

Gleason took out his belt knife and whittled a pile of wood chips from a driftwood tree branch so they could start a cook fire. Fettes took out his cigarette lighter and soon they had wisps of smoke rising from the pile. Within minutes they had a crackling fire that would fill the bill for their picnic. Barton took out his grill rack and fit it over the fire propping it up on each end with rocks.

Manckowicz was first, "Hey I thought this was supposed to be swim call!" He splashed out a few yards into the crystal blue water and began to swim along the beachfront. The others joined him and they splashed each other laughing and playing in their private water playground.

"Ron it's too bad we didn't bring a ball along to play with."

"Yeah I know, Ted a good game of water polo or beach volleyball would be fun. Hey I'll race you back to the boat!"

It was a close contest, Manckowicz's powerful arms and shoulders made him a strong swimmer but Carter was no slouch either. They finished in a dead heat.

Wilson laughed, "It's just like old times seeing you two guys working out together. I remember watching you on the football field and wondering where you both would go to college. Gosh you were both my big heroes back then!"

Carter grinned and slapped Manckowicz on the back, "This big guy was the key to our whole offense. When he pulled and led the charge around end there wasn't a team in our whole conference that could stop us. He could have gone to any school in the Big Ten and been a starter as a freshman. Instead he's a 'knuckle dragger' on a submarine. But, his Command Master Chief told me he's the key to the sub's offense too! They wouldn't be able to breath without him."

Manckowicz blushed from the praise, "Hey, I just do the job they gave me. Same as anybody else in the navy."

"Not true Ted," Wilson grinned at him. "I always thought you were pretty special."

They all gathered on the blankets to rest and dry off after the swim. Stanfield took the little tourist brochure and opened it to check out the island's features. She could make out most of the Italian words and she began describing things to her companions. "It says here the 'Grotto Azzuro' is one of the principle sights on the island. That's Italian for 'Blue Grotto' and people can ride a boat into the cave when the sea conditions allow. You transfer from a bigger boat into a tiny rowboat and the guide rows you into the cave. I think that boat with the blue and white canopy we saw when we were leaving the harbor is the boat that takes visitors to the grotto."

"Dorothy what other things are special here on the island?"

"Let me see Artie," she flipped to the next page. "It says the palace of the Emperor Caligula is open for visitors in the summer from nine o'clock 'til five in the afternoon and the grounds and play-ing fields are open all year round."

Carter and Gleason exchanged looks, "Artie what the Hell is this? I thought you checked everything out with the Quartermasters just before we got underway. This has got to be Capri not Ischia!"

"Holy shit you're right, Ron. That ferry boat had 'Marina Grande' on her counter that must be that seaport town we stopped in when we first got here. Jesus don't I feel like an idiot, we're on the wrong damned island!"

Stanfield joined the discussion, "Well, Mr. almost-a-Second-Class-Boatswain's-Mate you get high marks for getting us here safely but you surely bilged the figure-out-where-to-go part of the equation. I guess there's no real harm though, one island is as good as another as far as I'm concerned."

Carter shook his head, "I should have caught it before, I was too busy shootin' the shit with Ted. This makes us all look stupid, not even getting to the right place. Oh what the Hell, lets break out the Peronis and have a cool one. Who wants a beer?"

Barton looked up from checking his fire, "There's a church key hanging on the side of the cooler. Hey, Ron it's no big deal, we had permission to use the boat this afternoon. Who cares if we went to Capri instead of Ischia? So it was a couple of miles further away, so what? It just gave the new boat a better workout. Nobody has to know we were really going to one island and ended up on another. Who did we hurt?"

Carter shrugged, "I guess you're right. We didn't kill anybody and we didn't break anything or any rules. Even better, we have this - what was the word Dorothy; 'splendida' - beach all to ourselves."

Barton picked up his long fork and stirred the charred wood at the base of the fire, "The fire is hot enough to cook now so what do you wanna do, Ron? We could eat now or swim for another hour and eat then, your call."

"John put some more wood on and we'll swim for a little while more. Then we'll eat and have enough time to relax for a bit before we have to field day the place and make our retreat to the boat and we can head back." He checked the time on his wristwatch, "It's 1630 so let's swim 'till 1715 and eat then. That gives us plenty of time to square away and head back to Naples. We'll have to drop Sam off so I'm allowing a few minutes for that before we make the run from *Ike's* anchorage to Fleet Landing."

Stanfield pulled out her little transistor radio and fiddled with the frequency knob trying to pick up some music. Most of the dial was filled with static and she switched from AM to FM. That was better but the only music she could find was an opera, a tenor singing sweetly something that must be a love song. She quickly turned it off before her friends could complain.

Manckowicz surprised her, "Hey, Dorothy that's alright I kind of like opera music. My uncle is an opera buff and he taught me a little bit about it. That was from *Carmen* it's called 'the flower song', I think that was Pavarotti. The songs are pretty cool and some of the greatest love stories of all time are the librettos."

Wilson giggled, "Ted that's the most incredible thing I can imagine! You're such a big, tough, gruff looking guy and to hear you talk about operas and love stories is just so directly opposite from what I picture about you! I can remember seeing you all muddy and bloody after those home games and then seeing all the senior girls gushing because they all had crushes on you, the big famous football star. You even had your own car! Do you have any idea how many times I wished you would ask me out? I was the poor little sophomore girl just trying to make it onto the cheerleading squad and you never even knew I existed. God I can't believe I'm actually telling you this but it's true!"

Carter laughed, "C'mon, you two lets swim before it's too late and we have to call it a day."

Afterward they gathered on the blankets and Barton pulled out the paper plates. He cooked up the hot dogs and hamburgers and they ate hungrily.

Fettes laughed, "Hey, John how come we never get chow like this on board? It seems to me that this is the first medium rare burger I've ever seen from *Porter's* galley and this potato salad is as good as anything my grandma ever served!"

"It's the fire man." He started laughing, "Fire man, Fireman Fettes! It adds flavor. Aboard the ship all we've got is electric stoves. You can't get to the flavor of an open fire with an electric stove. Hey if the Supply Officer would let us we'd grill on the fantail and then you'd see some real burgers!"

Wilson picked up her towel and began drying her hair, rubbing briskly at her short blonde curls. "Hey, Dorothy do they have a decent hairstylist on *Porter* or do you get your hair cut ashore?"

"Sam it's one of our biggest problems aboard and I don't know how to fix it. The Ship's Servicemen can cut the men's hair just fine but we six women have to cut our own. I usually trim one or two of the girls and Chief Kahl trims mine but it's a hassle and it probably won't get fixed until a woman actually takes over and becomes the first CO and makes it a priority. In port it's no problem of course but it's been two months and I'm tired of feeling shaggy and pretty soon the XO or the Admin Officer is gonna yell at me."

Wilson offered, "We've got a pretty strong Ship's Serviceman's group. There are a couple of really great hairdressers in our barber shop. Hey, why don't you come and get a haircut on *Ike* before we get underway next week! It would be fun, I'll show you around and you can see my own 'private office' and meet my boss and we can have lunch and everything!"

Manckowicz jumped in, "On *Monty* we've got nothin'. No Ship's Servicemen and no trained barbers. If I want a haircut I have to sit on a stool in the crew's head and the COB waves a clipper over my head. Pretty rudimentary if that. Hey, Sam can I come on *Ike* and get a haircut too? I'll even belt out a chorus from *The Barber of Seville* if I can get a decent haircut!"

She laughed at the thought, "Sure, Ted come aboard and I'll set it up for you! I know a certain Ship's Serviceman who would love to get her fingers in that blonde mop of yours!"

Barton finished wrapping up the few uneaten hamburgers and hot dogs and put them back in the ice chest. They collected the paper plates and empty beer bottles and put them in a plastic bag ready to drop in the trash when they got back to Naples. The fire had died down and they heaped sand on the coals. The grill rack was lying in the sand and had cooled enough to be put into the ice chest with the leftovers.

Carter looked over the area and saw that it looked almost like they had found it, only the charred remains of the little fire and some footprints by the water's edge gave evidence anyone had even been there since the smugglers had made their cardboard heap. "Okay, Artie let's get started back. We still have half the beer and both bottles of wine but we can polish off the beer on the ride back. John can give us the bread and cheese on the way too. It sure was a great swim call!"

"Alright, Ron it'll only take a second. Jimmy let's get her started and we'll push her off the shoal before we board everyone."

Fettes clamored over the gunwale, stepped to the stern and checked the oil level in the engine before opening the fuel cock. He gave Gleason a thumbs up as he climbed onto the Cox'n's flat. "Here we go, firin' her up."

Gleason hit the starter button and held it for five seconds. During that space of time one spark occurred; not the starter, it refused even a feeble attempt to spark. The spark was in his mind, when he realized they were in big trouble.

"Jimmy check the battery and make sure the connections are good." He turned to look at Carter standing over on the sand. "This thing ran like a champ from the time we picked her up this morning until now so I'm hoping it's just something that vibrated loose on our way over here."

Carter nodded, "Okay, Artie can we help you do anything?"

"Don't know, Ron let Jimmy look over the electrical system."

Manckowicz waded out alongside the boat and leaned over the gunwale to give Fettes a hand. "You got some tools aboard, Jimmy?"

"Tool box is under that thwart, Ted."

Manckowicz pulled himself into the stern of the boat and opened the box. "Empty as shit, Jimmy."

Gleason heard the exchange and fear raced through his neurons with the speed of light. "How's it look Jimmy?"

"I pulled on all the wires and the ground seems tight. The battery looks brand new. Try turning it over again, Artie."

Gleason knew what would happen before he even pushed the

start button. The silence that followed broadcast to the others the seriousness of their situation.

Carter waded out alongside the boat and looked into the engine compartment to see for himself. The engine looked newly painted and there was no oily smell. "What's the verdict, guys?"

Fettes was leaning over the balky hunk of iron sitting coldly in its housing. He had a blank look on his face and to Carter he looked confused and frustrated. "I don't know what it is, Ron we have plenty of fuel and everything looks okay it just isn't getting any juice from the battery, has to be a problem in the wiring harness."

Carter looked at his wristwatch; 1830. He could recall Ensign Wheeler's instructions, they had an hour and five minutes until evening colors when they had to be back. He knew that wasn't possible. Even if they got the engine going in the next five minutes, there wasn't time to make the run back to Fleet Landing. Worse, it would be dark shortly afterward. Fettes and Manckowicz wouldn't be able to work on the failed wiring harness.

"Artie let's get everyone together up on the beach; we can figure out what we've got."

The men waded back to the sand and Carter sat them all down in a circle near the dead fire. "Okay everybody here's the problem as I see it. First the boat has a problem and we can't get it started. We're stuck here in this cove until we can fix it and head back or until someone comes and helps us. There's no way we'll be able to get back tonight. It will be dark in an hour and a half and we'll need to make ourselves comfortable here overnight. Let's all gather up everything we have, in the boat and amongst us, and see what we have to work with. Dorothy you be in charge of the collection. John, better see if we can get another fire going. We still have some water and beer but we better ration the rest of the food. It will get to be real hungry around here by breakfast time."

Stanfield spread a blanket and they piled everything on it. The second blanket, a first aid kit, two battle lanterns, some plastic boat bumpers, two pocket knives, nine damp towels, a dozen life preservers, a small flare gun with two red flares, one portable bridge-to-bridge radio, Stanfield's transistor radio, Barton's kitchen knife, long handled spatula, fork and grill rack, their sneakers, dungarees, hats, a hairbrush, half a roll of paper towels, a fire extinguisher and a tube of red lipstick. They had seven dollars and eleven hundred lira between them.

Barton inventoried the remaining food, "We have four hamburgers, six hot dogs, a couple pounds of potato salad, some buns, two loaves of Italian bread, and the round of cheese. The ice in the chest is mostly melted but everything should keep 'til morning."

Wilson counted the remaining beers, "Ron there's one for each of us with two leftover. The Thermos is half full of water and we have the two bottles of wine."

Carter had already looked over the beach site and concluded that they couldn't climb their way out of the rock cove. The walls slanted inward making their beach haven a wide crescent-shaped chimney with its vent 60 feet above the sand. Any attempt to climb it in their sneakers would be doomed to failure. Even if they had climbing equipment it would be a tough climb.

Gleason tried the bridge-to-bridge radio, "Any station this net, this is *USS Porter* motor whaleboat number one, over."

There was no response except for static. Either no one was listening or the sides of their rock prison interfered with their transmission. Gleason tried every channel for fifteen minutes and then turned it off to save the battery.

CHAPTER 8

POTABLES

WILSON NEEDED TO GO TO the head, "Dorothy, I don't know about you but I need to go pee. Ron can the women's head be down there past the boulder and that big driftwood tree trunk?"

"Good idea, Sam. It's pretty dark you'd better take one of the battle lanterns with you. Dorothy you wanna go with her just in case?"

She nodded, "Yeah, Ron I'll go along and while we're there I'm taking off this wet swimsuit and putting on my dungarees."

Wilson picked up her dungarees too and they started off down the beach together, the battle lantern's beam swaying and undulating with their movements.

The fire had been rebuilt carefully and a stack of splintery driftwood was nearby so they could keep it going all night. Carter took off his wristwatch and hooked it around the handle of the second battle lantern. "Alright here's the plan. We share the blankets and towels. We'll split the night into regular watches rotating alphabetically. The watch will have this battle lantern and my wristwatch. Every hour on the hour the watch will attempt to contact help on the bridge-to-bridge radio. Artie you teach everyone how to use it correctly. Call for 5 minutes and then secure it to save the battery. Also he'll stoke up the fire when it gets low, everyone got it? In case there's anything wake me up, okay?"

There was a chorus of understanding voices pierced by a woman's shriek from the far end of the beach. The men got up and began running toward the scream. Carter was yards from the frantically waving light beam when he made out Stanfield on her hands and knees, sneaker in hand wildly flailing at the sand. Wilson was holding the battle lantern trying to point the beam at the action. "Kill it! Kill it Dorothy!" Wilson screeched, "It's horrible. Oh, Ron, Ted it's an ugly thing. It was in Dorothy's shirt and it bit her!"

They saw that Stanfield's dungaree shirt was flung on the sand and she was naked from the waist up, her breasts bobbling as she flailed away wildly with her sneaker. There was a wound on her abdomen and the culprit was trying to make an escape, scuttling away toward the water's edge. It was a five-inch sand crab which had made its way into her shirt as it lay on the sand.

Carter played the beam of his battle lantern over the wound, "Dorothy let the sonofabitch go! C'mon get your shirt on and I'll put some antiseptic on that and get a bandage on you. You okay otherwise? How about you, Sam are you okay?"

Wilson nodded and stooped to pick up their swimsuits.

Manckowicz picked up the dungaree shirt and handed it to Stanfield. "Thank you, Ted." She shuddered as she shook it out, put it on and buttoned it. "That ugly little monster scared the living daylights out of me!"

They walked back up the beach toward the fire together, Carter leading the way with his battle lantern. "Jesus, Dorothy when you screamed like that I was sure some shark had snuck into the cove and bitten your leg off! You scared me out of a year's growth!"

She dropped down on her blanket, "My stars I was so scared. I'm sorry everyone I didn't mean to be such a baby but that really scared me and it hurt me too!"

She started to cry as Gleason got the first aid kit open and dug out the tube of antiseptic. Manckowicz knelt next to her, held her and patted her shoulder as if she were a hurt puppy. She rose to her knees and he hugged her, consoling her as her tears wetted the sleeve of his t-shirt. "Oh, Ted it hurt me," she sobbed.

"It's okay, Dorothy," he whispered as he stroked her hair, "I'm here now. I'll take care of you don't worry. Please don't cry"

She stopped sobbing eventually and Gleason checked her wound with the battle lantern. It was a two-inch-long jagged cut that was bleeding superficially. He dabbed some of the antiseptic on the cut and covered it with a pair of band aids. She let go her hold on Manckowicz's arm. "Thanks, Artie. Thank you, Ted. I feel better now but I'm still a little shaky. Ron what happened to that bottle of red wine? I could use some after the evening I just had!"

It was pitch dark by then but the fire cast a glow all around and they could make out each other resting on the blankets. Fettes used the corkscrew blade on his Swiss army knife and pulled the cork on the first bottle of wine. He wiped the rim on the sleeve of his shirt and passed it to Stanfield. "Here you go, Dorothy."

She took it from him and tilted it back taking a healthy swig of the sweet fruity wine. "Whew! This is wonderful stuff." She took another pull at the bottle. "Mmm I love this wine and I deserve a good drink after giving all you guys a free look at my boobs!"

She passed the bottle to Wilson as the men convulsed with laughter.

Wilson took a swig and began laughing too. The wine dribbled out of her nostrils. "Dorothy! Look what you made me do! Now I'll have to wash my shirt!"

Barton chuckled, "And a great look it was too, Dorothy!"

It made them all laugh even harder. It wouldn't become politically incorrect for sailors to make those kinds of comments for another decade or so.

Barton turned down his pull at the bottle, he had the first watch. They passed it around until it was empty and Fettes opened the second one. When it was gone they were all ready for sleep.

"RON WAKE UP IT'S TIME for your watch." Barton handed him the battle lantern and wristwatch. "Nothing on any of the channels on the bridge-to-bridge when I made the calls and I didn't see any lights passing the mouth of the cove. It's a starry night and I haven't heard any noises other than the wind and the surf breaking out there." He gestured to the outline of the cut in the outer cliff wall. Carter could see stars on the horizon outside the tunnel it made.

"There's still plenty of firewood, Ron. Everyone else is asleep."

"Thanks, John get some shuteye it's sure to be a long day tomorrow."

Carter got up and put some dry driftwood on the fire. He walked to the boat and sat on the bow, turned on the bridge-to-bridge with the help of his battle lantern and made the calls. Not one resulted in a reply. He turned it off just as footsteps approached him. "Ron, it's me Sam."

"Sam you should be catching some ZZs. I just told John it's going to be a long day tomorrow. Jesus, I feel terrible getting you involved in this. Now you're missing from your ship too and it's all my fault. I should have checked with the Quartermasters myself and I should have had them give us a chart!"

"Ron stop blaming yourself, it was only a mistake is all."

"You don't see it do you, Sam? Because everyone thinks we went to Ischia, that's where they will start looking for us. We can't raise anyone on the bitch box and the only local who can even help them find us is the waiter Dorothy talked to this afternoon. This could really get out of control and we're all in it together. This stupid trip for fun could be a disaster with far-reaching effects."

"Ron listen to me. You are not to blame for this. This disaster you think you have is nothing compared to the problem we have in the Battle Group. Two Captains stand the chance of losing their commands and their careers. Even worse I'm not there to help get my Captain ready for the Court of Inquiry. I know he'll need my help to finish everything and I'm not there to help him!"

She began to cry and he put his arms around her. "Don't cry Sam. We'll get something going in the morning. If push comes to shove I'll swim out and find a fishing boat."

"Oh, Ron I know something will happen but not tomorrow, it's Sunday. All the fishermen will be in church in the morning. In the afternoon they'll all be having their big family dinners." She had learned a lot from Chief Berg.

"It's okay, Sam please don't cry. I'll think of something," and then he kissed her ... and she did stop crying.

CHAPTER 9
MORNING QUARTERS

"ENSIGN WHEELER THIS IS THE Quarterdeck Watch, you wanted to be called if the motor whaleboat wasn't back by 2035, and there's no sign of it yet, Sir."

"Thank you, any sign of the Captain or the XO yet?"

"No, Sir I'll announce him when he comes up the pier."

"Very well."

Wheeler turned back to the other three officers sitting in the wardroom with him, "Damned idiots went off to Ischia this afternoon and I told them to be back by now, I'll have their asses if they aren't back by quarters in the morning. Whose deal is it?"

The XO returned at 2200 and Wheeler told him that the boat hadn't come back as he had directed.

"That's just great, Mr. Wheeler. Who was in charge and who went along in the party?"

"Gunner's Mate Carter was in charge, XO and there were four others, wait a minute though Carter had a friend with him from one of the other ships, Manckowicz I think his name was, he was from the *Montpelier*."

"Well there's nothing we can do about it tonight. They're all probably still picnicking. We'll see where we stand in the morning. Do we have a way to contact *Montpelier?* It would be a good thing to let them know this Manckowicz is among the missing."

"Gee, XO I don't know let me see if there is a shore phone listing. If not I'll try to get ahold of them through the SOPA Duty Officer."

"No don't do that, if you can't call them on the phone try getting them on the secure radio."

"Aye, aye, Sir." Wheeler found that there was no telephone listing for a submarine in the SOPA phone listings and the Duty Radioman was unable to raise them on the secure radiotelephone. The XO told him he would take care of it in the morning.

AT 0800 THE DUTY CHIEF on *Montpelier* picked up the 1MC, "Divisions muster on station, make all muster reports to Control."

The Chief of the Boat listened to the reporting stations' calls and shook his head. "We're gonna have a problem, guess I should go find the XO with the bad news."

"What the Hell do you mean Manckowicz isn't back from a boat trip! What boat trip, COB?"

"He went with a friend of his from *Porter,* XO I met the guy, a Gunner's Mate and he said they were taking a friend named Sam with them, from the *Eisenhower.* The Topside Watch overheard them say something about going over to Ischia for a swim."

"Let the Engineer know he's missing, COB that O2 generator isn't going to be ready to support underway and we've got a big problem. I'll go let the Captain know."

The XO went to the wardroom with the bad news just as the Captain was finishing his breakfast.

Commander Cushman thought for a moment and turned to the Duty Officer, "Brad check the SOPA Manual. I'll bet there's a specific procedure dealing with sailors missing from multiple ships and we'd better get the report out as soon as possible. I'll give the Submarine Group Headquarters a call and let them know too."

"Aye, aye, Captain." Lieutenant Akers pulled out the SOPA Manual and found the number to call and made the report specified to the SOPA Duty Officer. It was 0815 and *Montpelier's* was the first report of the problem.

BMSN HOLDEN GOT OUT OF her bunk and pulled on her uniform. She saw that her friend Wilson's bunk hadn't been slept in, her little brown and white stuffed cow was right there in the center of her pillow, and she was worried. It wasn't like Sam to miss anything and she remembered seeing her going ashore and coming back aboard to give Bad Billy his money. Hadn't she also gone with the sailors from that tin can that had collided with them? She called the Admin Office and asked for Chief Thomas. The Yeoman who answered said he would have the Chief call her back when he came in after his late morning breakfast.

At 0811 Holden answered the compartment phone. Two minutes later Chief Thomas passed the word to the CDO that they might have a missing sailor problem. Five minutes after that Captain Christensen was made aware of the fact that his favorite Captain's Yeoman was among the missing. "Thank you Commander, send everyone who knows anything about this to me in the Captain's Mess and call the SOPA Duty Officer right away."

In the meantime he called the Battle Group's Chief of Staff to let him know what was amiss, he knew the Admiral was still in London and wouldn't return until Tuesday. At 0823 *Eisenhower's* report informed the SOPA Duty Officer that the problem was bigger than he had originally thought.

PORTER'S CDO WAS HAVING BREAKFAST with the XO when the shore phone rang and the nice quiet Sunday morning they both had planned went to Hell in a hand basket. "This is the SOPA Duty Officer. There are reports from *Montpelier and Eisenhower* of men missing and they indicate that *Porter* has one or more missing men and a ship's boat missing as well. Come up on the secure harbor net and report your personnel status."

Lieutenant Commander Marlowe put down his knife and fork, "Mister Wheeler wake the Captain, I'll call the SOPA Duty Officer."

Porter's report came in at 0858 and it made the Duty Officer at SOPA's command center want to shoot somebody.

BY 0930 SOPA HAD BEEN informed. Admiral Winstead was 'triple hatted', as Commander Fleet Air Mediterranean (COMFAIRMED) he was responsible for all the Navy Air in the Mediterranean as CTF 63, he also oversaw all Coordinated Anti-Submarine Warfare in theatre as CTF 67 and of course he was SOPA. He was at home in his villa high on the hillside overlooking the Bay of Naples and his Watch Officer's call spoiled his plans for the day. He quickly digested the information and it was apparent that there were gaps in it. "Bill let's have the COs of the three ships assemble at the Headquarters, I'll be there as soon as I can drive in.

We'll lay out a plan to conduct a thorough search of the bay and the environs. Get the Fleet Weather Central guys to give us the tide and current data and the predictions for the next week. It's just not acceptable for seven sailors to be missing. Make all preparations for a full scale search and rescue. Get the VP Squadron in Sigonella on the hook. Launch the ready unit and have it search the area seaward of Ischia and Capri for the next six hours. I want every craft bigger than a fuckin' shingle overflown, plotted and identified. We're gonna find those sailors, and we're gonna find them today!"

"Aye, aye, Sir!" The Watch Officer hung up the local phone and turned to his watch team. Ketchmark start your plot. Chief Benevides get me a secure connection with *Montpelier, Porter, Eisenhower and* Sigonella Ops!*"

"Aye, aye, Sir" The response was almost in stereo as the young sailor and the grizzled Chief got to work.

"Commander I have Sig Ops on the hook."

"Very well," the Watch Officer took the handset and keyed it, "Six Three Two this is Six Three ...." Four minutes later the Opera-

tions Officer of VP 44, the Patrol Squadron at Sigonella, had his marching orders and fifteen minutes later the first P-3C Orion was taxiing to the runway. When airborne, Papa Two Yankee was vectored to a search area that covered the Tyrrhenian Sea between the "toe" of Italy's "boot" at Reggio Calabria and the "shin" at Civitavecchia. He would fly at 2000 feet and conduct a rigorous visual surface search for the motor whaleboat. They would be working for CTF 63 on this mission instead of their usual CTF 67, but since both were the same Admiral it probably didn't make a difference. The Ops Officer just hoped it wouldn't get more confusing.

"Sir, I have the three ships on harbor secure."

"Thank you, Chief," he picked up the handset, "Six one point numeral, this is Six Three, Admiral Winstead requires your attendance at Six Three Headquarters for a search coordination meeting as soon as possible. All units acknowledge."

"Six Three this is Six One Point One. Roger out."

"Six Three this is Six One Point Five. Roger out."

"Six Three this is Six One Point Seven. Roger out."

COMMANDER CUSHMAN PUT THE HANDSET back in its cradle and turned to his XO. "Thank God we were first to report this fuckin' flap XO. Get the Duty Driver for me I want to be first getting to the Headquarters. I'll take the Ops Officer with me."

COMMANDER GAVIN CAME OUT OF his stateroom and ordered his XO to get *Porter's* Duty Driver ready to take him to COM-FAIRMED's Headquarters. "I want you to come with me and get the Ops Officer too. I want to leave in 5 minutes."

CAPTAIN CHRISTENSEN CALLED THE FLAG Watch Officer and informed him that he was on his way to COMFAIRMED's

Headquarters momentarily. The Flag Watch Officer thanked him and asked to be kept appraised of the situation. As the Captain was grabbing his hat to leave his phone rang. It was the Chief of Staff, he wanted to go along and would meet him at the Quarterdeck.

Eisenhower's gig got underway 5 minutes later with both Captains embarked. The flag sedan was waiting for them at Fleet Landing.

ADMIRAL WINSTEAD WALKED INTO HIS COMFAIRMED OPCON center where the three ship Captains and the Battle Group Chief of Staff were already assembled. The Watch Officer reported that Papa Two Yankee had just arrived on station and so far had not found any sign of *Porter's* missing motor whaleboat. He briefed them on the weather data and the tide and current information he'd received from the Fleet Weather Center.

The Admiral cleared his throat, "How long has the boat been missing and who are the men in it?"

Commander Gavin began, "The boat left at about 1330 yesterday with 5 of my people and a Petty Officer from *Montpelier* aboard. I'm told his name is Manckowicz. My people were Gleason, the Cox'n and Fettes the boat engineer. Also one of my Gunner's Mates, Carter, a cook Barton and a Second Class Personnelman a woman named Stanfield."

The Admiral was aghast, "Don't tell me we have a woman to find too! This will be headline stuff and I don't want to mess this up."

Captain Christensen winced, "Admiral it's worse than that. My missing Seaman is a woman too, her name is Samantha Wilson and she's my Yeoman and a Cracker Jack sailor. Apparently *Porter's* boat picked her up yesterday at about 1400. GM2 Carter came to my Quarterdeck and collected her to go along with him. He told my OOD that they were going to Ischia on an authorized swimming and picnicking excursion."

The Admiral looked like someone had just run over his favorite dog. "Insanity! This keeps getting worse and worse. The Goddamn press is gonna have a field day with this if it gets out that we screwed this thing up. If one hair on one of those women's heads is so much as mussed up every damn one of us is gonna get his ass handed to him in two inch boldface and no matter what the facts are we'll be lynched for sure."

The Watch Officer interrupted them, he was holding a message blank in his hand. "Admiral I'm drafting an OPREP-3 to put the chain-of-command in the know, Sir. I'll have you chop it when it's ready to go. I think we should just state the facts and what we're doing about it."

"Good, Lieutenant. Don't put in the names in the initial message. We'll add that when we have some search data to report."

"Aye, aye, Sir."

The Battle Group Chief of Staff had an idea, "Admiral I'd like to take over responsibility for the search. I'll have my Air Group Commander coordinate with Sigonella for the long range search effort, but I have a whole helo squadron sitting on *Ike* and they could be off the deck and searching in twenty minutes. We'll break Naples Bay into search areas and fly so low we'll be able to identify the *Porter's* boat by reading the name on its side."

The Admiral thought for a second, "Ray that's a good idea. I'll provide the backup you need from Sig and from here in Naples. You've really got more assets than I do anyway for this kind of search. You are hereby designated the Officer in Tactical Command, I'll continue to exercise OPREP responsibility until Admiral Townsend returns from London. When do you expect him anyway?"

"He's due back on Tuesday evening, Sir and we're slated to get underway Wednesday morning."

"Got it. Thanks, Ray. Anyone have anything else." He looked at the COs. Commander Cushman spoke up, "Yes, Sir my Third Class Machinist's Mate Manckowicz is vital to the operation of *Montpelier* I don't think I can get underway without him. He's the guy that makes our O2 generator run and without that I'm not capable of sustained submergence."

The Admiral shook his head, "The shit just gets deeper and deeper doesn't it!" He looked at Commander Gavin, "You have any magical equipment that can't run without your five sailors, Commander? By the way, when did you first discover that your boat was missing?"

Commander Gavin looked at his XO, "The Petty Officer in charge was ordered to bring the boat back by 2035 last night, Admiral."

The icy silence following that statement was the longest moment in Commander Gavin's career.

"Do you mean to tell me that they've been missing for over fifteen hours already?" The Admiral was visibly angry over that piece of information and he scowled at *Porter's* officers, then he turned to the OTC. "Ray I'll bring out another P3, our primary search area just got one Hell of a lot bigger."

"Thank you, Admiral. Can I ask your Watch Officer to put me through to my Flag Watch Officer and *Ike*? I'm gonna scramble the helo squadron and they'll need every man and every minute to shift the flight deck around to get off the deck." He looked at Captain Christensen, "Chris I'm sorry, this is going to screw up *Ike's* liberty big time."

"Don't worry about that, Ray one of mine is out there lost too. Hey if you need them, I'll give you my gig and all my boats. My boats don't get lost and they don't break down." He shot Commander Gavin and his XO a sour look.

The Watch Officer gestured for the Chief of Staff to join him at the radiotelephone. "The Flag and *Ike* are up sir."

THE CHIEF OF STAFF SPOKE for only fifteen seconds giving his crisp orders and put the phone down after they were acknowledged. Then he turned to his ship Captains. "I want you all to guard the tactical nets both secure and clear voice 'til this thing is over and when it is, no matter how it turns out, I'll see you all again at the green table. Now let's go find our sailors."

Captain Christensen rode back to Fleet Landing in the Flag sedan with the Chief of Staff. They were friends who had served together several times before. Captain Mallory started first, "Something happened on *Porter* last night for the word not to be passed along and I'm going to find out what it was. And if it turns out to be another people problem on top of the collision fiasco I'm going to make it my personal business to roll some heads."

"Ray I don't know, but there was something unsaid between the CO and his XO. Hey, I'm staying out of it, I've got my own problems. My Yeoman went ashore to work on my Court of Inquiry package and I'll bet she ran into that *Porter* Gunner's Mate who came to get her. One of my other Seamen told me she went to high school with him. If anything has happened to her I'll … ." He didn't finish his sentence.

The sedan pulled up to Fleet Landing and the Captains could see that *Eisenhower* was already a beehive of activity. Her forward elevator was lowering a gray jet. The Air Boss was moving it out of the way to make room on the flight deck for the helos, their hope of the day. The gig was running and the Cox'n smartly got them away from the molo and cranked up the speed as soon as he could. They made it back to the boom in half the normal time and the two Captains took the ladder two steps at a time.

The CDO and the Flag Watch Officer were both waiting on the Quarterdeck when they arrived and it took only moments to bring them up to speed. They would be able to launch the first helo in 5 minutes and then one every ten minutes until all 8 of the working Sea Kings were airborne. They had recalled every man in HSL-87. The helo squadron's liberty was cancelled.

The Chief of Staff invited Captain Christensen to join him in Flag Plot where the Operations Officer would direct the search. "Thanks, Ray I'll be up as soon as I pull the string on something. I'll be there soon."

He took the CDO aside, "Round up all the sailors who were with me in the mess this morning and have them meet me there again at 1300."

CHAPTER 10
THE SONOFABITCH

IT WAS LIGHT ENOUGH FOR them to see by 0630 and Gleason awoke thinking how totally screwed he was. He had the duty this morning and he was sure Chief Groves would be pissed off to the max. Instead of triumphantly showing him the gleaming new motor whaleboat and impressing him with his mature and responsible handling of the boat exchange the Chief would see that he hadn't made sure the new one was reliable. He was sure he could kiss his new Second Class crow a fond, foiled and fucked farewell.

Carter awoke at first light with mixed feelings. Nothing in his navy training or his life experiences equipped him to deal with this situation. On the one hand he was the senior man and responsible for the lives and fortunes of everyone here. On the other he was so crazy about the pretty blonde Seaman sleeping at the other end of the blanket he didn't know what to do. How would he be able to get all these sailors to safety, let alone back to their ships; and how would he be able to get her to love him as much as he loved her?

Barton opened the ice chest and found that the ice had all melted and there was only water left inside. The package of meat was floating in it and the bread was sitting on top of the package of meat. He had the wheel of cheese separate. Breakfast would be pretty meager for all of them. "Ron what do you want to do about our rations? I have enough meat for everyone to have a burger or a dog and there's a portion of potato salad apiece. There's bread and cheese too."

"John let's hold off on chow until noon, we'll give everyone something then and we'll crack open the rest of the Peronis. We'll save the bread and cheese for tonight if we have to. I'm hoping they can get the damn boat running this morning and we can have evening chow on something that's big and gray and not underway."

Barton chuckled, "Okay Ron, I'll pour off the water into our Thermos, the ice is gone."

Carter turned to Gleason, "Artie as soon as it's light enough to see good we need to find the problem with the engine and fix it if we can."

"I know, Ron. As soon as the sun is high enough I'll have Jimmy take the whole cowling off. Dammit I just wish I had looked in the toolbox when I signed for the boat yesterday."

Gleason was able to start the inspection of the engine at 0900. The sun's angle grazed the opening above the cliffs and bathed the boat in its rays. Fettes and Manckowicz worked together going over every inch of the engine compartment, talking in low voices as they wiggled every piece of wiring and felt every connector. It was almost noon when Fettes finally called out the diagnosis to Gleason.

"Artie here's the problem, I think the sonofabitch wiring harness is fried! Looks like it all melted down because of the heat of the engine and I didn't catch it because of the smell of the new paint. The diesel was running the whole time so it didn't matter then, but after we shut it down we couldn't get any juice from the battery to the starter."

Fettes felt like an idiot in front of his shipmates. How had he missed the fact that the heat of the engine had melted the jacketing on the harness and killed their whole electrical system? Manckowicz had actually found the problem when he squeezed his massive shoulders into the tiny space between the engine block and the housing.

"Got it, Jimmy. Can you fix it with what we have?"

Fettes rubbed his neck and looked at Manckowicz, "What do you think, Ted? Maybe we can pull the harness off and strip the insulation back and see where the wire is messed up then we could splice it."

Manckowicz pursed his lips and thought for a moment, "That's possible I guess, we've got pocket knives. We'll have to rip the cabling off the cowling and the block but first let's yank the connections to the battery and get it out of the circuit. We don't want to get our asses shocked off."

"Good idea Ted."

They worked at loosening the battery terminals with their fingers. It was a tight fit with both their hands in the tiny battery compartment and they both grunted wiggling the stout cables back and forth. Manckowicz's clamp finally slid off and he bent it back so the clamp wouldn't flop forward and touch the post, giving them a surprise as they worked in the crowded space at the stern of the little boat. Fettes started prying the fasteners holding the wiring harness to the side of the engine compartment loose with the screwdriver blade of his Swiss army knife. He managed to pry one completely off and was starting on the next one when the blade snapped off. "Goddamn it, Ted the sonofabitch is trying to fight back! My damn knife just broke."

"Here, Jimmy move aside and let me at it," Manckowicz reached past him and grabbed the steel-jacketed cable with his big ham fist.

"Alright here goes." The sinews in his neck, shoulders and biceps stood out like nylon cordage as his muscular arm tensed up with the pull he exerted. He let out a loud bellow with his effort, "Eeee-yeaahh!"

The blast of his yell in its booming baritone made Carter jerk up from his thinking position as he sat cross-legged on the blanket. Stanfield looked up quickly from checking the band aids on her abdomen and the bunch of seagulls surveying them from the rock ledge over the channel cut sprang from their aerie screaming as they flew away from the startling sound.

Carter got up and quickly splashed out to the boat to check on his friend, "Ted you okay, man? Listen the last thing we need is for one of us to hurt themselves trying to fix the damn thing. Take it easy! Hey it's just after noon now why don't we all cool it for a while and have the last of the meat John has for us? We'll have the beers too. Maybe it will be easier if we all get a breather and go at it fresh in a little while."

Manckowicz pushed himself up onto his knees and leaned back. His face was red from the effort and he was dripping sweat from his chin. Steaks of dried sweat ran into the corners of his eyes. "Ron this sonofabitch is hard but I know I can yank the damn cable out and then we'll find the break and fix it. Maybe you're right, my damn stomach is growling like a grizzly bear!"

"C'mon you guys lets go get something to eat, John's got the grill over the fire. It won't be much but if we don't eat it now it'll all spoil."

Fettes and Manckowicz helped each other up and over the side. They waded to the sand and joined the others at the blankets. Stanfield sat down by Manckowicz and looked at his big hand. "Goodness, Ted you're bleeding look there's blood all over your hand and it's dripped onto your dungarees!"

He turned his hand over and she could see he had big chunks of skin missing from his right ring and middle fingers where a sharp edge on the metal jacketing had torn into his flesh. "I'll get the first aid kit, Ted just don't move. You helped me last night it's my turn to help you now."

Stanfield retrieved the kit and dug out the antiseptic and some gauze pads. She wiped the blood off his fingers and dabbed them with the antiseptic then she applied the gauze and wrapped it with adhesive tape. "See, Ted it's as good as new," she smiled.

"Thank you, Dorothy you make a great corpsman."

She giggled, "I've had some practice you know what with paper cuts in the ship's office; and my battle station is in the Crew's Mess assisting the corpsman if there are any wounded."

Barton cut into their discussion, "No paper plates today but you can each have one of the paper towels for your burger or dog and I'll give each of you a scoop of the potato salad. Jimmy if you can pop the caps on those Peronis with your opener we'll have our lunch. I wish I had brought double now but hey we didn't know."

He passed out the makeshift meals, "I've got two more hot dogs, who gets them?"

Carter eyed the franks on the paper towel, "Cut 'em up and div-vy a piece to everyone."

Stanfield shook her head, "Not for me, give my piece to Ted he's the biggest and he needs more food."

Wilson agreed, "Yes give him my bite too, he needs it more than I do."

Manckowicz tried to take tiny bites of his hamburger to make it last longer and he scooped the mound of potato salad up with his fingers a little at a time relishing the last of their food. Barton handed him a whole hot dog and passed the last one to Carter. "That's the last of it Ron. All we have for tonight and tomorrow is the cheese and the round loaves of bread. We have two more Peronis and a full thermos of water."

"Thanks, John we'll have to ration the water too. A half cup for each of us every six hours."

Manckowicz finished eating, "I think I'm gonna take a quick swim, I must smell like a wet dog. Then I'll get back at the wiring with Jimmy. Hey, Ron we have the flare gun maybe we should try that tonight after it's good and dark. I wonder if you can shoot one out the top of our cove here."

"I don't know, Ted but I was thinking the same thing. We've got two flares so we can try it but I was thinking I would swim out the cut between the rocks and shoot the thing from out there a few yards off. I'll use a life jacket and keep steady and aim the thing straight up in the air. Evening colors is 2035 so it should be good and dark by 2130. That's when I'll give it a try unless we get the en-gine going before then."

Gleason nodded his head, "Good idea, Ron and if it works I

think you should get the two remaining Peronis!"

Wilson finished her burger and got up, "I'm going to put my swimsuit on and I'll join you Ted. I can take my shirt off and wash the wine out from last night too."

They all went in the water except Fettes. He was shoulder deep in the engine compartment when they climbed back out of the cove, refreshed and clean. The men had built a makeshift drying rack out of pieces of driftwood and their towels had been hung on them since early morning. They were able to dry off and change into their dungarees again. Wilson and Stanfield began walking down the beach to "their" area when Manckowicz called out, "Hey, Dorothy be careful okay? No more self-induced wounds please and no more 'free shows'. Sam make sure she doesn't find another little surprise visitor!"

Wilson laughed as they waved and walked the length of the beach together, "Well, Dorothy it seems you have a conquest! I think Ted would just about kill for you."

Stanfield looked at her, "Oh, Sam please don't tell me you have a thing for him too? I kinda got the feeling there was something there when you and he were talking about the opera stuff yesterday."

"No, Dorothy he's not on my dance card now but when I was a kid in high school he just seemed so larger than life to me. Our football team wouldn't have been anything without him. He was the best player in the state and I'm still amazed he didn't go right to one of the big colleges. Also he was the hardest working guy in our whole school. I rode on the same school bus as he did. His little sister Margie was in my class in school. His parents own a big stock farm and he did most of the work on it. Just look at the shape he's in! He's quite a catch!"

Stanfield laughed, "You know, Sam I never pictured myself as the farm-wife type but there just might be something to it! So what about you and Ron Carter? I can tell there's some heat between you two."

"In school I was just the little girl from the country who lived on a farm and had to ride the bus to school. He was the big man on campus with a nice car and nice clothes and nice everything. He didn't even know I was alive until right before he graduated and I started dating his younger brother. He came home on leave after boot camp and wore his blues to school and around town and he and his girlfriend went with us to the movies. You see our town was so tiny if you wanted to go to a movie you had to drive 40 miles to the county seat. That was the nearest theater. In fact, just how big is the crew on your ship?"

Stanfield knew exactly, "Three hundred and six enlisted and twenty four officers as of Saturday morning, Sam."

Wilson laughed, "Well in our town we had enough people to man *Porter* with ten people left over, that's how small a town I'm from. It seems like the odds of three people from there meeting in Naples are like a zillion to one!"

"Well it seems like Ron's head over heels for you. Let me tell you something. He's a very smart guy and he's very highly thought of on *Porter*. I know the Weapons Officer is impressed with him because he came to the ship's office last week and got the Bupers Manual to look up officer programs. I know it was for Ron too because he took his service record with him."

"Gosh I sure hope this boat disaster doesn't put a black mark on his record and spoil his chances. I don't know about you but it seems like he is really doing an excellent job of keeping us all working together and getting us safely out of here and back to the world."

"I know, Ron has always been great aboard ship too. He's our ship's fitness coordinator and he has other collateral duties too. He's the Captain of our ship's softball and baseball teams and he's the ship's Planned Maintenance System Coordinator. We had a PMS inspection just before we got underway for the Med and Ron got us a perfect score. The Captain was very impressed."

"You know, Dorothy there aren't any bad sailors along on this trip. I was impressed by all your guys. Artie is nice and he seems very conscientious, I don't think the problem with the boat is his fault or Jimmy Fettess's either. That harness thing would have given out sooner or later anyway and it could have been really bad, maybe with the boat full of people and in the middle of a busy harbor."

"Exactly, or in the middle of a fog bank."

They finished toweling off and put on their dungarees, Wilson's shirt was still damp from her having scrubbed it with a handful of sand. "This shirt didn't turn out that badly, Dorothy I hope my ship's laundry can get the rest of the stain out."

They rejoined the men in time to hear the result of the renewed work on the wiring harness. Fettes and Manckowicz had managed to pull out more of the fasteners and had worked one end of the cabling free. Fettes was working to remove the end so they could strip off the steel jacketing. He worked the metal end back and forth trying to make it break off by fatiguing it and was making some headway.

Manckowicz was anxious to help, "Here, Jimmy let me break the damn thing off, I have more hand strength than you and it already messed up my hand. It's managed to piss me off and it's not a good idea to piss off the Mank!"

It took him another few minutes but at last the end cracked and he was able to start peeling back the metal exposing the wiring insulation within. Fettes began the slow tedious work scraping off the hard rubberized plastic, slicing away with the good cutting blade on his knife. Manckowicz sat up to get out of his way and called out, "Hey, Artie let me use your knife. Jimmy's got it started and your blade will let us go twice as fast."

Gleason waded out to the stern of the boat and handed his belt knife to Manckowicz, "Good going guys, looks like you two will get the Peronis."

Fettes laughed, "Were gaining on it that's for sure but it isn't over yet. We'll have it licked when we find the break and make the splice."

Gleason waded back to the blankets to talk with Carter, "Ron, they're stripping off the insulation now and it's going better than I thought it might. I just hope there's enough daylight left to get it all cleaned off so we can find the break before it gets too late to see."

Carter couldn't make up his mind whether to wish for a later sunset or an earlier one. If the cable problem couldn't be seen by nightfall he was planning on his swimming foray to shoot the signal flare. For that he needed it to be pitch dark. "Artie one way or another we're gonna make something happen today."

The sun won the race and a dejected Fettes and Manckowicz waded ashore. They would have continued working with the light of a battle lantern but already one of them was very dim, its battery all but depleted. Carter was saving the other one for emergencies.

They fed the fire more driftwood and the glow from it played on their faces as Barton cut the first loaf of bread with his chef's knife and passed the slices to the others. The round loaf of chewy Neapolitan-style bread was just large enough for them each to have a thick slice. They chewed in silence as Barton divided the cheese wheel in half and carefully cut one of the halves into seven wedges.

Gleason took a bite of the cheese, "Hey, this is really a great tasting cheese, it's tasty and not crumbly. I've never had anything like it, what kind did you get Ron?"

"I dunnow, Artie but I think the sign on the counter said 'formaggio de caprone' or something like that."

Stanfield laughed, "Ron that's Italian for 'goat cheese'. It's almost the same in French. You picked out something quite good, this and the bread are a great meal! It's too bad we drank up all the wine last night or this would be gourmet quality! And just think by the firelight on the sand; if we were anywhere back in the States having this right now we'd probably pay a pretty penny for it!"

Manckowicz chuckled, "Yeah, Ron imported cheese, imported bread, it's like our whole evening was planned for this."

Carter winced, "Shut up, Ted the only thing that was planned was a one day thing, only that one afternoon. This is all just bad luck or bad karma or something."

Wilson touched his hand, "Ron I think Ted was just complimenting you on the food, not trying to make you feel bad about the way things worked out."

"I know, Sam. Ted just likes to mess with me whenever he can, he's been that way since high school but he's still my best friend."

Carter had a thought, "Listen everyone I'm going to swim out through the cut after it gets dark. I'll take the flare gun and shoot the flare out there in the open. I'll need someone to keep sight of me from the beach here. Then after I shoot the flare they'll have to turn on the battle lantern and shine it out through the cut so I can see to swim in the right direction to get back here."

Gleason showed concern, "Why can't you just use the flare gun right here in the cove, Ron? I'm sure the thing will go high enough to get seen."

Carter had an answer, "If we shoot it here there's a chance it will smack into one of the cliff walls and bounce right back here in our laps. I don't want to put anyone in danger of getting burned. Besides there's a lot more visibility if I shoot it out there about a hundred yards out past the rocks. There's a clear sight line all the way to downtown Naples."

Manckowicz volunteered, "I got it Ron. I'll be the lighthouse for you to steer toward."

"Good thanks, Ted. John save the other loaf and the rest of the cheese wheel for the morning. We'll need breakfast before either someone comes to check out the flare or we get the engine going."

Carter was sure he was right and his conviction had a calming effect on his shipmates.

CHAPTER 11
WHERE ARE THEY?

THE SECOND P-3 ORION FROM Sigonella was searching the Tyrrhenian working at 1000 feet. The pilot called his squadron mate on the tactical circuit to find out if he had any luck. "Papa Two Yankee this is Alfa Six Bravo, situation check, over."

"Six Bravo this is Two Yankee, we've been searching for three hours now, no joy. We're at 1000 feet and I have the whole crew on surface search, no eyeball isn't busy and if I fly any slower pigeons will start building nests on the wings."

"Roger that Two Yankee, we'll stay at 2000 feet and search along east-west race tracks offsetting South between legs. The current predictions show a floater would move that way."

"Roger Six Bravo, call out if there's any joy. Who are we searching for anyway?"

"Roger Two Yankee, I'll blow the horn if we find them. It's a ships boat off the *Porter* and 7 sailors, sure hope they're alright."

"Roger Six Bravo, I've got four more hours on station then someone else comes to take over. Have a good search Two Yankee out."

CAPTAIN CHRISTENSEN STOOD AT THE head of his mess table and invited them all to sit down. YNC Thomas, BMSN Holden, BM3 Martin, BM2 Bates, the Admin Officer and MS1 Sims, his

Mess Supervisor, the Command Master Chief and the XO. "Alright everyone I suppose you've all heard the scuttlebutt by now about our missing shipmate and the six sailors from *Porter* and *Montpelier*. I have to tell you that we still have no idea where they are and whether or not they're safe.

Thank you all for the quick action this morning when you figured out Seaman Wilson was missing. Because of that quick thinking we managed to get the word out and the ball rolling to find her and them. Now I need you all to do something for me and here it is. I see her every day at least twice a day when she's doing her job and keeping me straight with correspondence, but I know absolutely nothing about her other than the things I observe. Those things are: she's very smart, she's punctual and reliable, she never needs to be told twice how to do things and she's polite and respectful but when she sees something she thinks I could have said better she is quick to suggest it to me. She is serious but has a sense of humor and she believes in pulling her own oar. She has an outstanding attitude and of course she's very attractive.

What I want to know is what you know about her that I don't. I'd like to have a total feel for this Seaman that we're searching for. I think if we have a good picture of what she is and what she would do in the present situation, the better we'll be able to look for and find her. So, you are the shipmates that know her best and I want you to tell me about her. Let's just go around the table and one at a time tell me the things you know."

THE CHIEF OF STAFF PUT down the secure phone and turned to the Flag Operations Officer. "Alright, Marv I filled in the boss on what happened and what we're doing about it. He was sitting in a meeting with both Admiral Wilkins and Admiral Morton so they're both cut in as well. Get the Watch Officer on the hook to the CNO Duty Captain after you tell me where we are right now in the search."

"Yes, Sir. We've split the whole Bay of Naples into eight pie-shaped sector 'wedges', their points intersecting here on *Ike*. We've got one chopper from HSL-87 in each of those zones with orders to fly slow and low and search out every wavelet, and every nook and cranny from Naples out past the offshore islands. There are two P3s on station and searching out past the offshore islands covering the whole of the Tyrrhenian. All aircraft are on the tactical circuit with orders to sing out immediately when they see something that looks like our people. So far we've received nothing but "no joy" whenever I've polled them."

"Thanks Marv. I'm going to call the Italian's and let them know we have a full-blown SAR underway. I won't ask them for any search assets. I'm going to give them a heads up that we may extend the port visit here for a while. The boss said to sit tight until we get every last one of our people safely back."

"Aye, aye, Sir."

He turned to the Watch Officer, "Commander Biddle get me the CNO Duty Captain on the 'steam valve' and poll the search team again."

"Aye, aye, Captain."

CAPTAIN MALLORY WAS HUNCHED OVER a chart of the Bay of Naples when Captain Christensen joined him. "Look at the coasts of those islands, Chris all kinds of navigation hazards here and here."

He dragged his fingertip along the northern coasts of Ischia and Capri fronting on the bay. "These are the places they would have been making for in that whaleboat, there and there. They're closer than going around to the seaward sides. I'm betting that's where they would have gone to swim and picnic."

"I agree with you, Ray that's where I would have gone to swim too. I think if we focus the search between where we are here on *Ike* and those beaches on Ischia we're using the assets to our best advantage. Also I have a suggestion, you and I are both pilots and we see things from the viewpoint of a pilot, our judgment is 'air biased' I think you should get someone to sit here and help your Watch Officer who can see things from the view of a 'smallboat guy'."

"That's a damn good idea, Chris! I'll get one of my Surface Warfare Officer qualified guys in here right away and we'll double the watch so to speak."

"Ray I wasn't thinking a 'ship driver' I was thinking a qualified small boat Cox'n. I'll give you some of mine and they can go right on your watch bill around the clock until we find our sailors."

The Watch Officer called out, "Got the CNO Duty Captain up on the 'steam valve', Captain!"

The Chief of Staff took the handset from him, "This is Mallory, Chief of Staff CTG Sixty point Two. I know you probably have Sixty Three's OPREP there and I want to send you an AMP as soon as I figure out whether or not we need help on the search but I'm using everything we have available now. I gave the Italian CNO a heads up and he stands ready to help on a bi-lateral basis. I need you to get with the people in the State Department and grease the skids for an extension on the port visits here in Naples. I'm talking about *Eisenhower, Montpelier and Porter.* I don't want to effect the other ships' schedules yet but there is a potential for keeping *Ike, Monty and Porter* here 'til we get this all resolved."

He listened as the CNO Duty Captain 'rogered' for the request, said he would get the word to State right away and wished him luck finding the sailors.

The Chief of Staff nodded as he heard the response and turned to the Watch Officer, "Commander give me the list of our sailors' names."

In a moment he was reading off the names, rates, and Social Security numbers of the seven unluckiest sailors in the Mediterranean. When he was done he added, "I recommend we keep the names of those sailors from the press until after we inform their next of kin and let them know we will work day and night until we find them and bring them back safe and sound. That's right thanks, Charley and give my regards to Sylvia."

He put down the handset and turned to the group. "Alright that's done, where are we in the search?"

There had been no change since he was last briefed three minutes before.

He knew they were doing everything they could at the moment and he reached over to pick up his coffee cup. "Who the Hell are you sailor?"

"I'm Bo'sun's Mate Bates, Captain. I'm here to help you find my friend Sam Wilson and the rest of our sailors, Sir."

"Good, Bates. Glad to have you, son. Now tell me where to look. Where the Hell are they?"

Bates assessed the question, "Well, Captain it's for sure they aren't where you're looking for them right now because if they were, you'd have found them."

The Chief of Staff smiled, "That's the only thing anybody has said all day that makes any fuckin' sense at all! Carry on, Boats work with the watch team here and figure out our next move."

He turned to the Watch Officer, "I'm going to take a shower and get something to eat. I'll be back for a briefing at 2100. Call me in my stateroom the moment we know anything more."

CARTER FINISHED THE LAST CRUMB of his bread ration and lay back on the blanket to rest before he started out on his swim out of the cove. Wilson was sitting next to him holding his hand. In the low firelight no one could see. She was concentrating on the sound of the surf breaking on the jagged rocks just outside the cut. All at once she started, "Ron I think I hear something. Does anyone else hear that? It sounds like a helicopter!"

Gleason scrambled to get up from the blanket, "Yeah I hear something too, maybe they know we're missing by now and they sent someone out to look for us. Jesus this is the perfect time for the flare, Ron!"

Carter stripped off his dungarees and grabbed the flare gun. He had loaded the flare during the day when he could see well and left the breech opened. It was all securely wrapped inside the last of the plastic wrap that had held their hamburgers. He would swim out through the cut wearing a life jacket, roll on his back, tear off the plastic and snap the breech shut. It would save fumbling around in the starlight trying to load the flare. Then he would fire the red Very round straight up in the air.

He quickly waded out past the boat into the little cove, struggling into the straps of the life jacket as he went. Then he began swimming, holding the gun over his head with his left hand and using his right to help his powerful kick. The sounds of the surf, the wind and the night birds didn't distract him from his effort. He steadily pulled his way through the dark tunnel cut in the rock and the stars added light and perspective as he emerged. Just a few dozen more strokes and he would be far enough out to make the shot. He flipped over on his back and feverishly tore open the plastic, slamming the breech shut. A quick prayer; "Oh God please help me do this!" and he pulled the trigger with every ounce of his might.

"SEARCH BOSS, THIS IS SEARCHER Six. I'm over the west end of the island in Bay Zone Six. No joy over."

"Who was that, Sir?"

"Boats that was the helo down here."

Commander Biddle put his pencil point down on the western edge of Capri and drew a circle the size of a dime on the chart, "He's right about here and he's holding until I call him off."

"That's where I would have put in, Sir. It looks private and like the sea would be fresh there, no crap from the town there and off the beaten path of the friggin' touristas."

"Thanks, Boats I was hoping for something there too. It makes a lot of sense when you lay it out like that. Jesus we're burning a lot of gas and manpower in this damn search."

Bates grimaced when he heard the comment, "I know, Sir but just think about it. Wouldn't you want to have somebody looking hard if it was you or one of your kids who were missing at sea, Sir? Let me tell you what I heard from those whining pissants in the helo squadron at chow while I'm at it. Some of them were bitching about having been recalled and missing out on a day of liberty to look for our people. I told them I would be pretty damn reluctant to search for even one of them if their damn helo went down."

Biddle was chagrined, of course he had been out of line, he had been fatuous and outright thoughtless when he had mentioned manpower and fuel costs. "Boats thanks for putting it in the proper frame of reference for me. It's seven of our own out there."

A P3 ORION NEWLY ARRIVED from Sigonella relieved Papa Two Yankee on station and the fatigued crew flew back to their home field feeling dejected. They had passed the bad news to their relief. No joy in the search. Three hours later Alpha Six Bravo made the same report to its relief.

THE CHIEF OF STAFF WALKED INTO Flag Plot just after the watch team's relief was completed and Commander Biddle reported the results of the day's search. Zero.

"Alright, let's bring in the choppers and rest the crews. I want to be ready to launch them again at first light. Same zones and same mission."

Biddle passed the orders on to the team and the tactical circuits crackled as the tired helo pilots acknowledged and began heading back to *Ike's* welcoming flight deck. The chopper crews would get some chow and take showers finally hitting their bunks knowing they would be roused at 0500 so they could go back to doing the same thing at dawn. No liberty for them nor for the *Eisenhower* sailors who handled the choppers, fueled them and fed the crews. Spirits were not good and crewmen began looking for someone to blame for their getting the short end of the stick.

CAPTAIN CHRISTENSEN FINALLY HAD A moment to himself and sat down at his desk. His whole day had been spent wrapped up in the search for his missing Seaman and his plan to go over the Court of Inquiry package had been totally overtaken by events. He shuffled some of the paper sitting on the desk and pushed the routine stuff aside. And then he saw it. A neat package of typed paper fastened carefully on the top with a 'bulldog clamp' and with a yellow 'sticky note' stuck on the first page, Wilson's note offering her suggested alternative ending to the missive. He called the Chief of Staff with an idea and then he called the CDO. "Have the First Lieutenant and the Command Master Chief come and see me in my stateroom."

By the time they arrived the Captain and the XO were mulling over the facts. "Here's the situation as I see it; a 19 year old Seaman is missing and half the Battle Group is looking for her and the other six sailors who through some accident, incident or just old fashioned bad luck have managed to lead her astray with them. The afternoon and evening search has found nothing but that's not all bad news. The fact that they came up with zero means they didn't find any wreckage, no floating debris and no floating sailors. I think that means they aren't at sea and they aren't in the Bay of Naples.

I think they are ashore someplace. In the morning we send out our boats searching the shoreline. It has to be the islands where we'll find them, not the open ocean. First Lieutenant, I want the gig and three other boats manned with search teams and portable radios and in the water at 0600. Master Chief I want you to hand pick the boat crews, make sure we have medics in them. Two boat pairs, one heads for Ischia the other to Capri. I want people who speak Italian in each of the boat crews too. I want them to talk to the locals. Find out if anyone at all saw them or knows anything about the Saturday visit from the American sailors. Anybody got any other ideas?"

Nobody did.

"Good this is where *Eisenhower* takes over and gets the hard part done."

The Master Chief and the First Lieutenant left to get things organized and going at the level where it really counts, at the shipmate level.

CARTER WAITED TWO WHOLE SECONDS after he pulled the trigger and heard the snap as the firing pin snicked home on the red flare round. Nothing, no reaction from the round at all. No whoosh as it left the muzzle of the gun. No brilliant upward flight and no bursting rosy red plumes of the star shell. No noise at all. He opened the breech and quickly shut it recocking the gun. One more try.

Click, then nothing.

Searcher Six was on its way back to *Eisenhower*, he could see its navigation lights only half a mile away. He slumped on his back and watched the helo as it got smaller and smaller, headed home to its welcoming carrier.

"Sonofabitch! Damned flare! Damned gun! Damned helicopter!"

He couldn't even see the beam of the battle lantern that Manckowicz was shining out through the cut in the rock that led to the tiny cove. His homing beacon. Obviously the current had moved him away from the cut and he would have to swim parallel to the shore until he found it. But which way to head? He waited conserving his strength and looking up at features on the island.

"Come on, damn it! There must be some Italian people at home with the lights on tonight!"

And then he saw it, a light in a farmhouse or a villa high up on the mountain. The current was taking him slowly out to sea. He pulled the flare round out of the chamber, dropped it into the sea and stuck the flare pistol down the top of his life jacket. At last he could use both arms to swim. He began his slow crawl stroke back toward the cut in the rock.

"Just keep it slow and steady," he thought. "Don't try to push too fast. It's only a few minutes I've been out here. I can't have drifted more than a hundred yards. Nice easy pace, just keep kicking. Stroke, stroke and stroke again. Gotta keep going. Gotta keep going to stay warm."

GLEASON KNEW SOMETHING WAS WRONG. It had been too long since Carter had disappeared down the cut. Everyone else could sense it too. There had been no flare. Surely they would have seen the thing fly up, or the burst, or heard the bang or something. Something was wrong, he should have been back by now.

Gleason turned to Stanfield, "Dorothy I'm going after him. Something must be wrong."

Manckowicz disagreed, "No you're not. I'm a lot better swimmer than you are and he's my friend, *I'm* going after him."

Stanfield said, "Nobody is going after him. He's fine, give him a few more minutes, he'll be right here I know it. He's the fittest most athletic guy on *Porter*. He'll be swimming back in here in three minutes, just wait and see." She had faith in him. Right then that's all she had faith in.

CARTER WAS EXHAUSTED BUT HE kept reaching and pulling and he kept lifting his head and rolling it to the left as he swam. One more stroke, and then another and another, and then finally the white-yellow beam of the battle lantern shining weakly through the cut in the rock. "Thank God!"

They heard him first as he entered the narrow channel; the splashing as his hands stroked plunging into the water, the sound amplified as it reflected off the solid rock walls. "It's him! He's back, he made it!" Gleason shouted as the rest of them hurried to where he and Manckowicz were crouched with the battle lantern. "Here, Dorothy hold this while I help him ashore."

Stanfield took the battle lantern and aimed the light beam at the water ahead of Gleason as he and Manckowicz ran out into chest deep water and grabbed Carter's life jacket. "Easy man we've got you now."

The other men hurried to help support the exhausted sailor as they laid him on the blanket nearest the fire. Wilson ran to the Thermos, filled the silver cap and brought it to him. He drank from it gratefully as the others toweled him off and removed the life jacket. The flare gun fell onto the blanket and Barton moved it out of the way.

Carter caught his breath after a few sips of the water, "The Goddamn gun misfired. I don't know if it was the round or the gun but it didn't work. I even recocked it. I could even see the lights on the chopper! Damn it I feel like a fool. Holy shit my leg is stinging like fire!"

Stanfield played the beam of light up and down both his legs. Jellyfish tentacles were wrapped around his left calf. She motioned to Barton, "John go wet one of the towels in seawater get it good and soaked. Here, Sam hold the light while I get the gook off him and wash his leg in seawater. Ron this will hurt for a while but if you aren't allergic to the toxins you should be alright."

Barton brought the soaking wet towel over to the little group, "Here's the towel Dorothy."

She put it down, grabbed a dry one and used it to pull off the tentacles and then rubbed the welts down with the seawater-soaked towel. Manckowicz knelt down beside her. "Dorothy I thought you were supposed to use urine to treat jellyfish stings."

"No, Ted that's an old wives' tale. We don't have any vinegar or I would use that; seawater is the next best thing for this."

"That's too bad I've been wantin' to piss all over this guy since the third grade!" Even Carter had to laugh, painful leg and all.

Carter thought a moment, "Who has the watch now?"

Wilson said, "I do, Ron. I haven't been able to raise anyone on the bridge-to-bridge and the battery is really down on it, there's hardly any squelchy noise anymore."

"Alright, Sam leave the thing turned off tonight and let's save the battle lantern too. Just keep the fire going and I'll think of something for tomorrow. The good news is that they are looking for us and amazing as it may seem; they seem to think we might be here on Capri too. I think that's good. I don't want anyone to lose heart, we are going to be alright and we are going to get back."

THE PUBLIC AFFAIRS OFFICE WAS normally a soundless tomb on weekends and Lieutenant Barnard had been very surprised to be called in to the office by a Watch Officer who said she was recalling him as directed by the CNO Duty Captain. He pulled on his uniform and drove in from Tyson's Corner, outside the Beltway, where he shared a town house with his girlfriend an Air Force Captain who also worked In Public Affairs. It took him an hour to arrive and find a parking space. The Duty Captain's assistant handed him a message that listed the names, social security numbers and the ships that the seven missing Sixth Fleet sailors were assigned to. "Sorry to drag you in on a Sunday afternoon but the Duty Captain wants these people's families called ASAP and informed that they are missing and the navy is searching for them."

It was an IMMEDIATE precedence message that provided amplifying data to information previously sent and identified the missing by name. "What good is this? These are the missing sailors, it doesn't tell me who to call at all. Somebody over at the Bureau of Personnel probably has their next of kin information. I don't have access to any of that!"

"Look, Lieutenant your name is on the recall watch bill. It's your problem. Call in whoever else you need but I'll expect a report from you by 2000, a full report of who you contacted and who you couldn't."

Barnard's needed information was filled in by the helpful First Class Personnelman at the Bureau of Personnel who maintained the file of navy personnel's next-of-kin and their contact information. She was actually quite cheerful on the phone and he made note of her name. Someone helpful *and* cheerful on a Sunday afternoon was a good person to know. It was she who first saw the anomaly too. Three of the social security numbers began with the same three digits, "Lieutenant this is weird, three of these sailors are from the same little town in Iowa. Two of them even live on the same road! I'll bet they're neighbors."

MRS. BARBARA WILSON WAS JUST setting the kitchen table for Sunday dinner when the phone rang. She put down the water goblets and went to answer it just as her husband walked in from a day of hard work. Running a 1600 acre stock farm wasn't easy. He went to the sink to wash his hands and saw that his wife had the phone to her ear.

THREE AND A HALF MILES down the road Mrs. Helen Manckowicz had already put the phone back in its cradle. Tears were streaming down her cheeks and her husband began trying to calm her. "Who was that and what did they say that's got you all blubbery?"

"Oooh, Jack it was a navy officer in Washington. He said Teddy is missing from his ship and they're looking for him!"

"How the Hell can he be missing from a submarine? I thought submarines were watertight, how could he be missing?"

"His submarine is at Naples, Italy and he was with some other sailors on a picnic, somehow they got lost at sea in a little boat! Oh my God what are we going to do?"

He took her in his arms to comfort her and patted her trying to get her to stop sobbing.

"Don't worry, sweetheart Ted is tough and he's levelheaded he'll figure out what to do. He'll be fine. You just wait and see, he'll be fine."

MR. AND MRS. CARTER GOT the same call as the others but Mrs. Carter was more stoic. She knew that Ronnie was just fine. He had always been so bright and resourceful as a boy and she had every confidence that he would come out of the present situation with flying colors. She would see Helen tomorrow at the club meeting and see if she had heard from Ted.

THE FLAG WATCH OFFICER MADE one final proofread on the message he had drafted, the AMP that would update the whole chain of command as to the status of the SAR effort so far and laid out the search plan for the next day. They would fly again and keep looking for the seven unlucky sailors who by now were famous throughout the Sixth Fleet. He initialed the yellow flimsy, signed the RE-LEASED BY block, and handed it to the Communications Watch Officer, "Get it on the air right away Mr. Conklin."

"Aye, aye, sir." Two minutes later it was gone and communications personnel at the headquarters of every echelon of the navy were making copies of the message. It would be distributed to their staffs and talked about at morning briefings.

EISENHOWER'S DECK GANG WORKED WELL into the night. They lowered two more fifty footers and fueled them, stocked them with food for the search teams and every last item the Command Master Chief and the Master Chief Boatswain's Mate could think of. They took one of the big launches out of the liberty shuttle rotation and made it ready for the search effort too. The gig was already set to go of course, Bad Billy Bates had made doubly sure of that.

CHAPTER 12
SAR, DAY TWO

THE TOWER AT SIGONELLA GAVE Bravo Charlie Four permission to go and the big P3C Orion sub hunter started its roll down the runway, its crew fresh and anxious to begin the day's search. They would be retracing the path of yesterday's VP searchers and cover the Tyrrhenian with every eyeball straining to find the missing seven sailors. Back in the electronic equipment bay Naval Air Crewman First Class Alec Mather finished his coffee and sighed to his friend AC Second Class Norton, "All this sophisticated gear, probably eight million dollars' worth, and it's all useless for the job they've got us on today."

Norton groused, "Yeah I know, we should be out searching for the damn Commie submarines that are screwing around here in the Med, not straining our eyeballs looking for a bunch of idiots who were out on a joyride in a Goddamn little boat."

"Hey give 'em a break. It's not their fault they're lost at sea. From what I heard in the preflight brief they've been lost for two days."

Norton still wasn't buying it, "Maybe it isn't their fault but that doesn't change the fact that they called us in off liberty yesterday to go out and spend the whole day on a wild goose chase."

Mather had had enough, "You know, Frank if you ever want to make First Class you'd better start working on that attitude problem of yours. Those lost sailors may be an unexpected nuisance but right

113

now they are what the whole navy is concentrating on. And oh yes, someday they may do you a favor. So quit bitching, there are eleven other guys in our crew and they aren't, so let's squeeze some eyeball."

THE HELO SQUADRON HELD ITS preflight brief at 0540 and they would begin their long dogged search as soon as the light conditions allowed them visibility. The weathermen promised another day of good visibility with a very low probability of rain. Surface visual search would be optimum. The wind was nil and the seas a flat calm, the surface of the Bay of Naples was as smooth as the top of the Chief of Staff's desk.

CAPTAIN CHRISTENSEN WAS JUST COMING out of his shower when the phone rang. He wrapped a towel around his middle and padded to the desk. "Captain."

"Chris it's Ray Mallory where do you stand on your small boat search detail?"

"Mornin', Ray I was just on my way to brief the parties myself before they shove off. How long 'til the helos take off?"

"Chris I just got a quick call from Washington. Apparently someone on the Potomac is antsy about sending out search boats. They think it will alarm our Italian hosts too much, especially on Capri if the navy descends on them in force. I told them it wasn't going to be like that at all but it didn't seem to matter. Some damn politically correct politician somewhere has a bug in his bonnet about it. They probably have a copy of the Landing Party Manual in the office somewhere and are afraid we'll have our sailors all wearing leggings and brandishing cutlasses. But I can't let you go. Even though I agree with you that the boats are the best way to find our people, I can't let you send them."

"I understand, Ray. Hey, can you get whoever it was that made that stupid decision to put it in writing and send it out as a naval message? And while I'm thinking about it, make them put in writing just exactly what I *can* do with my boats!"

"Good thinking, Chris. That'll sure make the idiot sit up and think about it! I'll send a message up the chain and ask for detailed guidance right from the top!"

"Thanks, Ray in the meantime I'm off to hold up my boats; if you hear any yelling you'll know that some of Seaman Wilson's shipmates don't think any more of that stupid order than I do."

The Chief of Staff chuckled, "Or I do. Oh and by the way, I called Admiral Townsend and he thinks whoever pushed out the edict is a, let me remember his exact words; ah yes 'a landlocked Potomac pussy who has forgotten his roots'. Well, let me see to the choppers. Good luck with your boat crews, keep me posted."

"Thanks, Ray." Captain Christensen put on a fresh uniform and went to the Quarterdeck where four six-man boat search teams were patiently awaiting his arrival.

The Command Master Chief ordered, "Attention on Deck" and the group snapped to, ready for the Captain's words.

"Stand easy everyone. Gather in here so I don't have to yell." He waited while they all moved in closer around him.

"We're holding off on the boat search until it's been cleared by whoever has to clear boat searches in foreign waters. So, Master Chief stand down the crews of the launches for now. Which crew was lined up for the gig?"

The Master Chief detailed them, "Captain it's Bates, Holden, Petty Officer Martin, Chief Thomas, Sims because he speaks Italian, and Chief Peterson is their corpsman volunteer."

The Captain nodded, "Good three men and three women. Here's what we're going to do. Get that crew into civilian clothes, hand every one of them a camera and dig up any tourist guide books you can find. We're sending the gig on a 'liberty party tourist excursion'. Have them come see me in my mess when they're dressed for their 'holiday'. Everyone else, thank you for being ready, if we get word from the elephants I'll let you know."

The Master Chief sent the rest of the volunteers off to their duties and saw to the 'outfitting' of the gig's party. They joined the Captain in his mess just as he was finishing his toast and bacon. Bates was wearing a windbreaker and khaki slacks, Sims and Chief Thomas looked equally casual and the women all had colorful skirts and tops. So far so good.

Captain Christensen briefed them, "So here's the plan, get over to Ischia first, it's biggest and will take the most time. Get ashore and quiz the locals, the story is you're relatives of the little navy group that was seen heading there on Saturday, You were planning to meet them today for a beach party and you can't remember where they said to meet. Find out from the locals where they are or at least the best places to look for them. How much money do you have?"

They had almost two hundred dollars in cash between them. The Captain asked them to give him a moment and went to his stateroom, opened his desk drawer and took out his wallet. He gave them another two hundred. Four hundred dollars was about three hundred mille lira, a decent search fund.

"Whatever you do, try not to stand out as sailors on a search mission. We have to be incognito about this. But find our sailors and bring them back safe and sound. Use the radio to check in with us but don't use search language or navy terms. Call the search 'the party' and make things up as you go along. Stay out of trouble," he turned to grin at Bates.

"Now get going and find them."

The gig was underway 5 minutes later just as Captain Christensen was calling the Chief of Staff to let him know that his gig was off on a 'party' excursion to Ischia.

Captain Mallory chuckled, "Good idea you crafty SOB, you know nobody back in Washington is ever going to release that 'detailed guidance' message and remove all doubt that he's an asshole. Let me know how they do. Who did you send anyway?"

"Ray, the Cox'n is the Bo'sun's Mate I gave you last night and there are five of Wilson's shipmates with him. Three of them are women."

"Shipmates. Good choice, Chris."

CARTER WOKE UP WITH A growling hunger and a fierce thirst. He could see well enough in the light from the early dawn to make out the rest of his party, spread on the two blankets by the dying fire. In another hour or so it would be good and light and they could get back to fixing the electrical harness. Manckowicz was only half effective because his bandaged fingers made it hard to use his right hand. Fettes was clearly not very talented in an electrical environment and none of the rest of them had any training in electrical repairs. Besides, the space to work in was so tiny it only allowed for a couple of arms and hands to fit inside.

He was glad Gleason was the Cox'n, he was a steady guy and smart. Barton was good too, he could be trusted to get done whatever he was directed to do and he was a good shipmate. Stanfield, now she was a Godsend. Smart and handy in medical emergency things. His calf hardly hurt at all this morning. And then there was Sam. She had given up her water ration so he could drink when he'd made it back last night. He didn't know what to do about her.

Barton was stirring and sat up.

"Hey, John we still have half the cheese and the other loaf of bread right?

"Yeah, Ron what do you want to do for breakfast?"

"Equal shares, same as yesterday but let's hold off eating until noon. It can't be helped. I'm hoping the snipes can get the engine going by then. They didn't have all that much left to strip when they finished yesterday. Maybe they'll be lucky."

SIGONELLA TOWER CLEARED FOXTROT ROMEO Seven and the second P3C lumbered off to join the search between Sardinia and the 'shin' of the Italian boot.

The VP Squadron Commander got on the secure 'hook' to his boss in Naples right after the launch. He explained that at the rate he was pushing men and materiel into the SAR effort he would exceed his monthly fuel budget in two more days. He was already providing one anti-submarine P3C search unit in the air in the eastern Med round the clock. That meant that it took two planes to maintain the search, one on station for searching with its sonobuoys and one either on its way to relieve it or on its way back to Sigonella. It was pushing the men and the machines too hard. No patrol squadron could support having four planes in the air for long. Something was bound to break soon and they both knew it.

COMFAIRMED knew his squadron skipper was absolutely right. "I know it, Ernie it's bad business and that's why we're making an all-out effort to find them today during daylight. I'll also tell you that tomorrow I'm cutting back your SAR sorties to one unit in the air during daylight hours. And I'm bringing in some help from the squadron at Rota. That should ease the burden on your troops. In the meantime keep their spirits up, there is light at the end of the tunnel."

Commander Perkins grunted, "Aye, aye, Sir. Thank you, Admiral that is some good news but the best news of all would be that we find them safe today."

"You're right, Ernie that's what I keep praying for too."

THE HELOS LIFTED OFF AT 0800 with the same search routine they had used the day before. Immediately Flag Plot could tell it was going to be a long day. It was Monday and all the fishermen who had been celebrating Sunday with a nice leisurely day in port devoted to Church and family dinners were back to practicing their trade. There were hundreds of fishing boats the size of a dory littered about the Bay of Naples. The chopper pilots couldn't even take advantage of the fact that the ship's whaleboat they sought was gray. It seemed there must have been a sale on battleship gray paint at the local stores.

The tactical circuit was a constant stream of reports from the helo pilots. It didn't pay to plot all the 'possible' contacts. The search board and the Plexiglas status board would have been inundated with possibles.

Captain Walters picked up the handset and made up his mind, "All Searchers this is Search Boss, continue to check each contact closely but belay reporting each one. Report only the ones that contain multiple people or appear to be in real distress. Search Boss out."

Unintentionally he had just told eight very motivated search crews to keep their mouths shut.

FETTES AND MANCKOWICZ FOUND THE break after an hour of scraping away the hard crumbly insulation. It was just a very tiny disruption in the copper. It was so narrow Manckowicz thought the damned electrons should have been able to jump across it with ease. It didn't matter, they'd found it and all they had to do was splice the two ends together and then, oh shit! How were they going to keep the four feet of now-bare copper wire from touching the engine block and shorting out the whole circuit?

Manckowicz sat back in the sternsheets and wiped the sweat out of his eyes, "Well, Jimmy another fine mess you've gotten us into! Any ideas on how we can splice this pig and then not have it touch the block and short us into kingdom come?"

Fettes pulled himself upright, "I guess we fell right into that trap, Ted. I haven't any idea, I just wish we had four feet of spare cable somewhere that we could replace this whole mess with. I'd better get Artie to come and look, maybe he or Ron have some ideas."

"Yeah I agree, we need some plastic or rubber or something to serve as good insulation."

Fettes sat up and called to Gleason. He waded out and the quick conference resulted in just what Carter feared most; another damned problem.

BRAVO CHARLIE FOUR GAINED CONTACT on a small auxiliary ship just after noon and something didn't seem quite right to the pilot. "You know that thing looks a lot like that Russian AGI we flew over a couple weeks ago. Let's drop on down and take a closer look. TACCO lets fire up everything we've got, maybe we'll get lucky!"

Ten minutes later they were at 300 feet making a wide pass around the little vessel. AC-2 Norton was just covering a cough when he saw the flicker on the O-scope on the Magnetic Anomaly Detector's instrument panel and an instant later the little indicator went off the chart. He turned to his buddy Mather, "Alec holy shit look at that! I've never seen the MAD go that high before, it's like we just ran over a trainload of pig iron!"

Mather scooted over to look at the scope, "Jesus you're right!"

He hit the mike to communicate with the Mission Commander, "Madman! Madman! Sir we've got a sub down there as sure as I'm here talkin about it!"

This was at least something exciting, bored and tired eyes perked up at once as the Mission Commander tweaked the pilot. Another pass over the suspected sub told the story. "Make an immediate contact report Mr. Kiley, give our current position and tell them the AGI is here and we are suspending the SAR to prosecute the sub. Now let's get some buoys in the water!"

THE COMFAIRMED WATCH OFFICER TOOK the stairs from the seventh deck to the sixth, three at a time. He raced down the passageway to the blast-reinforced blue steel door to COMSUBMED's spaces and frantically mashed the button summoning a Petty Officer in the Communications Center to the video camera monitor.

"Mr. Randall the Airedale Watch Officer is pounding on the door. Should I let him in?"

"Go ahead, buzz him in. I can guess what it is already."

Lieutenant Wagner pushed open the heavy door and ran to the COMSUBMED OPCON Center. Inside Lieutenant Randall welcomed him, "What can I do for you, Mikey?"

"Rich I have a P3 who's reporting a hot contact right here, he's got the AGI right there too." He walked to the giant wall chart of the Mediterranean stretching 30 feet across the front of the briefing room and pointed to a deep spot in the Tyrrhenian, midway between La Maddalena, Sardinia and the upper part of the 'shin' of Italy's boot.

"Do you have one of your guys there?" He took the proffered grease pencil and made a red X on the hot spot.

Lieutenant Randall shook his head, "Mike it isn't one of ours, let me make sure it isn't one of the NATO boats." He grabbed the big 3-ring binder that held every one of the SUBNOTEs: the submarine exercise areas which had been scheduled, reserving ocean area for NATO nations to conduct their own training exercises. It worked just like the system most organizations set up to allow individuals or small groups to reserve scarce conference rooms. Just sign up for the room in advance and respect the rules governing its occupancy and use. COMSUBMED held the submarine signup book.

Lieutenant Randall flipped through the pages of current message SUBNOTEs shaking his head, "No, Mike I've got all these plotted on the OPCON chart and the spot you show is nowhere near any of them. It's all yours my friend, prosecute away!"

Lieutenant Wagner was panting from exertion as he flung back the door and reentered his own headquarters. He yanked open the drawer containing the preformatted blank RED report message blanks and started filling in the information. Forty seconds later he handed the form to a Petty Officer who converted the paper message into a FLASH precedence outgoing and input it to the AUTODIN system. Electrons began jumping immediately as the information leapt through the airways and cableways connecting all of the two hundred or so headquarters, Intel centers, support activities and bureaucratic recipients who got the news that a navy P3C aircraft right smack dab in the middle of the Tyrrhenian Sea had solid contact on a Soviet submarine and was tracking him with sonobuoys and magnetic anomaly detecting gear.

REAR ADMIRAL TOWNSEND WAS SITTING in the opulent office at CINCUSNAVEUR's headquarters at Grosvenor Square in London thinking about where he would come down on issues that were the subject of the morning's meeting. Rear Admiral Bevins, Commander Task Force Sixty, Vice Admiral Wilkins, the Sixth Fleet Commander and Admiral Morton who called the polished walnut conference table 'his' rounded out the group. The agenda included far reaching subject matter having to do with the pace of naval operations in the Mediterranean, ship safety and the morale of the 45,000 or so sailors who counted on them for leadership.

They had tackled the really knotty item on the agenda first and decided that Admiral Townsend's Chief of Staff had a handle on it. There were still no headlines related to the missing seven sailors. Halfway through the meeting a staff officer knocked on the door and brought in the RED message passing it to Admiral Morton. He scanned it quickly and exclaimed, "See! This is the kind of thing I've been talking about, now we've got the Goddamn Soviets popping up and getting in the way of us solving our own fleet problems. It's almost like they have a magnetic attraction to us! First the Goddamn AGI sticking its nose into all of Tommy Townsend's Battle Group's ops and then that Goddamn plane buzzing him in the Adriatic two weeks ago and now they send us a Goddamn submarine to gum up the works finding our sailors!"

He passed the message to the Fleet Commander. "COMFAIRMED is going to be stretched damned thin if he has to expend a lot of assets on this damned sub. He'll be reaching into his next month's fuel and sonobuoy allowance very soon and it's only just past middle of the month."

The two task force Admirals nodded in agreement and Admiral Bevins spoke for both of them, "Cold War my ass. The only thing 'cold' about it is the temperature of this coffee."

The meeting was interrupted again a few moments later as the staff officer entered again, "Admiral that word from the State Department you were looking for is in, the Italians have approved a three day extension of the Naples port visit."

"Well at least the Italians understand, thank you Commander."

Admiral Morton looked across the table at rear Admiral Townsend, "Tom that gives you a couple more days to find them and after that you still have to figure out what to do about that collision glitch."

Admiral Townsend knew what he meant and made his move, "Yes, Sir. I'm confident we'll find our sailors but I'm gonna need help on the collision problem. I was swinging from a high line transfer cage when it happened and damn near got my ass crushed between the two ships. I don't think I would be the objective arbiter conducting a Court of Inquiry. In fact I'll probably be called as a witness. I'm going to need someone to help out."

He looked across the table at vice Admiral Wilkins who grimaced and nodded, "You're right Tommy. My fleet, my problem. I'll convene a Court of Inquiry on my flagship Thursday." He turned to Admiral Morton. "By then we'll have the people problem resolved and I can concentrate on the other. All the participants are right there in Naples and we'll chopper them to the flagship in Gaeta."

ELAINE CARTER WAS SITTING IN the lobby of the community center building in downtown Corning Iowa when her friend Helen Manckowicz walked in with a concerned look on her face. Their book club meeting could wait. They each had a question for the other.

"Helen we got a call from a navy officer in Washington last evening, Ronnie is missing at sea somewhere have you heard anything from Ted?"

She was aghast, "Elaine we got a call too, and they don't know where he is either. I was hoping you had heard from Ronnie!"

The two friends hugged each other for mutual support as Helen thought of something, "Let's call Barbara Wilson, her daughter may have let her know something about it."

Five minutes later they had their answer; something was amiss with the three sailors from Corning Iowa and someone had damn well better be doing something about it!

Elaine said, "The call we got was from the Navy Department I wrote down the man's name and phone number."

Barbara Wilson caught up with them thirty minutes later at the Woolworth's lunch counter across the street and they pooled their information. Helen pursed her lips, "Let's call the number Elaine got and ask if there is any news. I think Europe is six or seven hours ahead of us so it should be almost nightfall there. Surely they must have found them by now."

They walked the two blocks to the Carter home where Elaine invited her friends to sit down in the kitchen while she dialed the number she had written down.

The phone rang once before it was quickly answered, "Navy Department Public Affairs Office, Lieutenant Spooner speaking, Sir or Ma'am."

"Hello this is Elaine Carter calling from Corning Iowa, is there any news of my son and his friends? They were missing from their ships in Italy."

Helen and Barbara watched Elaine's face as she listened to the reply from the navy's centralized fountain of information. Elaine listened for perhaps fifteen seconds, her features showing increasing signs of worry and frustration until finally she cut the conversation short, "Lieutenant If you have no further news of my son and his friends would you be so kind as to forward my call to whoever it is in the navy who *does* know anything?"

The hapless Public Affairs Officer was at a loss for an answer, as far as she knew no one in the navy at that point actually did know anything.

Elaine put the phone down and Barbara spoke up, "Not a good call, I can tell. Well, why don't we call someone who actually can help us? Here's the number for Senator Gressley".

THE SENATOR'S OFFICE IN DES MOINES was coolly efficient and the plight of the three Corning sailors was passed on to the Senator's office in the old Senate Office Building just as he was headed to his luncheon with several visiting constituents who had come to talk to him about the upcoming vote on the Farm Bill. His look of concern shook his receptionist, "Mrs. Reid, put in a call to the Secretary of the Navy at once. I'll wait in my office for it."

He turned to the waiting delegation, "Three of our Iowa sailors are missing. This may take a few minutes, make yourselves comfortable. I'll be right with you."

THE PHONE WAS ANSWERED BY a staffer who quickly grasped that the senior Senator from Iowa was in no mood to banter about niceties. He wanted answers and he wanted them now. He couldn't understand why three of his constituents were missing. He couldn't imagine how an organization as big and costly as the navy could lose three people, call and alarm their families but fail to update them on the progress of finding them and getting them safely back to their ships. He wondered if perhaps the navy had altogether too many people to lose and too many ships to lose them from. Perhaps the Secretary ought to take charge of the situation or else the next time he came in front of his committee looking for funding for the next generation of aircraft carrier or submarine or whatever; it wouldn't all be sunshine and lollipops.

THE PHONE LINES HUMMED FOR the next few minutes as questions, threats, expostulations and promises were exchanged at every level of the navy inside the 'beltway' and message traffic kept the AUTODIN system in hyper drive as communications personnel on both sides of the Atlantic raced to copy the queries, responses and status reports that by then had been distributed to triple the number of interested headquarters and activities than the report of the Soviet sub had. Sailors all over the Sixth Fleet's area of responsibility now knew that seven of their own were lost and that the elephants were concerned and trumpeting about it.

THE CHIEF OF STAFF HUNG up the secure phone and turned to the Flag Plot watch team. "Still nothing from any of the helos?"

The Watch Officer nodded, "Still nothing Captain Mallory, and the P3 that is searching the Tyrrhenian relayed a 'no joy' via CTF 63 about fifteen minutes ago."

"Sonofabitch, yesterday the Potomac couldn't have cared less about this situation; today the heat is on and we can't tell them enough."

He had just gotten off the phone with the CNO Duty Captain and moments before that he'd updated Admiral Townsend. He put down his coffee cup, still half full of his sixth beverage since lunch. "Lieutenant how long until sundown?"

"An hour and a half, Sir."

"Good, start recalling the search helos, have the one with the most fuel remaining make one more pass over the area right here."

He touched the chart at the western edge of Capri, "I just have a feeling is all. Let me know when everybody is back aboard and call the CTF 63 Duty Officer and get the latest status on the Russian sub that's prowling around there waiting for us when we get underway. *If we ever get underway!*"

WILSON AND STANFIELD LISTENED AS Manckowicz and Fettes explained the problem. The wire was spliced but how could they put the juice to it without shorting the whole damned thing to the engine block?

Wilson asked, "Couldn't we make insulators to hold the wire away from the engine? My dad's electric fence has these white ceramic things that keep the wire away from the fence posts but his Herefords feel the shock. It always seems to work too."

Carter knew what she was talking about and it made a lot of sense to him, "Ted I think we can make something to do that, let's see what we have for insulators."

Wilson said, "Couldn't we cut pieces of the plastic bumpers and make them hold the copper wire away from the engine?"

Carter knew she was more than just the pretty girl he was crazy about, she had listened in those physics classes in high school!

"Hold up there guys, she's got a point. John see if you can slice some chunks of plastic from one of those boat bumpers. Let's give it a try!"

Barton took out his knife and walked over to the pile of things they had amassed on Saturday evening. He selected the least scuffed and grimy of the pair. Five minutes later they had enough chunks of the thick rubbery plastic to try it out.

Fettes and Manckowicz connected the makeshift harness and fit the pieces of plastic between the bare wire and the engine making sure no part of the wire was in contact. Manckowicz nodded as Fettes twisted the connector back onto the positive terminal on the battery.

Gleason hopped up onto the Cox'n's flat and Fettes gave him the thumbs up sign. Gleason hit the start button and the stillness almost made Carter want to weep in frustration. Back to the drawing board. Fettes took the connector back off the battery terminal and began the hunt for the next break in the harness. He and Manckowicz knew there had to be one, maybe even more than one.

Carter called them all to come and meet with him at the blankets. They had delayed having the last of the bread and cheese hoping they would be leaving and they could satisfy their hunger at the little café in the town so nearby but still so inaccessible. Carter had the rations handed out and they ate in silence. The end of the food meant they were really in trouble.

BATES CALLED *EISENHOWER* AFTER SIMS came back from his walk along the waterfront querying the locals to see if their friends had been seen there Saturday afternoon. No one had seen them and he had asked every fisherman, every waiter, and every shopkeeper he found. They had cruised close inshore along the northern and eastern coasts of Ischia all morning and afternoon and found nothing. They entered the harbor and tied up at the quay afterward and Sims spent an hour making his circuit. Not even the ticket agent at the ferry boat terminal had seen anything and his window had a commanding view of the dock area. It was almost dusk and they had just enough fuel to return to the ship.

Captain Christensen nodded when the CDO reported the information Bates had passed them and reluctantly ordered him to have the gig return. They would search Capri next. He went to find his friend in Flag Plot with the news.

ELAINE CARTER RETURNED TO HER kitchen with the big atlas that usually sat on the bookshelf in her husband's study. Helen Manckowicz and Barbara Wilson were sitting at the kitchen table sipping coffee. The phone had been busy in reaction to their call to Senator Gressley. No less than five calls had been received in the last hour with callers between the ranks of ensign and rear Admiral.

Each had been polite and solicitous but none had any idea concerning the whereabouts of the three missing Hawkeye sailors.

Elaine opened the book to the "Italy and the Mediterranean" page and the ladies poured over the maps of the area, observing that there were several islands of note in the Bay of Naples. Elaine's copy of Frommer's *Travel Guide to Europe* provided some useful information too but the ladies would need to peruse the town's library for anything recent. They called the librarian who agreed to stay an extra hour and let them look at everything she had in the building that had "Naples" or "Italy" in its title. The *Michelin Guide to Italy* had a wealth of information on the islands in the Bay of Naples.

It was getting dark when Barbara Wilson got up from the library table, "I'm going home girls, Wally is probably wondering where I am and he's probably hungry for his supper too."

Helen Manckowicz knew that her Jack would be ravenous, all the Manckowicz men were big eaters. "I'd better be getting along home too Barbara. Let's agree to meet somewhere tomorrow morning and call each other if there is any news."

It was all they could do. The navy was not letting them know anything new.

THEY HEARD A HELICOPTER BRIEFLY, just at sunset, but it was too far out for them to try the last signal flare. It was dark in the cove. They still had some of the driftwood left but Carter didn't order the watch to bank the fire brightly as they had done the last two nights. They had to conserve what little was left and one of the battle lanterns was dead too. They had managed to delay eating the last of their food until 1800 and Wilson and Stanfield had given part of their bread and cheese ration to Manckowicz and Carter. They were down to almost a pint of fresh water in the thermos. Carter prayed that the last break they had found in the cable harness would be their last impediment and that they could start the engine in the morning.

He lay back on the blanket and felt Wilson next to him curled up and asleep, her rhythmic breathing was somehow comforting.

He whispered to the watch, "Artie just poke the fire every couple of hours. When Dorothy comes on watch tell her the same thing. We'll conserve the wood as long as we can."

Gleason understood, "I've got it Ron. I'll pass on the word and I'll see you in the morning."

He woke Stanfield for her midwatch and drifted off to sleep immediately. They were all tired. Something had to happen soon.

Stanfield was glad when she held the wristwatch near the glow of the fire and saw that it was time to call Wilson for the 04 to 08 watch. She knelt on the blanket and touched her shoulder lightly, "Sam it's me Dorothy." She murmured it softly so as not to wake the others. "You have the four to eight, don't let the fire die out but we're conserving the wood. Here's the wristwatch. Ron wants to be called at 0600."

Wilson rolled over rubbing the sleep out of her eyes and sat up. Carter was sleeping soundly next to her and she could just make out Stanfield by the fire's glow. "Thanks Dorothy, I've got it. Get some sleep, we're getting out of here in the morning. You've been a wonderful friend."

She clasped her hand in the darkness and they exchanged places. Stanfield lay down on the place Sam had warmed on the blanket and Wilson moved over to sit by the fire. She just had to wait a little while now, sunrise wasn't far off.

She took off her sneakers and pulled out the laces. Then she shucked off her dungaree pants, folded them into a doubled-over length of denim, rolled her sneakers up inside them into a tight roll and tied it with the shoestrings. She wore her dungaree shirt over the tank suit she had put on the evening before. She made a loop in the shoestring she could slip up her arm; she would tow the little bundle behind her. She knew that Ron had been swept seaward the night before by the current but it was a new day and the time was offset by nine hours. The current should be running toward Naples now. It would be helping her instead of trying to push her out to sea.

This couldn't be any worse than the meet when she had swum the 800 free right after kicking Ruthie Evans's skinny little ass in the 400 free, and then she had anchored the 800 medley. Ribbons and medals mattered during her school days; the safety of her friends and shipmates mattered now.

CARTER AWOKE TO THE SCREECHING of sea birds returning to the cove. They were hungry and looking for crabs on one of their favorite beaches. They had left days ago when the people came and built their fire but now the smoke was gone and surely the crabs would be abundant.

It was very light and he sat up with a jerk. Sam must have let him sleep. He felt guilty and jumped to his feet, it was bright enough to see the whole cove. He looked toward his sleeping shipmates and saw they were beginning to wake up too, all five of them and something clicked in the back of his mind. "Where's Sam? Who had the watch before hers?"

Stanfield sat up and rubbed her eyes, "I did Ron, she relieved me at 0400 I told her to wake you at 0600."

"Well she didn't. Where the Hell can she be?"

THEY SEARCHED ALL OVER THE cove. She wasn't at the 'women's head' at the end of the beach past the broken boulder and the driftwood tree trunk. She wasn't over by the pile of discarded cardboard. She wasn't in the motor whaleboat and she wasn't in the water. Seaman Samantha Wilson was gone.

NINE THOUSAND MILES AWAY THE light was on in Barbara Wilson's kitchen. She had awakened at midnight with a weird sense of foreboding and couldn't get back to sleep. She sat alone at the kitchen table looking through picture albums at photos of Sam they had amassed over the nineteen short years of her life. Pictures that showed her with her first tooth, her little tricycle, her first Hereford calf and her first pony. She flipped another album open and there was Sam leading a heifer around the show ring at the State Fair holding her big blue ribbon and smiling so brightly. Wally came in and found her, "Barbara what are you doing in here?"

"I was just looking over some of Sam's old pictures, I'm scared Wally. They should have found them by now. It's been three days!"

She began to sob and her husband hugged her trying to sooth her, "You know she's fine. The girl is smart and a hard worker. For her size she's as strong as an ox and when she makes up her mind to do something, she does it. Remember when she broke her foot and the doctor said she would be on crutches all year? She worked so hard in rehab and healed so fast she made the cheerleading squad that fall. That girl is nothing but tough and determined. She'll find a way to get back to her ship. Mark my words, she will."

CHAPTER 13
HOW DID WE MISS THAT?

NAVAL AIR STATION SIGONELLA, SICILY is the forward deployed 'home' to the Mediterranean's P3C Patrol Squadron. The Patrol Squadron based at Rota Spain also scouts the Mediterranean, but the 'Sig' squadron does the lion's share of the 'Med' work. Commander Ernie Perkins sat with his maintenance personnel on Tuesday afternoon while they updated him on the status of each of their planes. The Commander already knew that of their nine P3s, one was a notorious hangar queen and it could be relied upon for nothing. If it wasn't a bad engine or two it was a problem with some half million dollar chunk of its avionics package. That left eight other planes to handle their tasking requirements.

The squadron had over half its flyable aircraft in the air at that very moment. One plane was tending a sonobuoy search barrier in the eastern Med and a second was on it's way to relieve it. Two planes were involved in the SAR looking for the seven missing sailors and one was in contact with the Soviet sub in the Tyrrhenian. His relief was just doing pre-flight checks and would be airborne in half an hour. They would conduct a 'hot-turnover' and the relieving plane would take over "Commie watching" for an eight hour stint.

Materially speaking they were chockablock; all it would take was one tiny thing going wrong and they would have no backup for any emergency. Commander Perkins looked at his worried and harried Squadron Maintenance Officer and decided to share some good news with him. "Bart the Admiral told me that we'll be backing off on the SAR. Today we'll only be tasked to fly one daylight search mission."

The Maintenance Officer's level of concern didn't appear to ease at all. Instead his teeth seemed to grit even more and he eyed his boss tiredly, "That's good news I give you that but when can you tell me the Goddamn commie subs will stop popping up all over the Med and I can give my troops some rest? My Chiefs haven't had a weekend off in over a month." Morale in the Maintenance Divisions was in the toilet.

Commander Perkins was in no mood to broach prima donnas so he launched into his hip pocket spiel, "Bart you can tell your Chiefs that I couldn't care a damn whit about their liberty! Our aircrews are in the bitching mode too and what I have to tell them I'll certainly be happy to put out to your maintenance Chiefs! We need to all pull together on this, I know it's tough and Admiral Winstead appreciates that more than anyone. We just happen to be the ones in the limelight right now but think of the three ships those sailors are missing from. Those ships are really under the gun, at least we're getting some credit for finding and holding onto the Commie."

The Maintenance Officer was onboard with that. At least he had stated his case and warned the boss that they were holding onto the last straw.

NORTON, MATHER AND THEIR TAO were going over the strip charts from their afternoon mission at the Tactical Support Center with the analysis team. Their LOFAR grams were a thing of beauty and the squadron analysts were excited to the point of giddiness as they examined them together. The senior analyst turned to them, "This is the same 'voiceprint' as the Commie sub we picked up over in the east Med two weeks ago and the bastard gave us the slip! There's a flight out there right now trying to turn him up! You guys did really well!"

"Yeah you sure did," said his assistant. "You guys just made two plane crews for today and tomorrow morning real happy and I suspect that the Maintenance Officer'1 be happy enough to kiss you all!"

COMMANDER ERNIE PERKINS DIDN'T WANT to kiss anyone but he was the happiest man in the whole Mediterranean. With the revelation that they had the Commie sub nailed in the Tyrrhenian they would be able to wrap up the barrier flights in the eastern Med. That was half their current effort and the knowledge that it was over was like a dose of euphoria. Now if only the SAR would turn up the missing sailors he could cut back the pace of things to just the prosecution of the sub which had been unlucky enough to get himself caught.

ADMIRAL WINSTEAD WAS THE NEXT-HAPPIEST man in the Mediterranean and his shot of jubilation occurred when his CTF 67 Watch Officer called him right in the middle of dinner with his wife and their guests. The Watch Officer knew that the local phone system was probably being tapped by every enemy agent living in Italy but he wanted to let the Admiral know what had happened so he devised a 'code' on the fly, made up of homey sporty-sounding terms. "Good evening, Admiral I thought you'd like to know that the horseshoe tournament on the east side of Carney Park is cancelled because the stake got lost this afternoon and I'm having the horseshoes put away. It turns out that the stake is really being used in the tournament on the west side of the park."

The Admiral quickly discerned that he was addressing the ASW effort and that the sub in the eastern Med had followed the Battle Group to the Tyrrhenian. He was frequently called at home by his Watch Officers who seemed to compete with each other in devising obfuscating gibberish. He had also played horseshoes in Carney

Park. "Well, Lieutenant I'm happy to hear we've sorted that out. Make sure we let all the tournament observers know and let's make sure the participants know too. And while you're at it see if someone in the recreation department can figure out how the stake was misplaced to begin with and why we didn't know which stake was which from the beginning!"

The Admiral returned to the table and brought the third and fourth happiest men in the Mediterranean up to date on the Commie sub situation. Admiral Townsend and Admiral Wilkins had flown in from London earlier in the evening and had arrived for cocktails and dinner with the Winsteads at their villa, "We've dropped the prosecution of the Russian 'Echo' in east Med. He's confirmed to be waiting for you off the 'shin' Tommy. We've got him cold. The only thing that bothers me is why it took us so long to figure out he'd given us the slip over there and set up housekeeping in the Tyrrhenian, it's like they had access to your port visit schedule! I don't know how we missed it."

Admiral 'Tommy' Townsend had relegated the importance of the missile-firing nuclear submarine to the third slot on his give-a-shit list. It was a 'cold war' fact of life that wherever an attack aircraft carrier went, some skulking soviet sub wouldn't be far behind. There were still sailors to find and ship collisions to deal with but he listened politely as 'Willy' Winstead passed the information. Then he attacked his pasta course, spaghetti ala carbonara, Missy Winstead sure knew how to throw a lovely dinner party!

Admiral Wilkin's wife had driven to Naples to go shopping and for her appointment at the Naval Hospital on the hill overlooking the NSA. She sat across the table from Admiral Townsend. "Tom your poor sailors have been lost for two days now and they are the talk of the NSA. People at the hospital were saying you have helos searching all over the Bay of Naples. I think that's pretty scary. Do the mothers and the wives of your sailors know that you are doing everything humanly possible to find them?"

He frowned, "Sally, I only know we *are* doing everything possible to find them but I don't know what the mothers have been told." He made up his mind and went on, "But I'm damned sure gonna find out!"

THE CNO DUTY CAPTAIN PUT down his secure phone and sent two of his Watch Officer assistants to answer the question that had just been asked by the man responsible for the seven missing sailors in the Mediterranean. That question was, "I want to know what the navy 'mouthpiece' is saying to my sailors' parents." It was such a good question that he lit a fire under the Chief of Naval Information's action officer to find out.

IT WAS JUST AFTER WALLY went back to bed when the phone rang in the Wilson's kitchen startling Barbara and making her spill some of the snapshots she was laying out on the table, onto the floor. She quickly got up, lifted the receiver off the hook and placed it to her ear, "Hello, Wilson residence."

"Mrs. Wilson my name is Townsend and I'm calling you from Naples, Italy. I want you to know that I'm the man responsible for your daughter being lost and I don't know what the navy's shore establishment has told you, but I'm doing all that's humanly possible, and I'm going to find her and her friends and get them back safe and sound."

He talked to her for almost half an hour and Barbara had the feeling that she had just heard the right words from the right navy man. She was comforted for the first time since the ordeal had begun. She could feel a sense of rightness and hope after two days of scripted blather.

She knew she would be able to meet with Helen and Elaine in the morning with a fresh outlook and a new fix on the horizon.

CHAPTER 14
COCKAMAMIE IDEAS

BMC GROVES SAT UNCOMFORTABLY AT the table in the wardroom as Commander Gavin asked the questions he had jotted down after the Battle Group's Chief of Staff had given the *Porter's* officers his piercing 'this-bunch-of-idiots-just-lost-five-shipmates' stare during the Sunday morning meeting at CTF 63's headquarters.

"Chief tell me why you set up the boat exchange for Saturday and not Monday or Tuesday."

"The First Lieutenant told me to get the boat swap done this weekend, Captain. I was under the impression he wanted it done as soon as possible."

"Thank you, Chief," he turned to the First Lieutenant, "Mr. Anders why did you want it done Saturday?"

"Captain I wanted to get rid of the damaged boat because it was a reminder of the collision and I knew the XO had posted the picnic outing in the plan of the day so I had the exchange happen in the morning so we could support it with the new boat."

Commander Gavin had the feeling that they were on shaky ground but he went ahead anyway. "Chief who did you assign to the boat swap?"

"I put Gleason on it, Sir. He's the leading Third Class and he pins on BM2 next month. He's been a qualified Cox'n for over a year and he's conscientious."

What the Chief didn't say was that the only alternatives to

Gleason would have been the First Class Boatswain's Mate or himself … and they were both ashore on liberty.

Commander Gavin had a bad feeling about the boat exchange, "Alright, Chief what instructions did you give Gleason about checking out the new boat?"

Chief Groves was only a little more uncomfortable after that question, "Captain I told him to check the boat carefully and to be sure it had all its gear and safety equipment with it before he signed for it."

Commander Gavin nodded and turned to his XO, "Exec get in touch with the maintenance facility. I want you to go talk with the Officer in Charge and find out what happened there when the boat exchange was made on Saturday.

Now I want to find out all about what went on aboard getting ready for that picnic excursion. Who was the Command Duty Officer?"

The XO looked at his copy of the watch bill, "Ensign Wheeler had the duty Captain. There was a delay while the XO went off to find the young Ensign and the Captain excused the Chief and the First Lieutenant in the meantime. When the XO brought in Ensign Wheeler the Captain began, "Mr. Wheeler tell me everything you know about the liberty boat and the picnicking excursion that happened on your watch Saturday."

Wheeler was unprepared for the question but he responded quickly, "Captain I put everything in the Deck Log, the Navigator has it now, I'll go get it from him and then I'll be able to answer your question."

"Very well, Mr. Wheeler go get the log sheets."

Ten minutes later the Captain had all the information he needed. Wheeler had meticulously recorded the personnel in the party, the order he gave regarding their return by 2035, and Gleason's assurance that he had conducted a thorough test of the new boat before signing for it. He documented that the Cox'n had ensured him that the proper safety equipment was aboard. Finally he indicated the boat's destination and that they planned to stop at *Eisenhower* to embark a "Sam" enroute their Ischia beach party.

The Captain paused in his reading, "And what was the response to your order to return by 2035, Mr. Wheeler?"

"Captain, Petty Officer Gleason said, 'don't worry, Sir we'll be back by colors.' There were two quarterdeck watchstanders who heard the exchange, Sir."

"What happened when they didn't get back?"

"I was in the wardroom, Sir and the quarterdeck called to inform me that the boat hadn't returned. I logged it and I looked for the XO to report the fact to him. He returned aboard at 2200 and I made my report. He told me to try and contact *Montpelier* on the shore phone or the secure radio telephone to let them know that their sailor was with our party and hadn't returned. I was unable to find a shore phone listing for them and they didn't answer the radio telephone call. I reported that to the XO and he told me he would take care of it in the morning."

The Captain was uncomfortable, "Did you attempt to contact the SOPA Duty Officer?"

"No, Sir. The XO told me not to."

The Captain felt a rushing in his ears when Wheeler made that cockamamie statement and he looked toward his XO for a response.

Lieutenant Commander Marlowe's pulse was pounding as he began, "Captain I didn't want to let the whole harbor know our ship's troubles. There was nothing that could be done during the Saturday night hours anyway."

Commander Gavin looked at him disdainfully, "We'd better hope that Admiral Townsend sees it that way, XO and we'd better find those sailors damn quickly, or I'm afraid he won't."

CAPTAIN MANFRED PICKED UP THE ringing phone just after his staff meeting and found that Admiral Winstead was very interested in how his Naval Support Activity operated, especially on weekend days and definitely as it pertained to refurbishing small boats. Well, he was SOPA, he had a right to be concerned. His was a significant tenant command and Bill Manfred was always attentive to his best tenants.

"Yes, Admiral I'll be in your office in two minutes, Sir!"

Their three minute meeting resulted in two immediate things; the Captain would personally familiarize himself with the workings of his small boat refurbishment efforts, and every single sailor in Saturday's duty section would provide CTF 63's Investigating Officer with a written statement detailing any contact they'd had with any sailors from the Battle Group.

By 1800 the Investigating Officer had collected a quarter-inch stack of written statements, a fairly good idea of the movements of Seaman Samantha Wilson of the *USS Eisenhower* but absolutely no clue as to the whereabouts of her or the six other sailors who had been missing since Saturday afternoon.

IT WAS STANFIELD WHO FOUND it, "Ron! Look it's a note from Sam!"

Carter hurried to where she knelt by the pile of emergency gear they had collected on Saturday. She had the second plastic boat fender in her hands and she handed it to him. The message was written in red lipstick on the scarred white surface, "I'm swimming for help. Hold on, it won't be long. Sam."

Carter felt a chill at the base of his spine and his calf began to tingle and then throb again as he thought about the jellyfish and God knew what other dangers she was braving … for them. He almost started to sob as he hung his head in anguish and Stanfield put her arm around his shoulders. "Ron don't worry, she's a fantastic swimmer; she beat both yours and Ted's asses yesterday right here in this cove! She told me she was the top high school girl swimmer in Iowa in the 800 meter freestyle two years running! If she can't swim around the point and save us nobody can!"

"Dorothy, it's a Goddamn cockamamie idea. We're right there! She's risking her life for us and it's only a couple of hours and we'll have the damned boat working and be done with this!"

IT WAS ACTUALLY FAIRLY WARM in the water. The seabirds were swooping down screeching at something a few hundred yards away but she paid no attention to them, she was intent on making her way through the broken rock spires and then rounding the point as it jutted into the sea ahead of her. She smiled to herself as the yards fell to her lithe strokes and she could see that the first rays of sun over her right shoulder were in her favor, if she made it to the breakwater she would find people awake and up and conducting business as they had been in the little port for centuries. It gave her confidence and with that came a second wind. She knew that she could make it. After that it was just a matter of remembering how to spell.

BATES WAS UP EARLY SO that he could make sure the gig was ready to go. It had been fueled and checked over by the engineers and they had pronounced it in tip top shape. He saw Chief Thomas coming down the gangway, the last of their search team to embark. The Chief Corpsman was already below with Sims; they had coffee and some breakfast pastries they had taken from the mess. It was time, almost an hour until sunrise. He signaled to Holden and she took in their bow line and he backed them away from the boom.

Holden joined him at the wheel, "Where to first, Billy?"

He had looked over the chart carefully and had a hunch, "We'll swing by the section of the island near where the Blue Grotto is. There have to be local boat people there, they may know something. Then we'll pull into the harbor and get Sims talking to the shopkeepers and fishermen. We'll be there in less than an hour at this speed. Take the helm and keep her headed on 165. I'm gonna grab some of that coffee, I'll be right back."

SIGNORE GIOVANNI BONCORE WAS JUST arranging the stacks of the different denominations of lira notes in order in his cash drawer when some movement down by the jetty caught his attention. It was still too early for it to be one of his fisherman friends, they would all still be at the café enjoying the last of the strong coffee and a 'graffa', one of the delicious giant donuts the pasticiaria next door was famous for, before loading their nets and heading out after the morning's catch. He adjusted his spectacles and looked harder at the point of land guarding the harbor entrance. Hopefully it wasn't something floating in the water that would be a hazard for the ferry boat he expected in an hour. The tourists who had spent the night in the hotels and at the world famous thermal spas looking for the 'cure' would be arriving shortly to buy their ferry tickets and he needed no distractions, but still there was something there.

Wilson was nearing exhaustion when she finally reached out and touched the rounded boulders that made up the base of the jetty. It was low tide and she had to deal with the gooky, slippery algae growth on the huge lower rocks. As she began her climb it turned into a smelly black and green mess that stung her nose and made her want to throw up but she managed to control herself and stay focused, pulling herself up past it, breaking fingernails and skinning both knees on the immense barnacles in the process. As she climbed she scared the nearby gulls and terns who sprang into the air and screamed shrilly, causing a great commotion.

SIGNORE BONCORE LOOKED UP FROM his cash drawer tidying at the first shriek of the gulls and saw them hovering and swooping excitedly near the end of the jetty and then he saw the painfully slow climb of someone who was exhausted but determined to survive and finish her mission.

WILSON PULLED HERSELF OVER THE top of the jetty and flopped down on the rough wooden planking that ran from the point to the beginning of the waterfront where the fishing nets were hung and the boat oars were stacked waiting for the fishermen. She rolled onto her back to catch her breath before untying and unrolling her bundle. Slowly she pulled on her dungaree pants and slipped on her sneakers.

SIGNORE BONCORE HAD NEVER SEEN a girl come out of the sea, put on her clothes and walk up the jetty to his ticket window before and he stood with his jaw agape as the lovely, short-haired blonde began speaking English to him in an excited manner. He of course only knew enough English to make change for his customers but he knew someone who spoke it very well. He picked up his telephone to call his English-speaking friend when the girl smiled and made the dialing motions with her hands that showed she wanted to use his telephone. Politely he held out the handset in her direction. She took it and moved closer looking down at the face of the dial on the cradle, and shakily began to dial: 5693552374, lowellberg. She was sure that was it.

SIGNORA EVANGELINA BERG WAS EXPECTING a call from her sister to discuss their upcoming shopping trip to Rome and she picked up the phone on the second ring, "Pronto?"

"Hello Ma'am is Chief Berg at home?"

'Vangie' quickly shifted from her native Italian listening process to the English process she had so painstakingly tried to learn since marrying her American sailor. "Si hello, yes this ees the Berg residence but Lowell is no home right now. He go to work early to finish beeg printing job. May I take a message for heem?"

THE TELEPHONE IN THE DOCUMENT center rang and one of the junior sailors picked it up, he caught the Chief's attention, "Chief it's your wife on the phone, she says it's urgent."

The Chief took the phone and Vangie gave him the information about the missing sailors in the desperately-fast, excitedly-emotional way that Neapolitan women speak when they are advising their husbands to be careful while driving in heavy downtown traffic.

He had to slow her down several times but over the course of the next minute he got all the essential information. He thanked her and hung up, then he tried to call the CTF 63 OPCON Center. The number was busy.

The Chief ran to the elevator and mashed the UP button. When the car came he pushed the SEVEN button and rode the four decks upward in silence. At the OPCON Center door he rang the buzzer and a Petty Officer admitted him. COMFAIRMED and his staff officers were in a briefing and the Chief overheard them discussing the Soviet sub that was being worked over by the P3s. The Admiral was about to ask a question when the Chief burst out, "Sir, I know where the seven missing sailors are!"

The Admiral was immediately attentive. By now every single sailor in the European Theatre of Operations knew about the missing sailors and now at last somebody could answer the question he had asked the packed briefing room on Sunday morning. Two minutes later the Admiral was on the 'steam valve' with the Battle Group Chief of Staff. A minute after that Captain Mallory was on the phone with his friend Captain Christensen.

THE RADIO ON THE GIG crackled and Bates answered, "This is the party boat".

He could make out the unmistakable voice of the Captain, "Party boat this is the number one partier, our missing little sister just used the telephone at the ferry boat ticket office on Capri to call home. Go get her, Boats and bring them all back safe."

BATES SWUNG THE BOW NINETY degrees to the left and headed directly toward Marina Grande. He passed the word to the rest of the party below that Sam was there and he jammed the throttle to the stops. They would have her safe and sound by the time his coffee cup was empty.

SIGNORE BONCORE OPENED HIS OFFICE door and called out waving excitedly to his friend Antonio DiGiuseppi who ran the bar next to the waterfront café where he always had his noonday lunch. He usually spent two hours over his lunch because the ferry schedule was arranged to allow ferry company personnel their traditionally lengthy midday meal. Even the ferry crews were afforded time for a lengthy repast. "Antonio viene y porti alcuno spirito de vino! Presto, Presto!"

The barman hurried inside and emerged with a bottle of strong red wine spirits and sprinted across the street to the ticket office. He could see the problem as soon as he opened the door. The soaked and exhausted young woman was huddled on the wooden bench outside the ticket window grille and shivering violently as the water dripped from her clothes and pooled on the floor boards by her sneakers. Signore Boncore found an empty cup and DiGiuseppi uncorked the bottle and poured some of the strong spirit offering it to her shaking lips with fatherly tenderness. "Biba signorina, biba!"

Wilson opened her mouth and a tiny rivulet of the potent stuff ran down her throat. She began coughing as the raw spirit burned its way down her gullet and made her retch. This certainly wasn't soda pop! She jerked up and put her hand over her mouth, after she stopped coughing she smiled up at the men, her hands making 'enough thank you' motions.

BATES EYED THE APPROACH TO the breakwater and cut the corner as closely as he dared. The gig sliced through the narrow passage in the breakwater at maximum speed, its bow wave causing the little fishing boats tied to the molo to porpoise wildly as they were bounced against each other and the rocks of the molo. He gauged the range to the ferry slip and counted the seconds before he slammed the transmission into reverse and hit the throttle with full power. Every seam and fastener in the gig shuddered and groaned as he brought the boat to a stop at the ferry slip. Seaman Holden leapt down onto the molo and threw two hitches around a pair of bitts. Then she ran toward the little building with the 'BIGLIETTI' sign.

SIGNORE BONCORE HEARD THE ROARING of the navy boat's engine and looked up just in time to see the gray and white gig churn to a sudden foamy stop right outside his office window. Sims and Martin ran to the weatherbeaten building and they took their young shipmate into their arms. "Sam, we're here and we've got you!"

Chief Petersen ran in and checked her vital signs and they helped her up. Bates and Holden rushed in as Sims was thanking the ferry ticket master and his amici for their kindness to their missing shipmate.

Bates picked her up into his arms as if she were a poor lost hurt kitten and carried her tenderly back to the gig. Sims gave the barman five dollars and took the bottle of wine spirits with him. Chief Petersen thought it was a good idea because the others might need a stimulant when they finally found them. They put Wilson on the padded naugahide bench in the sternsheets. Chief Peterson and the other women stripped off her soaking dungarees and her tank suit and dried her with towels, rubbing some warmth into her limbs. Holden had even had the foresight to bring along clean socks, underwear and fresh dungarees. Chief Peterson cleaned her raw knees and put antiseptic on them before taping gauze over the abraded skin.

Bates backed them clear of the ferry slip and steered for the mouth of the breakwater. Dried, cleanly dressed and exhausted, but eager to finish what she'd started, Wilson struggled to her feet and climbed up on the Cox'n's flat with him. "Billy it's to the left outside the breakwater. It isn't far but the mouth of the cove is hidden you'll have to be close to the base of the cliffs to find it. Oh, Billy thank you for finding me. Thank you for saving us all!"

She clung to Bate's arm to steady herself and tears began rolling down her cheeks as Martin caught up with her and handed her a coffee cup full of hot soup. Bates patted her arm gently, "You did it Sam. The Captain radioed me where to go, I just drove the boat. Besides, we still have to find your friends."

FETTES COULD SEE THAT THE last break was a big one and he pointed at it so Manckowicz could see. "Somehow we need to jump that gap when we try it Ted. If we only had a damn screwdriver we could make it without getting our asses shocked off."

Manckowicz could easily see the problem too. Carter and Gleason were standing outside the boat looking down at them when Manckowicz had his cockamamie idea. "Hey, John," he yelled to Barton. "Does your cook's knife have a Bakelite handle?"

"Yeah, I'm pretty sure it does, Ted."

"Bring that puppy out here, we're about to start this big hunk of iron up and your knife is the tool we need to do it!"

Manckowicz could see the light at the end of the proverbial tunnel. They were almost home free. "Artie I think we're ready for you to hit and hold the start button. I'll close the circuit with John's knife. If we get this sucker running, keep it running. The electrical system is totally shot but the diesel should be fine, we just need to fire her off with the starter. Jimmy cut in the fuel and push the connector on the battery terminal we're gonna do this!"

Gleason climbed up on the Cox'n's flat and waited as Barton waded out and passed the big knife to Manckowicz. He said a silent prayer as Manckowicz bent down to make the makeshift circuit. "All ready, Artie fire 'er up!"

THE NOISE OF THE ENGINE rumbling to life was the music they had missed for the past three days. Manckowicz and Fettes pulled the cable back out of the way and shut the cowling cover. Then they jumped down and waded up onto the sand to give the others a hand loading the things they had unloaded on Saturday night; the boat's equipment and their cooler and blankets. That took only seconds as willing hands made short work of it. Then they lined up at the gunwales to help push the boat off the sand. Gleason gunned it in reverse and moments later it was free and afloat.

Manckowicz lifted Stanfield into the boat and climbed in behind her. He put his arms around her and they cuddled in the bow as Fettes, Barton and Carter climbed aboard. Gleason swung the boat around and lined up on the cut intent on leaving their idyllic beach, secret cove and impromptu prison behind forever. They shot out into the open sea past the jagged rock spires just as the *Eisenhower's* gig came into view 200 yards to starboard.

WHEN BATES SAW THE MOTOR whaleboat with the six sailors inside he grabbed the mike and keyed the radio, "Great big party boat this is the little party boat. Tell the number one partier that all of our vacationing friends are here and I'll be bringing them back safe and sound."

Gleason pointed toward the handsome white-topped craft and shouted, "Look it's Sam with the cavalry!" He throttled back and shifted to reverse as the two boats drifted down on each other. Manckowicz took his arms from around Stanfield and stood up with their bowline in his hand. When they were alongside Gleason nodded and he passed the line to a sailor on the gig who made it fast to a cleat.

Bates called down to them, "We have food, water and clean clothes and our Chief Corpsman is with us, you guys have got to be starving! Come aboard and get some chow then we'll figure out what to do."

Gleason stayed with the boat while the rest of them climbed up onto the gig. He was determined not to let the engine die and he was gonna get the boat back to his ship and report aboard with his head held high. He was starving and it was only when Holden stepped down from the gig and handed him three chocolate frosted donuts that he could even think of anything else. "Holy shit! You mean you *Eisenhower* guys get chocolate donuts?"

Holden laughed, "Yeah we 'bird farmers' get lots of things you 'tin can' sailors don't. Now shut up and eat. I'll mind your boat for you."

Gleason wolfed down the donuts while cautioning her to keep the engine running at all costs and Holden gave him a bottle of water to wash them down. It was the first food and decent drink of water he'd had in over a day and he was grateful to his new bird farm friends for their thoughtfulness. Bates passed him a plastic bag containing clean socks, skivvies and a new pair of coveralls. "The Master Chief figured you'd all want to get out of the clothes you've been in for all this time."

Gleason scratched his chin and felt his whiskers. He realized he hadn't noticed the stubbly growth while he was trapped inside the cove, he knew he must look like Hell. His dungaree pants were filthy and he realized he must smell horribly. Holden was polite to pretend not to notice it, maybe she would mind the boat while he changed. "Hey could you keep her runnin' while I climb up forward in the gig and change clothes?"

She smiled and nodded as he stepped up onto the gig. Stanfield was below in the sternsheets changing and the other men were in the bow changing into the coveralls *Ike* had provided. He stood beside Bates waiting for the others to finish so there would be room for him to change too. "Gotta tell ya we got it going just two minutes before you showed up. Sam is the hero in all this. She was crazy to risk that swim but she sure is the hero."

Carter finished changing and gave his space up forward to Gleason. Manckowicz had a baloney and cheese sandwich in one hand and a cup of hot coffee in the other. He was wolfing down sandwiches so fast that the others just watched in awe. The coveralls he had shimmied into were the largest ones they had brought along but his arms and shoulders were in danger of bursting the seams.

Stanfield finished changing and came looking for Manckowicz. She started laughing as soon as she saw him, "Ted you look like Popeye with that get up on! The coverall company didn't have you in mind when they decided to make these one-size-fits-everybody jumpsuits!"

It was particularly comical because her tininess resulted in her swimming in her coveralls even though the sleeves and pant legs had been rolled up. Manckowicz gave her a sandwich and they sat in the sternsheets laughing together as the Chief Corpsman checked over the rest of them before they headed back to *Eisenhower*.

Wilson looked over the spit and polish, the fancy knots and Turk's heads and the handsome naugahide seat cushions in the gig and gestured to Carter to come and stand with her next to Bates. When he hopped up on the Cox'n's flat with them she said, "Do you like my Captain's boat Ron? He was going to have it take me in and then pick me up on Saturday morning when you saw me at Fleet Landing. Just think, if I'd done it I wouldn't have met you and I would have missed out on this whole thing!"

Bates started laughing, "Yeah, Sam and you wouldn't be the most famous sailor in the Sixth Fleet right now either, along with the rest of this bunch!"

She was incredulous and Carter was perplexed, "What do you mean, Billy?"

"There isn't a sailor in the Med who doesn't know your names by now. They're even calling you 'the Sixth Fleet Seven'. There's been messages back and forth between every Admiral there is, asking if you'd been found and what was being done to search for you. They even got our port visit extended so we could continue the search until we found you. The Admiral told the Chief of Staff not to go anywhere until we got our sailors back and that's almost a direct quote, I know 'cause I was there. The whole Helo Squadron got recalled to search for you and they had VPs in the air looking up and down the whole Tyrrhenian basin.

The Captain figured it out though and he was gonna send all our boats to search both Capri and Ischia but something happened and that got nixed from way up on high. But the Captain sent me with our search party on the sly and yesterday we nosed all over Ischia 'cause that's where you were supposed to be headed. This morning we checked the other side of the island and I was just about to turn back and head into that little town where we found you. If we'd gone to Capri first we'd have found you yesterday."

Carter listened to Bate's narration of the search effort and shook his head, "All those people, the choppers and the planes. I'll bet they spent a ton of dough on fuel alone and all that screwed up, cancelled liberty. We're all in some pretty deep shit!"

The gig and *Porter's* motor whaleboat made it across the Bay of Naples and back to *Ike* by 1100. Bates had the gig secured as Wilson kissed Carter and said goodbye to her companions who departed for Fleet Landing. The *Porter* sailors sheepishly made their way to the brow where Manckowicz shook hands with them all. Then he kissed Stanfield and turned to begin his walk back to the Italian navy base. He was welcomed aboard by the COB and told to get a shower and get squared away. The work on the O2 generator could wait until after he had a chance to meet with the Captain.

WILSON REPORTED TO THE OOD that she had returned to the ship and Chief Thomas told her to go ahead and get squared away and get some chow. He would check with the Admin Officer and see what had to be done.

She wanted her shower to go on forever and she reveled in the hot water, the soapsuds and in the shampoo. She dressed in a clean uniform and put on some lipstick before hurrying to the Captain's stateroom. She knocked, "Captain it's Yeoman Wilson, Sir."

"Come in, Yeo. Welcome back how was your picnic?" He grinned up at her as she entered and stood by his desk at attention.

"Captain I'm so sorry, I know I messed up. I should have found a way to get back to the ship so I could be here and do what you needed me to do on the Court of Inquiry package. Did you see it, Sir? Sims told me he would make sure you got it when you got back aboard. How did it go, Captain did the Admiral let us off the hook, is it going to mess up your career or the Captain of the *Porter's*, Sir? Am I on report, Captain?" She was keyed up and emotional and it all came out in a torrent as tears welled up in her eyes.

Captain Christensen took off his reading glasses and waved her to the chair beside his desk. "First of all, you'll be on report *only* over my dead body and from what I hear from the search team I sent out to find you, there's probably a reason for us all to pat you on the back. Secondly, I did read the package and there's nothing more to do on it. It's perfect thanks to your very prescient alternate ending. Now as to the Court of Inquiry, it hasn't happened yet and it won't until Thursday. That's because the whole fleet and half the rest of the navy have been worried sick and searching for you and the other six 'lost lambs' that have been in the headlines for the last few days. Hopefully that's all over now and we can go about the business of the Battle Group but I've made arrangements for you to go and use the AUTOVON at COMFAIRMED's headquarters so you can call your parents and tell them you're okay."

Wilson had tears running down her cheeks by the time the Captain finished. He reached over and patted her hand. "Go ahead now,

Yeo. Go let your folks know you're okay, I know they've already gotten word but I know your mom and dad will feel better hearing it right from you."

MANCKOWICZ STEPPED OUT OF THE CO's stateroom and made his way to the Crew's Mess. Stevens was waiting for him there with the Engineer and the DCA. The Engineer looked quizzically at him, "Well Petty Officer Manckowicz, the Captain decide to keel haul you or are you back in his good graces?"

"I'm good to go, Sir. The Captain told me to get my ass in gear and get the O2 generator back together but he wants me to go over to COMSUBMED's headquarters and call my mom first. I was just gonna check with the COB and see if the Duty Driver can give me a ride over in the van. I should be able to have the generator on drop test by this afternoon."

"'Alright, Manckowicz better shake a leg then. Welcome back, I'm glad you're safe, and hey, better have the corpsman check out your wounded hook there."

"Thank you, Sir. Maybe you're right."

CARTER AND GLEASON BOTH STOOD in the Captain's stateroom as Commander Gavin listened to their brief description of the incident and made a few notes. His temper threatened to get the better of him as he tried to add up the stupid actions that had contributed to the incident. He decided it was better to let things cool off before deciding what actions he had to take. "Alright you two go get squared away."

He turned to his XO and the Command Master Chief, "Make sure everyone in the party gets over to the USO so they can use their phone exchange to call home, XO. I want to interview each one of them and then we're writing up a full report of the incident. I want to do that as soon as we can while everything is still fresh in everyone's mind and then we're putting it out by naval message."

Carter had an idea, "Captain my friend on *Montpelier* told me that sub crews get permission to use the AUTOVON at the COMSUBMED headquarters, that way they patch into the closest military base to wherever their homes are and it doesn't cost them a hundred dollars like it does at the phone exchange. They only get charged like it's a local call. Can we see if we could arrange something with them?"

Commander Gavin nodded, "That sounds like a good idea," he turned to the Master Chief. "Let's get someone to run them all over to NSA."

CHAPTER 15
HOW STUPID CAN WE GET?

THE QUARTERDECK WATCH AT THE NSA Admin Building pointed to the elevator when Carter asked for the way to the COMSUBMED headquarters. "Sixth deck, then press the button to the left of the blast door."

The five *Porter* sailors rode up in the elevator together. It only took a few moments and they stepped out into the passageway and saw the heavy blue steel door. Carter pushed the button under the RING FOR ADMITTANCE sign and they waited for a reaction. They knew someone was watching them on a video monitor some-where, the big stationary camera aimed at the door was evident to them all. Finally a First Class Radioman opened the door wide enough to ascertain they weren't terrorists. "What do you want here? This is COMSUBMED headquarters."

Carter was just thinking about how to respond as the booming voice of his best friend came from the other side of the door. "Ron c'mon with me. I've got permission from the Yeoman in the Plans Officer's office ta use their AUTOVON line. I was just makin' a head call when this guy asked me if I knew you guys. Hi Dorothy!"

Manckowicz turned to the Radioman, "I'll vouch for all these guys, they're all here to use the AUTOVON. They're off the *Porter* and got lost with me this weekend."

The door was held open and the group followed Manckowicz up the passageway to the little office where a Second Class Yeoman was just putting a cover on his typewriter and securing the unlocked safe drawers for the afternoon. He looked around as they entered, "Hey, people feel free to use any of the desks. My assistant just left for the day and the Plans Officer is on watch in the OPCON Center so it will be quiet here. There are three AUTOVON lines here in the headquarters so two of you can call at once, save the third line for official use okay? Manckowicz make sure you lock up when you leave and don't leave a mess in here. There's coffee in the other room and some spare cups here in my middle desk drawer. Good luck, I'm glad you guys all made it back okay, seems like you were in the news just about everywhere." He handed them a copy of the *Stars and Stripes* European edition. The headline screamed: "SEVEN SIXTH FLEET SAILORS MISSING AT SEA!"

They passed the paper around and Stanfield saw that it had been printed on Monday, the second day of the SAR effort but the third day of their ordeal. "It seems like the word we were lost got out pretty quickly and look they even got our names and ships all right."

Manckowicz was on the phone already. He had the operator at Camp Dodge on the line and he gave her the phone number of his parent's farm in Corning Iowa. A minute went by while the connection was made and the phone rang. Mr. Manckowicz answered it, "Hello, Manckowicz farm."

"Dad it's me Ted! I'm just callin' to let you and Mom know I'm okay. I'm back on *Montpelier* it was a bad couple of days but everything is fine now. Yes, Ron Carter and Sam Wilson are back too. Yeah it's 1600 here I think we're 8 hours ahead so it must be 0800 there. Ron is right here with me now he's callin' home in a minute too. Maybe we'll see Sam and we'll tell her to call her mom. Okay Dad, tell Mom I love her and I'll see you when I get some leave after we get back from the Med this fall."

Carter was already on the other phone line speaking with his mom. A wellness check. The others made their calls and worried parents in Texas, Oregon, Ohio and California were put at ease. The wire services had picked up the *Des Moines Register's* story and various navy spokespersons had been quoted as saying the navy was concerned about their missing personnel but had no further information as to their whereabouts. A search and rescue operation was being conducted in the area of the Bay of Naples.

The list of missing personnel was finally published in stateside papers on Tuesday morning and it almost floored the Stanfield family. They hadn't been home for several days and attempts by navy officials to notify them by telephone hadn't been successful. Mrs. Stanfield almost fainted when her husband handed her the morning *Pasadena Star News* with the screaming headline: "LOCAL WOMAN LOST WITH SIX OTHERS, NAVY STILL SEARCHING". When Dorothy called them her mother had been crying nonstop since she read it and her father was preparing to drive to Long Beach so he could choke the living Hell out of the first navy official he could find. Dorothy's call put a stop to both activities.

WILSON GOT TO THE ADMIN Building and signed in at the Quarterdeck. She took the elevator to the 7th deck and after showing her ID card was taken to the Personnel office where she quickly called her parents. She could hear her dad in the background crowing as her tearful mom began laughing gratefully. "See I told you she'd get back safe!"

"Mom it's okay, please let Mrs. Carter and Mrs. Manckowicz know we're all okay. We were never really in any danger and except for not having very much fun at all for three days and being pretty hungry for most of that time it was really nothing."

She put her mother's fears to rest and in the process made the light in her eyes shine like her husband hadn't seen in years. "Sam please take care of yourself, we love you and hurry home to us! Oh Brianna just had twin heifer calves!"

Wilson hung up the phone and thanked the office personnel for their help. She grabbed her Havelock and purse and headed for the elevator. When it came she stepped inside and was about to press the

ONE button when a man stepped into the elevator with her. He was wearing sneakers, tennis shorts and a sweater and his racquet bag was hanging from a strap over his shoulder. He saw the *USS Dwight D. Eisenhower CVN-69* patch on the right shoulder of her blues and smiled, "It must be good to have all your *Ike* sailors back aboard again safe and sound."

She pushed the ONE button and the doors slid shut as she smiled to him, "Oh yes, Sir it is. I'm so glad to be back and I just got a chance to call and talk to my folks and oh my goodness, I just found out one of my cows had twins!"

The man in tennis clothes chuckled, "You must be Seaman Wilson then, we were all plenty worried about you. What happened to you folks out there?"

The elevator stopped on the deck below and the door slid open to reveal the excited sailors from *Porter* with Manckowicz leaving the COMSUBMED offices together. Carter's face lit up with a smile when he saw Wilson inside the car and hers did too. The man in the tennis clothes noted the reactions as the other sailors entered the elevator. Wilson turned to him, "These are all my friends from the boat, we just got back to our ships this morning and we haven't even been able to compare notes yet. All I know is that the best feeling in the world is finally being able to take a hot shower and put on a fresh uniform."

They were all clean and squared away in their blues, and after being able to call home they were all feeling good about their ordeal. Manckowicz and Stanfield were standing together hand in hand. The man in the tennis clothes took it all in smiling.

As the elevator door slid open at the first deck the Quarterdeck Watch sang out, "Attention on deck!" and the few people milling about there snapped to attention. The man in tennis clothes turned to the sailors still in the elevator, "You know I had a bit part in the whole saga of your weekend adventure and I'd really like to hear what happened to you folks out there but I have a tennis game now and I'm running a little late. Could you all meet me at my headquarters in the morning, say at 0930?"

Wilson quickly put two and two together and spoke for them all, "Aye, aye, Admiral we'll be there, Sir."

Admiral Winstead chuckled, "Good, Wilson," he scanned the rest of them smiling. "I'm glad you're all safe. I'm gonna invite my tennis partner to sit in tomorrow morning too. I know he'll be interested."

He left them at the elevator and strode out of the building and down the steps heading off to the tennis courts in the park nearby. Wilson turned to her friends, "That was Admiral Winstead he's the one who got the ball rolling on the search for us. He's SOPA and also the Commander of all Mediterranean navy air, except for the carrier planes. I suspect he wants to know how this all happened so he can prevent it from happening again."

Carter thought a moment, "Artie and I told our Captain what happened but Ted you and Sam are on different ships and I don't know how this is all going to play out but like I said on the boat coming back, this was an expensive search and I think we're in deep shit. The Admiral could hang our asses."

Manckowicz shook his head, "He can't hang us, we didn't do anything really wrong."

Fettes wasn't so sure, "Hey we missed muster and we were all AWOL for two days."

Wilson knew how to reassure him, "Jimmy when I got back aboard this morning I went to see the Captain right after I took a shower and got into a clean uniform. I asked him if I was going to be on report and he told me I would be only over his dead body, so I think your Captain will see it the same way."

Carter was thoughtful, "Artie and I got called in to see the CO when we got back and we briefed him on the boat's electrical problem and a little bit about how everybody was involved and you swam to the town and called and how *Ike's* gig came and got you and you led them to us just as we got the engine going. I suppose each of us remembers the whole thing a little differently and with three ships involved it may be that we'll all have different 'receptions' if you know what I mean."

Manckowicz shook his head, "No, Ron my CO told me it wasn't my fault and as long as I got the O2 generator up and running, I wasn't gonna be on his shit list. Speaking of that though, I'd better get my ass moving back to the boat and somehow before 0930 tomorrow I have to get a damn haircut, the rest of you look fine but I'm a shaggy dog next to you!"

The Quarterdeck Watch heard Manckowicz's statement about his tonsorial problem, "Hey, Mac there's a barber shop on the third deck. The barber is an Italian guy and I think he's open for another half hour."

THEY RODE BACK TO FLEET Landing together in an NSA van and dropped Manckowicz off at the Italian navy base gate. Wilson rode back to the ship in the liberty launch and immediately went to find Chief Thomas. She needed to tell someone that the Admiral wanted her to come and meet with him and the others in the morning to discuss their weekend odyssey. He would know what to do. Surely the chain of command in the ship was being bypassed. Wilson found that Chief Thomas was on liberty. So was her Division Officer and she knew the Admin Officer was on leave. There was only one thing to do and she went to find the Executive Officer. She found him in the Captain's Mess having dinner with the Captain and the Battle Group's Chief of Staff. Sims told her they were having coffee, she could knock and go in.

"Good evening, Captain may I speak with the XO, Sir?"

The Captain smiled and nodded and the XO turned to listen to her question. She explained that her Chief, Division Officer and Department Head were unavailable and he was next in the chain of command and she wanted to do it right; she needed his advice.

"Go ahead, Wilson what do you need advice on?"

"Sir I went to the NSA to use the phone and call my parents.

When I was leaving, the others who were with me on the boat trip got on the elevator with me. Admiral Winstead was on the same elevator. He figured out who I was and then he said he wanted all of us to come tomorrow morning to his headquarters and tell him what happened. He said to come at 0930 and he said his tennis partner would come too, that he would be very interested."

The Captain turned to the Chief of Staff, "Admiral Townsend is back in Naples now isn't he?"

"Yes, Chris he is and he's an avid tennis player."

The Captain grinned, "XO give her some real good advice because she's representing the whole ship in this."

"Aye, aye, Captain." He turned to her with a smile, "Wilson just be calm and respectful and tell them the truth."

Wilson could see the Captain smiling and nodding as she thanked the XO and left the mess.

AFTER SHE CLOSED THE DOOR the Captain looked at his friend the Chief of Staff, "Ray I hope those sailors from the *Porter* come across to the boss as squared away, for their sakes. My Yeoman is a star and from what I hear she's the one who saved all their asses. I'd like to be a fly on the wall during that meeting tomorrow."

"Well I know the Admiral was concentrating on this collision business but he told me he's gotten the Fleet Commander to preside over the Inquiry because he expects to be a party but he has the morning free tomorrow. He may want us to come along, just so he can get the whole picture, I'll let you know."

"Good, Ray I'd really appreciate it, not that I don't have enough to do getting ready for the Inquiry but it would be a chance to see the whole picture, an across-the-board peek at an event that we should really learn something from."

"Chris I know exactly what you mean, I just hope the people from the other two ships can keep it together. This has to be the dumbest Goddamn thing that I've ever been involved in and I've seen some real doosies! I mean how stupid can we get? Hey, where'd you get that young Seaman from? She's quite something!"

He chuckled, "Ray, wait 'till she gets going!"

CHAPTER 16
THE GREEN TABLE

MANCKOWICZ CLOSED THE TECHNICAL MANUAL and put it back in the bookcase. He scrubbed his hands and went up to the Control Room and got the Equipment Tagout Log. He removed the sheet delineating the O2 generator's danger tags and took it to find the Duty Officer. "Mr. Henning I'm finished with the repairs on the generator, Sir. Request permission to clear the tags and commence startup. Here's the sheet, Sir you just have to sign to clear them."

The Duty Officer signed on the CLEARANCE PERMISSION line and Manckowicz was off to remove the tags and restore the valve and electrical lineup for the machine. He had finished his work and the machine had passed its pressure drop test at midnight. He would be able to get a few hours' sleep in his own bunk for the first time in four days. He put in a wakeup call with the Below Decks Watch for 0500. His blues were pressed and on a hangar in the Auxiliary Machinery Space all ready for him to pull on in the morning. He had already lined up the Duty Driver to run him over to the NSA, he would meet his friends at the Navy Exchange Cafeteria for breakfast at 0800.

CARTER AND GLEASON WERE UP and showering at 0600 they wanted to look their best for the meeting with the Admiral. The Captain had been surprised when Carter explained what had happened in

164

the elevator the day before and he was a bit unsettled with the idea that his boss was upstaging him by directly taking part in; Hell he didn't even know what it was, an investigation, a finding of fact or what? All he knew was that five of his sailors had been "asked" to attend a meeting with two Admirals. That suggested to him the potential for a huge downside. He wished he could be a fly on the wall at that meeting too.

Stanfield was ready to go at 0700. She had made arrangements with the Quarterdeck Watch to hold the ship's van for her and her four shipmates. It would take them to NSA and return to Fleet Landing. She had no idea how long the meeting with the Admirals would take but she didn't want to tie up the van for the whole morning. She would put in a call when it was time for the van to pick them up.

WILSON TOOK THE 0630 LIBERTY launch ashore. There she would check in with the SOPA office at Fleet Landing. Perhaps they had a vehicle available. She knew they made scheduled runs to NSA and to the airport at Capodichino. She had taken special pains with her hair and makeup this morning. Her blues were inspection ready and she put on a new pair of stockings even though her knees were still painful. Her shoes had a mirror shine to them. She even had a few minutes to kill before it was time to go to the Quarterdeck and she stopped in to her office to plan her next day's work. There would be a big stack of correspondence thanks to this port visit, thank yous to different people who had helped make the port visit a success and official correspondence both routine and unusual. Thank goodness the IBM man had come on Monday afternoon and fixed her 660. It would have been a pain to have had to type each letter individually. She found herself wondering again about the Court of Inquiry and what it would bring. But first there was this morning's meeting with the Admirals. And then she thought of something and dug out the binder with the information she needed.

THEY MET AT THE CAFETERIA in the basement of the Admin Building. They would have time enough for breakfast before heading up to the Quarterdeck to sign in and catch the elevator. Manckowicz ordered scrambled eggs and bacon and shared his toast and jam with Stanfield. Carter told them all what his CO's reaction was to the news of their meeting with the Admirals. "The Captain seemed squeamish about it. He seemed to have the feeling that anything we tell them that isn't good could come back against the *Porter* I think he was afraid we would say something 'incriminating', not necessarily about him but about the ship in general."

Manckowicz shook his head, "Ron that's malarkey if somebody had an axe to grind about any ship he was stationed on there are a million ways to handle it but not one of those ways would include shooting your mouth off in front of an Admiral."

Stanfield nodded and joined the discussion, "Ted's right, Ron and besides I don't think there was anything the ship did that contributed to our problem. Surely you and Artie, Jimmy and John all did wonderfully after we were marooned there. I guess the fact that we went to the wrong island and that might have made it a longer problem is one thing, but we could have broken down on our way out there and been washed out to sea, they had to cover all the possibilities in the search."

Wilson had the last say, "Listen all of you. When I got back to the ship last night I knew I'd have to tell someone about the meeting this morning so I went up the chain of command and our XO was the first person who was available and I went to him. He was having dinner with the Captain and the Chief of Staff of the Battle Group. I told them about riding in the elevator with the Admiral and that he wanted us all to come and meet with him this morning. His advice to me was to be calm and respectful and tell them the truth. By the way, I think Admiral Townsend is the 'tennis partner' so we're talking with two Admirals this morning and both of them were instrumental in finding us."

They decided that her 'calm, respectful and truthful' method was the right way to go. They policed their table and threw away the trash. As they were climbing the stairs toward the Quarterdeck Barton managed to say, "I'm damned nervous and I don't care who knows it!"

Gleason clapped him on the shoulder, "John he may not even ask you for anything, just keep calm like Sam said."

They reached the Quarterdeck and as they signed in the Watch there picked up his phone and dialed a number, "They're all here on the Quarterdeck, Chief want me to send them right up?"

He put the phone down, "Chief Maushak will show you where to go when you get to the seventh deck."

As the elevator's upward motion stopped and the door slid open, a woman Chief appeared and ushered them to a small conference room across the passageway from the headquarters "front office". She opened the door and signaled for them to file inside. There was a long table in the center of the room covered with a green baize cloth, five chairs lined each side with one on each end. "This is the Admiral's chair and these are for his guests," she indicated the seat at the head of the table and the two closest chairs on each side. "This is an informal meeting so you can all sit down when you speak with the Admiral but remain standing by your chairs until he invites you to take your seats."

They all chose their chairs, Carter, Gleason and Barton to the left; Fettes at the foot of the table with Stanfield on the right. Manckowicz was next to her and Wilson would be in the last seat on the right, she realized she would be sitting next to one of the Admiral's guests. When they were all standing by their chairs the Chief looked at her watch, "I'll tell them you're all here and ready to go. They'll be right in."

AS THE DOOR OPENED CARTER could see the Admiral in the passageway and sang out, "Attention on deck!" There was really no need to because they were all at attention already. Admiral Winstead strode in and stood by his chair while the others followed him. Admiral Townsend went to the chair on the left; they all knew him from his photo on the Quarterdecks of their ships and of course Wilson had seen him before when she'd hand carried something to the Flag Spaces to give to the Flag Secretary. The next guest took the chair to Admiral Winstead's right. He had two stripes above the broad gold band on the sleeves of his blues. Only Wilson recognized him, she had just looked over his bio sheet in her office. She knew he was vice Admiral Wilkins, the Fleet Commander. She knew the other two guests too, the Chief of Staff and her own Captain.

Admiral Winstead looked them over as he smiled and invited them all to sit down, "I want you all to know how seriously scared we all were when you turned up missing on Saturday and what we went through to try and find you and get you back. You know we even had to get the State Department involved so we could extend the port visit until we found you. We spun up a lot of people to search for you and believe me we all breathed sighs of relief when you were back safe. I just wanted you to know that because that's how we feel about our people."

He saw the looks of seriousness on their faces and went on, "I thought it would save a lot of time if you could tell us what happened to cause this whole thing and maybe we can figure out how to keep it from happening again. I thought you all should participate too. I know each of you remember parts of the event so maybe we can all just help the conversation along. Now can we start at the beginning and just cover the parts each of you remember best? Each of you has a start point and a view of this and they are all different, we understand that. Who wants to start?"

GLEASON TOLD HIS PART OF the story; being assigned to exchange the damaged boat for the new one, the reluctance of the NSA Petty Officer to allow him to put the new boat through a thorough test, his stupidity in taking them all to the wrong island and the ensuing attempts to fix the electrical system.

Admiral Townsend took out his felt tipped pen and a 3X5 card and wrote:

Notes on the saga of the "Sixth Fleet Seven" and then he wrote:

"Electrical systems unreliable." and **"Process for new boat testing?"**

Fettes went next. He talked about the lack of tools in the boat and said he thought he could have easily jumpered around the bad cable if there had been a spare harness available.

Again the Admiral noted on his card:

"Cost of a spare cable vs cost of SAR."

Barton didn't think his input was very important but his contribution of the cook's knife for the final jumpering certainly was.

Admiral Townsend wrote:

"Improvised! Used resources at hand."

Stanfield began by saying that her involvement started when at the direction of the XO she had put the announcement of the picnic and swim excursion in the Plan of the Day. When Carter told her another woman was coming too she had decided to go along, it had sounded like fun. She described the injuries that Carter and Manckowicz suffered and indicated she was happy to have been of some use to the others.

The Admiral smiled and wrote:

"Ship's sponsored outing." and **"Knowledge of first aid/personal readiness."** Then he wrote: **"Damn good thing she was along!"**

Carter went next, "Admiral it was all my fault. I was the senior man and I failed to make sure I knew where we were going and we ended up at an unfamiliar place and selected a dangerous beach we couldn't get away from. I tried to signal the helo I had in sight with a flare gun and it failed to go off. I put my companions in danger, Sir. It was all my fault, I even got Petty Officer Manckowicz and Sam, I mean Seaman Wilson involved in it."

Admiral Townsend wrote:

"Unreliable signal flare." and **"Petty Officer in charge not briefed on location of island."**

Admiral Wilkins had to ask something, "Carter how did you know Manckowicz and Wilson and why do you think it was all your fault?"

"Admiral I was in charge, I should have done more. I've known Petty Officer Manckowicz and Seaman Wilson for years, Sir we went to the same high school together."

Admiral Townsend wrote:

"Chance raises its ugly head!"

Manckowicz couldn't let his friend take the fall for something they had all had a hand in, "Admiral my friend Petty Officer Carter is being too hard on himself. We all went along on this thing and we were all to blame for whatever went wrong."

Admiral Townsend wrote:

"Shipmates shoulder the burden."

Wilson listened to them all and when it was her turn she was ready, "Admiral this whole thing started for me when I realized that there was work to do that I couldn't do aboard. I had an imperative package to complete and I had to get ashore to do it. When I finished

I was on my way back to the ship and Petty Officer Carter ran into me at Fleet Landing and told me about the outing. It was chance but it was an opportunity to see two of my heroes from high school days and I wanted to go along. I met everyone else and we began having a wonderful time. Then the boat's problem happened and we found ourselves marooned. First Dorothy, I mean Petty Officer Stanfield got hurt in the dark by a crab. The next day Ted Manckowicz hurt himself working on the boat. Then Ron Carter tried to swim out and use the flare gun and we almost lost him."

She had spoken faster and faster as she went along and she paused to collect herself before going on, "Admiral the truth is that Petty Officer Carter was the hero of this whole thing. His leadership kept us all together, focused and disciplined. He assigned watches and responsibilities and we wouldn't have made it out of there without his leadership."

Admiral Townsend smiled and wrote:

"Impressive!"

He was about to use his pen again when she looked up the table at Admiral Winstead, "Admiral I know you are all very busy but I thank you for the chance to tell you directly what happened when we were stuck out there. We certainly didn't want to be lost like that and I know there were a lot of resources used in the search, but I just want you to know that if I had been in your shoes and it was one of your kids that was lost, I would have ordered the search too."

ADMIRAL WINSTEAD'S SERIOUS FACE BROKE into a grin, "Tell me, Wilson how it came about that you called Chief Berg and told him where you all were?"

"Sir I met Chief Berg on Saturday when he gave me a ride from NSA back to Fleet Landing. He suggested I take a USO tour and I considered it. He told me if I had any questions about local things I could call him because his wife is a local girl and he gave me his home phone number. It was easy to remember and it's the only number I knew so he's the one I called. I guess if I had gone to Herculaneum I wouldn't be here now."

The Admiral smiled, "I think you may have left something out Wilson, how did you get to a phone?"

She thought about it for a moment, "Sir I had the watch and I knew we couldn't last another day. We had to get out of there, we were out of food and almost out of water and I wasn't sure if the men working on the electrical problem could conquer it so I made up my mind to do what I could. I'm sorry I abandoned my post but I swam for the town. I'm a strong swimmer, Sir and I was sure I could make it. I did and then I got to a place with a phone and I made the call. The next thing I knew, my shipmates were there and Bad Billy came and picked me up and carried me to the gig. I just had to tell him where to steer to reach the others in the cove."

Admiral Townsend wrote:

"Swam!" and then, **"Bad Billy?"**

Admiral Wilkins was perplexed, "What was so 'imperative' that you would work all Saturday morning on it in a liberty port, Seaman Wilson?"

"Sir it was my Captain's Court of Inquiry package. My IBM went down and I got permission to use the one at NSA. He needed it on Sunday and I wasn't going to let him down."

She could see Captain Christensen across the table leaning forward a trifle and he grinned and looked at her with what she always felt was his "soft and caring" look.

ADMIRAL WINSTEAD WAS CURIOUS ABOUT something too, "Can anybody tell me who the Hell this 'Bad Billy' is and how he came to save you?"

Captain Mallory started to chuckle, "Go ahead Chris, I'd like to know about that myself!"

CAPTAIN CHRISTENSEN LOOKED ACROSS THE table at the now grinning Fleet Commander and began his explaination, "'Bad Billy' Bates is Bo'sun's Mate Second Class Bates my sometimes Cox'n and full time excellent sailor. He fought Golden Gloves under the moniker 'Bad Billy' as a middleweight and won 13 fights by knockdown before he enlisted. I sent him out to search for Wilson here with a small party in my gig. He searched Ischia Monday with no success and he was searching Capri Tuesday morning when Admiral Winstead phoned the news to the Flag Watch Officer and Ray called me. I radioed him in the gig and he did all the rest."

ADMIRAL TOWNSEND GRINNED AT THE Fleet Commander and started chuckling, "Seems like I remember you were a middleweight at the Academy, Bob. That would be one for the record books wouldn't it?"

Wilson tried to keep her smile from showing but Admiral Townsend caught it as he was drawing a line through **"Bad Billy?"** on his list. "So you're a good swimmer, Wilson?"

"Yes, Sir in high school I was on the swim team and I won the 800 meter freestyle at the state finals in Des Moines each of my last two years in school."

Admiral Townsend smiled and wrote:

"Eligible for Academy?"

Captain Mallory pursed his lips, "I have to say something while we're on the subject of getting these sailors back safe. If we had been able to affect a boat search on the first day of the SAR we'd have found them Sunday afternoon. Some idiot in Washington is to blame for well over half the effort." He eyed Admiral Townsend and they seemed to pass some secret thought back and forth. The Admiral wrote:

"Find moron turd in DC!"

Admiral Winstead asked if anyone else had anything to add and then dismissed the enlisted sailors, "Thank you everyone I think this was a good meeting and I appreciate the opportunity to talk with you all. It's a whole lot better than reading about 'the incident' in some official report six months from now when everything is all cooled off and things that should get done can't get done because everyone has moved on to the next flap."

He smiled as he remembered something, "So you folks have another day here in sunny Napoli; what are you going to do with it?"

Manckowicz was smiling from ear to ear as he said the first thing that came to mind, "Sir I'm buying the biggest pizza they sell here and eatin' it along with havin' a few of those Peronis!"

THEY GOT UP TO LEAVE the conference room and as Wilson was filing past the Fleet Commander he looked up at her, "Wilson tell me about this package you made for your Captain."

SHE STOPPED AND LOOKED ACROSS the table at Captain Christensen. His eyes had the same look in them that she knew. "Sir it's a narrative that encompasses every single thing that was going on for the half hour before and after the *Porter* brushed against us in the Adriatic. All the actions, the personnel, the orders given and all the logged data too and there's even a package of charts and figures that sums up all the outside factors and where the AGI was at the time."

174

She could see the understanding in the Admiral's eyes as she went on, "Admiral if you saw it you would know immediately what happened, just as if you were there yourself."

He stood and shook her hand, "Thank you, Seaman Wilson, so you're a Hawkeye too eh?"

She grinned, "Yes, Sir a tiny town called Corning, I think there are 300 people in the population, nowhere near as big as Decorah."

His eyes crinkled then and a smile spread across his face, "So what did you raise; Herefords, Angus or hogs?"

She laughed, "I'm a Hereford girl, Sir. I was driving a tractor around our farm when I was seven."

He grinned and patted her shoulder, "Seems like a hundred years ago, Wilson but I was raised on a dairy farm outside Decorah. I'm a Guernsey man."

"Yes, Sir. The State Fair, making hay in the summers and all those big corn fields. Thank you, Admiral have a great day, Sir."

SHE LEFT AFTER HE PATTED her shoulder again and she found the others at the elevator waiting for her. "Hello everyone! Let's go somewhere and make sure that Ted gets his Naples wish!"

CHIEF MAUSHAK TOLD THEM ABOUT a place right across the street from the NSA where they could get the best Italian food they could imagine and at the tiniest prices. "Americans call it the 'hole-in-the-wall' but they speak English there and they really do make some wonderful things and it's all very reasonable."

ADMIRAL WINSTEAD WAS CONVINCED THAT half the problem was right here in the NSA boat rework facility. "I've asked the CO here at NSA to look into every aspect of how they get a boat ready for issue and I think the electrical problems are pretty well documented or at least that's what the boat users tell me."

ADMIRAL TOWNSEND LOOKED AT HIS 3X5 card and it seemed to him that something was missing; what was it his Chief of Staff had said about the *Porter* that day they discovered the seven were first missing? "Ray what's your take on *Porter* in this? Didn't you tell me they held off letting anyone know they had a problem for a whole day?"

"No, Sir they didn't say anything until the boat was missing for fifteen hours. I got the feeling that something went amiss and somebody dropped the ball on *Porter*. I think it would be a good idea if I ride *Porter* for a few days when we get underway, Admiral. I don't *know* something is wrong there, but I have a feeling and I think the easy way to find out is a nice leisurely ship ride."

The Admiral nodded, silently agreeing. If anyone could quickly get a handle on the 'turd in the punchbowl' without making big waves it was Ray Mallory.

ADMIRAL WILKINS STARTED TO GET up when he thought of something, "Captain Christensen I'd like to see that package your little swimmer girl mentioned. It might just save us all a lot of time tomorrow. By the way, she's quite something! She knew I was a Hawkeye and she knew Willy had kids in the navy. Hell she probably has all the dirt on Tommy too! And only a Seaman," he shook his head slowly as he smiled. "How'd you end up with her as your Yeoman anyway?"

Captain Christensen chuckled, "Luck of the draw, Admiral. I lost a First Class Yeoman to a drug problem three days before we got underway and she had just reported aboard fresh out of A-school. She took over the job and she's been Cracker Jack. I'd stack her up against the best Yeoman on your staff! I'll get the package to you this afternoon, Admiral. Where will I be able to find you, Sir?"

ADMIRAL WILKINS CHUCKLED, "I'LL BE playing tennis here at NSA with Willy at 1400, after that I'm at the mercy of Sally's shopping list. Somehow I think I may be at Madame Vacarelli's for most of the afternoon."

"Aye, aye, Sir. I'll get you the package this afternoon."

WITH THAT CAPTAIN CHRISTENSEN AND his friend left the conference room and headed toward the elevator, "Ray excuse me I want to find that Chief and see where my 'swimming Yeoman' went. I need to ask her a question."

Chief Maushak pointed him to the "hole-in-the-wall" ristorante across the street. "Ray, why don't you have my Duty Driver take you back to Fleet Landing? I'll get a ride back after I talk with Wilson."

WILSON WAS JUST EXPLAINING TO the group that one of her duties as Captain's Yeoman was to maintain the 'VIP Book' which held all the biography sheets on the Admirals and other notables that the ship might come in contact with and she passed it to the Captain to review whenever a personnel change occurred in their hierarchy. "Just like there is a photo of the Admirals on the Quarterdeck for recognition purposes, there is a sheet that tells about them that I keep track of, it's just common courtesy," she chirped. "If I didn't know Admiral Wilkins was a Hawkeye from Decorah I wouldn't have been doing my job."

THE WAITER CAME IN FROM the kitchen, bringing Manckowicz's pizza to the table just as Captain Christensen walked around the corner and Wilson saw him coming toward them. "Attention on deck!"

They all started to get up from the table and he motioned for them not to. "Go ahead and eat troops, I just came by to ask Seaman

Wilson a question."

She knew what he was going to ask already, "Yes, Captain I made a copy of the court package and I have it locked in a drawer in my desk. Should I go and get it for you, Sir?"

"Goodness no, Yeo I'll give him the one you gave me. Admiral Wilkins wants to look it over before tomorrow. Hey, how are you all getting back to Fleet Landing?" He took in the group of happy sailors who were just getting their first meal on liberty since the port visit began. They were relaxed and having a good time and he hated to disturb them especially since the food they'd ordered all looked so good. The big sailor, Manckowicz, looked mesmerized by the giant pizza in front of him and the little PN, Stanfield, looked like she couldn't get enough of the spaghetti she was having. He felt guilty bothering them at their meal.

Wilson smiled, "We'll find a ride back, Captain would you care to join us, Sir? This is the best Italian food I've ever tasted!"

"Thanks, Yeo but I really have to get back to the ship I have a window to get there and back and give the package to the Admiral. After that I may be able to squeak in a little late lunch. Thanks for asking and hey, you all have a good time on liberty. You did very well this morning."

TWO HOURS LATER THE CAPTAIN handed the package to the Fleet Commander who weighed it in his hands before slipping it into his briefcase. "Thank you, Chris. I've decided to stay in town tonight and we'll convene in Tommy's flag spaces on *Eisenhower* at 1000 tomorrow. All the participants are right here in Naples so it would be a waste of time and fuel to helo everyone up to the Flagship in Gaeta. We'll do it right here."

"Aye, aye, Sir. It'll be good to have it over with."

CHAPTER 17

A NIGHT OF LIBERTY

VICE ADMIRAL WILKINS KISSED HIS wife goodnight, "Don't worry sweetheart I won't be up long." He walked into the sitting room, shut the door behind him and sat down on the striped sofa. He adjusted the reading light and pulled out the package Captain Christensen had given him. Flipping through the pages he realized that the little Hawkeye Seaman had been right, it was as if he were there watching them right in the thick of the whole thing. It was as if he were the producer of a movie and his *Eisenhower* cast was performing their individual parts in the play. By the time he finished his read-through he had his mind made up. He picked up the phone, called the Sixth Fleet Staff Watch Officer and gave him an order.

The Admiral didn't often get a chance to get away from the business of the navy, stressful and mundane things weighed him down probably three hundred and fifty days of the year. It was always a treat for him and Sally when they could get away together and catch even a few hours of down time. They had checked into the *Hotel Excelsior* after their trip up the mountain to the famed pottery factory. Madam Vacarelli herself had come down to the showroom to demonstrate the intricate patterns of her masterpieces to Sally. He had no function other than to carry the heavy packages Madam's five assistants had wrapped in brown paper so that they could be transported to Gaeta in the trunk of their Alfa Romeo sedan. Thank God his driver was an expert on the local traffic, he knew where to find a fantastic out-of-the-way ristorante with Sally-satisfying main courses too. They had checked in after dinner, a two hour delight that had made them glad he had decided to take his orders to the Sixth Fleet when he might have gone to the Seventh, and lived in Japan.

MANCKOWICZ AND STANFIELD WERE ON the dance floor at the *Bluebird*, dancing to the old songs of the Beatles and the Monkeys. They were both good dancers and she was popular and pretty and one of only a few women there; it was only the intimidating size of him that kept the other two or three hundred male sailors from trying to cut in and spirit the diminutive beauty off to some dark corner of the dance floor for a close encounter of the very first kind. Any sailor making that mistake might be thought to be harboring a death wish.

An old slow song came on and he pulled her close and put his lips to her ear as they swayed together in the center of the crowded floor, "Oh, Dorothy your hair is so soft and silky, I love it and I love you! I don't know what I'm going to do without you when we get underway. You'll be on that tin can and I'll be in my boat and we won't be 5 or 10 miles apart but it will be like being on different worlds. Oh God I don't know what I'm gonna do not being able to see you! It's gonna be agony."

She clutched his big arms and pulled him tight against her, "Oh, Ted I know I need you too! Listen when we get back to the states I've got a month's leave on the books. I'll be transferring to Naval Station San Diego and we can have a whole month together before I have to report in. We can go anywhere you want, Ted."

"I want to take you to meet my folks and my sister in Iowa and I want to meet your folks too because I want to ask your dad if I can marry you. Dorothy I'm sorry I don't have a ring or anything but will you marry me?"

Her excited squeal and urgent kiss were the only answers he

needed.

CARTER AND WILSON SAT TOGETHER on the sofa in the living room of Lowell and Evangelina Berg's Neapolitan apartment. They were sipping the homemade wine that Vangie's father was so proud of as they chatted with their hosts. Wilson smiled, "Chief it's just so great this all worked out and your wife was home when I called."

Chief Berg chuckled, "I know, Sam when I got to the OPCON Center and told Admiral Winstead where you were it was like a heavy yoke was lifted off his neck and he passed the word to the Battle Group Watch Officer so fast it was like magic. The mood in that whole room changed and the Admiral even slapped me on the back he was so happy."

She laughed, "No, Chief I meant today, this afternoon when I called hoping I could thank you both for helping us."

Vangie picked up a plate of pastries and tried to pass it to Carter who politely smiled and held up his hand to wave it away, "Oh gosh no, Mrs. Berg thanks if I have one more bite of those cannolis I'll explode, but they're so delicious."

Vangie beamed when he complimented her desserts, "So how long have you two known each other?"

Wilson explained that they were from the same home town and that she had been his little brother's girlfriend before graduating from high school. But Vangie could see for herself that it was real between them. "Are you two engaged or anything?"

Wilson giggled, "He hasn't even asked me yet, but he will and when he does I'm gonna say yes but only after he finishes at the Naval Academy."

Carter's eyes widened to the size of teacups, "Naval Academy? How do you know about that? I haven't even been recommended for it yet and with this boat disaster I'll be lucky if I don't get busted!"

"Oh shut up, silly! Your CO is going to send you off to the

Academy this fall, you just mark my words! And next year maybe I'll be able to join you there. That is if I can manage to be a good enough sailor for my Captain."

IN *EISENHOWER'S* FLAG SPACES THE Chief of Staff and the Flag Operations Officer put the finishing touches on the sortie plan for the Battle Group. They would rendezvous, pass through the Strait of Messina and then operate in company in the eastern Mediterranean for three weeks before their next set of port visits. The whole effort was designed to show the flag off the Israeli shore.

Their port visits were already scheduled and their hosts would be a variety of Greeks and Turks while *Montpelier* was even slated for a layover in Ashdod, Israel. Captain Mallory offered his assessment of the plan, "It looks good and it will probably all hold together for just as long as it takes another one of our sailors to figure out how to tempt Pandora again. Maybe not with a motor whaleboat, but with something. By the way, send *Porter* a message saying that I will embark before they get underway. Tell them I anticipate arriving at 1800 tomorrow."

ADMIRAL TOWNSEND PUT HIS 3X5 card in his desk drawer and handed the message flimsy to his Flag Secretary. "Fill in the blanks here and here with the names of those two sailors and then release this with the distribution I've indicated on this sheet." He passed her a piece of ruled notepaper with ACTION addees that started with the CNO, Chief of Naval Material, the Naval Safety Center and every ship in his Battle Group. The INFO addees included every headquarters that had received the initial OPREP regarding his lost seven sailors and had grown by leaps and bounds to fill up the entire sheet of notepaper.

The Flag Secretary looked over the wording of the lead paragraph and shook her head, "Admiral are you sure you want to accuse someone in the CNO's office of 'unduly restricting the traditional initiative of the officers at the scene of action, interfering with the orderly search for my missing sailors, hazarding them for at least an additional day and exacerbating the situation leading to the needless expenditure of ...'?" Her voice trailed off as she recognized the set of his jaw and the determination in his eyes.

"Aye, aye, Sir I just thought there might be a more diplomatic way to tell the boss that there is an asshole on his staff who should be ...."

"Lieutenant this message says exactly what I want it to say. It's the equivalent of 'Fuck you! Strong message to follow'!" He was having just a little fun with it now and the reaction of his prim and proper Flag Secretary was icing on the cake.

"Yes, Sir and it's sure gonna get some attention!"

She found the missing names and filled in the blanks. The bombshell first paragraph was sure to be talked about at all levels soon but the follow-on paragraphs dealt with getting to the bottom of small boat electrical system problems and might even make for a standardized loading of tools and safety equipment on all small boats. That was a good idea she thought. And then there were the paragraphs praising the sailors involved; Carter for his steady leadership, Gleason and Fettes for their determination and knowledge of boats, Stanfield for her first aid skills and readiness and Barton for his care for them. Then the submariner, Manckowicz for his strength and determination and finally the *Eisenhower* Yeoman; wow he was putting her in for a medal for saving them with a 'superhuman effort both mental and physical'. All in all she thought it was one of the best messages she'd ever read and she hurried to the communications center to supervise cutting the final version. She would have it on the air waves by the time the evening movie was ready to roll in the Flag Mess.

THE DUTY RADIOMAN HANDED ENSIGN Wheeler the message board, "Sir three messages for *Porter,* one is IMMEDIATE and it requires action."

Wheeler took the board and saw that ComSixthFlt required the Commanding Officer to be aboard *Eisenhower* and to report to the Flag Spaces by 1000 tomorrow. Its Subject was "Inquiry". The second message was notification that Captain Mallory, the Battle Group Chief of Staff, would be embarking the following day prior to their sortieing. The last message was the Battle Group Commander's blast up the chain with the good words about the sailors who had been lost at sea. Wheeler almost flew to the Captain's Stateroom and knocked on the door. "Captain it's Ensign Wheeler, Sir."

The Captain was in the middle of brushing his teeth before turning in when the knock on his door startled him and he dropped his toothbrush on the deck. He looked up as Wheeler proffered the metal board with the paper sandwiched inside. "Thank you, Ensign Wheeler give me a moment please," he swooped down and retrieved his errant toothbrush, "Now let's see what we have to look forward to tomorrow."

The first message's curt frigidity in its summoning finality and the second's announcement of the imminent arrival of the Chief of Staff had a very unsettling effect on the Captain and all thought of a restful night's sleep and a leisurely day preparing to get to sea evaporated in an instant. "Mr. Wheeler ask the XO to come see me please."

LIEUTENANT COMMANDER MARLOWE KNOCKED ON the Captain's door 5 minutes later. "Captain it's the XO, Sir."

He entered to find the Captain fishing through his desk for a notebook he'd assembled that had many of the pertinent facts related to the collision. He looked up, "XO get the Deck Log from the Navigator and make sure it goes back to include the time of the collision. Look at this."

He handed him the message board and he quickly scanned the messages. To him it appeared that the Captain was in danger of being relieved of his command. That surely wasn't good news and since when a Captain got sacked it probably meant that the XO, Navigator and OOD all took a bath with him; that was *really* disconcerting.

"Holy shit, Captain this is right out of the blue! Nice of them to give you twelve hours' notice on it. I'll get the Deck Log and be right back, Sir."

He woke the Navigator and gave him his orders, "Nav bring me the Deck Log for this month!"

The Navigator turned out and ran to CIC where he had just reviewed the last two sheets of the Log. He grabbed the inch-thick stack of paper held together by brass prongs and left a sheet for the Duty Quartermaster that read; "See the Navigator for May's Deck Log though the 22nd, original pages provided to the Executive Officer this date." He signed the sheet and took the first three weeks of May's pages to the XO. "Here you are, XO May's Deck Log right up till midnight last night."

"Good thank you, Navigator. I'll let you know if there's anything else. The Captain has to go to the Flagship in the morning. I guess it's the collision thing come home to haunt us. Now that the search for the sailors is over the powers that be can focus on us again. I don't think it's going to be pretty."

MANCKOWICZ WALKED STANFIELD TO *PORTER'S* brow at midnight but he couldn't let her go, "Oh, Dorothy you don't know what you do to me! I wish there was a jewelry store open right now so I could buy you an engagement ring!"

She stood on her tiptoes and leaned against him pulling his face to hers with her hands. "Kiss me, Ted it's only a few more months and then we can be together. Don't worry my darling, I'll write you every day. Do you get mail often on your sub?"

"No but at least when we're working with the Battle Group we do get it from time to time. The carrier is good about it so I guess we probably get something about once a week. Gee I wonder if we'll have another port visit together! Wouldn't that be great? Maybe in Greece or someplace I'll have to check with the COB and see what they have planned for us."

CHIEF BERG DROPPED CARTER AND Wilson off at Fleet Landing just after midnight and Carter shook his hand as he opened the door. Wilson hugged him and thanked him for his part in their rescue for the fortieth time that evening. "Chief thank you so much and please tell Vangie thank you for me too. We might still be trying to get back here if it wasn't for you and her."

"Sam it's okay. We're just glad you got back alright, you and Ron and the rest of the 'Sixth Fleet Seven'. Maybe the next time you are all in Naples we can get together and we'll have you over to our apartment for a nice dinner. Vangie would love to show off a little of her cooking."

Carter thought that would be a fun thing, "I'd love to see Ted Manckowicz dig in to some of Vangie's cooking, that would be an epic event!"

Wilson thought the idea of that was funny too. She had watched him eat that whole pizza and then he'd ordered a mound of spaghetti and smacked his lips over the Bolognese sauce. After that he'd had some Italian ice for dessert. Ted Manckowicz could really *mangia*! She'd learned that word from Vangie earlier in the evening.

They walked down the pier together and stopped by the *Eisenhower's* idling liberty launch. There were a dozen sailors in the launch already, waiting for the Cox'n to shove off on schedule to return to the ship. Wilson recognized two of the sailors in the boat right away. They were from the rowdy crowd that had been shooting off their mouths about how much beer they would drink the night before they had anchored. They were from the helo squadron.

She took Carter by the hand and led him away from the launch toward SOPA's pier office. "Ron I don't want to leave you but we have to go. Those guys on the launch are from the helo squadron and I don't want them to see us kissing. They already know it was me who messed up their liberty and I don't want them mad at you too. Just kiss me and then we'll go to our separate ships and I'll write you and you can write to me and ... oh my goodness hold me! When this deployment is over, I want to take a couple of weeks and go home and I want you to come with me. I want to be with you and I want it to be perfect and I do want to marry you after you finish at the Naval Academy. Now promise to write because I'll write every day!"

He nodded his head in surrender, "Sam c'mon I'll put you on the launch and if anybody gives you any shit I'll break their face."

He kissed her again. They walked back down the pier and she said goodbye as she climbed aboard and sat down.

One of the Airmen recognized her right away, "Aren't you the bitch that got lost and got our liberty cancelled for three days?"

His buddy, a Third Class Petty Officer added fuel to the fire slurring, "Pretty friggin' bad deal we got too, stupid bitch."

Wilson was just ready to reply when the Cox'n stepped down from his flat and inserted himself between the bellyaching Airmen and the Seaman. "When you talk to one of my shipmates, Pal it better be with the respect she deserves and I demand on my boat. Now apologize and then shut up for the rest of the trip or I might just throw your ass right into Naples harbor. Got it?"

The Third Class opened his mouth and sneered, "That fuc ..." just as Bate's right fist lashed out so fast it was a blur and jammed the rest of his drunken statement back down his throat. The irreverent youth's jaw went slack and he slumped backwards against the gunwale.

Bates glared at his sidekick, "Better help your trash-mouth buddy there, Mac he seems to have fallen asleep." He turned to Wilson, "Sam you okay?"

She smiled up at him, "Hello, Billy! We can't go on meeting on boats like this. People will talk!"

He chuckled as he climbed back up onto his flat and signaled the Bowhook to take in their line.

ADMIRAL TOWNSEND PUSHED BACK FROM the table in the Flag Mess and turned to the Chief of Staff as the messmen put the reels of film in their carry case and put the projector away in its storage locker. "Ray no matter how it turns out in the morning, I want you to know it's been a pleasure serving with you."

"Admiral?"

"Somebody's getting fired in the morning I just hope it's the right guy."

"As far as I'm concerned Boss, I think I know the right guy."

CHAPTER 18
THE INQUIRY

BMC GROVES CHECKED OVER THE davits that supported Porter's gig, everything was ready. He signaled to his two Seamen and called out, "Lower away, easy there not too fast! I don't want to mess up this boat too."

When the gig was safely in the water he turned to the party, "Wrap it up and secure. The CO said he'd be back by this afternoon, we'll hoist in then and make it ready for sea. Go ahead now and get your breakfast, then up to the fo'cs'l. We still have plenty of work to do before we're ready to get underway this evening."

He called down to Gleason in the gig, "Take it to the pier and make her fast. The Captain will be down about 0800 so be ready, he's going out to *Eisenhower*."

"Right, Chief you need me up on the fo'cs'l too or have you got enough help up there? I need to get in a clean uniform after I make her fast. I'm not going out to the flagship in my dungarees."

"No, Gleason I've got plenty of help just make sure the gig is good to go before the Captain calls you away."

MANCKOWICZ GOT PERMISSION FROM STEVENS to go ashore for a few hours. "Just make sure you're back by the time we station the Maneuvering Watch, Mank. That should be around 1600 according to the Plan of the Day."

"Thanks, Steve I gotta get over to the NSA, I'm goin' to the Navy Exchange for somethin', and can I get you anything while I'm there?"

"No thanks, Mank be careful of the traffic, it's nice to have you back in one piece. Let's try to keep it that way!"

Manckowicz put on his blues and slipped his wallet into his pocket. He had just over three hundred dollars in cash and a blank check. He managed to flag a passing navy van headed towards NSA and within 15 minutes he was standing at the Navy Exchange jewelry counter. The clerk helped him pick just the right ring and he put half his money down on it. He wrote out the check for the rest of the eleven hundred dollar price tag and was out the door headed for Fleet Landing half an hour later.

COMMANDER GAVIN PACKED HIS NOTEBOOK and the deck log in his briefcase and looked himself over in the mirror. His uniform was neat and his tie was perfect, his ribbons and Surface Warfare Officer breast device were regulation and his gold Command at Sea device was correct. He checked to ensure the cover on his combination cap was snowy white and his black dress shoes were highly shined. He was as ready as he would ever be.

Gleason saluted him as he stepped into the gig then signaled the Bowhook to take in the line. When the Captain was seated he nodded and Gleason backed them clear, put the rudder amidships and shifted the transmission to go ahead. He steered for the boom on *Ike's* port side. He had been there before. At the Quarterdeck's hail he answered, "*Porter*" and idled in alongside. The Bowhook made them fast as the Captain stood and climbed out onto the platform at the bottom of the accommodation ladder. "I don't know how long I'll be, Gleason just stand by here and I'll pass the word when I know."

"Aye, aye, Captain." He shut down the engine and watched as he climbed the ladder. He could hear the *Ike's* 1MC as the word was passed, "*Porter* arriving."

"Okay, Rios better take it easy, the Captain will let us know when it's time to go. I'll stay with the gig if you want to go and check out their ship's store. Be back by 1000, I want you to watch everything while I go find a friend, okay?"

"Sure, Artie. I'll be here when you need me."

Gleason settled in as the Seaman ran up the gangway to experience the culture shock of meeting a crew twenty times the size of *Porter's*.

WILSON KNOCKED ON THE CAPTAIN'S Stateroom door and announced herself. She knew he only had a short time before the Court of Inquiry convened. She had heard the Fleet Commander's and COMFAIRMED's arrivals announced just moments ago and she thought it a good time to wish the Captain good luck and to check with him to see if he needed any more copies of the court package. She heard his familiar "C'mon in, Yeo" and opened the door. She was surprised to find another officer sitting there talking with him. She knew all the Department Heads and the COs of their embarked Air Squadrons but this Commander was a stranger. He stood up and turned to face her as she shut the stateroom door. Before she could apologize for interrupting them the Captain smiled, "Commander Gavin this is Seaman Sam Wilson. Sam this is Commander Gavin, Captain of *USS Porter*. He's here to say hello and we're going to report together to the Flag Spaces in about half an hour. By the way, congratulations on your award."

He handed her the message Admiral Townsend had sent the night before, "You did real good, Yeo. I just hope some of that rubs off on the rest of us, we're gonna need it this morning."

She took the paper from him but didn't even glance at it, "Oh, Captain I know it will all work out fine for you both. Nobody did anything wrong either here on *Ike* or on *Porter*. It was an unfortunate accident is all, and that stupid Russian pilot is to blame for everything. Sir I wanted to know if you want me to make any more copies of the court package and if there is anything else you need me to do to get ready."

He shook his head, "No, Yeo I gave the original to Admiral Wilkins yesterday and I have the other one you made to refer to if he wants to go over anything. That should be enough." He turned to Commander Gavin, "Do you need copies of anything made before we go to Flag Country?"

Gavin thought for a moment, "I brought the Deck Log with me but I have to take it back to the ship. If the Admiral wants to include part of that in the record I'd better make a copy." He opened his briefcase and took out the Deck Log.

Wilson smiled and took the package from him, "It'll just take me a few minutes, Sir. I'll be right back with it."

ADMIRAL WILKINS, ADMIRAL WINSTEAD AND Admiral Townsend finished their coffee as the white tablecloth was stripped off leaving the Flag Mess table bare. The messmen brought in the green baize cloth and smoothed it, transforming the convivial setting into one of formality. Admiral Wilkins had brought two of his staff with him for the event, his JAG Officer and the Flag Secretary they would be sufficient for his purposes. He could borrow anyone else he needed from Tommy Townsend.

WILSON FINISHED AND RETURNED TO the Captain's State-room, "Here you go, Sir. I didn't have any of the brass prongs so I used a bulldog clamp for the copy."

Gavin took the log sheets and the copy and thanked her, putting them into his briefcase.

She heard him ask Captain Christensen if he was bringing any-one with him to make statements during the inquiry. "No I've in-cluded all the statements from my Bridge, CIC and Air Ops watchstanders, and my high line transfer party in my package. If the Admiral wants anything else I'll be surprised."

CAPTAIN MALLORY WAS SATISFIED WITH the preparations for the proceedings. He had assigned several of the Battle Group's staff officers to support the Fleet Commander's needs. He had researched the requirements for Courts of Inquiry in the *Manual for Courts Martial* but the Admiral had wanted the event to be as informal as possible yet still retain the elements of naval tradition. There was no need for excessive pomp and ceremony, there was still a Battle Group to run and individual ships to get underway. They all hoped to have the proceedings concluded by early afternoon.

CAPTAIN CHRISTENSEN HUNG UP THE phone and got up from his desk, "We have to be there in five minutes, Bob. Let's go, my XO can handle the load while we're otherwise 'indisposed'."

WILSON HEARD THE CAPTAIN'S VOICE in the passageway and hurried to open the office door. She smiled as both Captains walked by, "Good luck, Captain. Good luck, Sir."

The Captain smiled and thanked her and Commander Gavin nodded but looked very grave. They turned the corner and vanished from her sight as they walked toward the Flag Spaces. Wilson finished typing the last page of the latest of the Captain's letters to Admiral Rickover and put it in a folder ready for him to sign out before they got underway. She got out her list of crew members whose families the Captain would write to next and took the first twenty five. Thank goodness the IBM man had fixed her 660. She would run off one of the personal letters for each of them on the Captain's stationery tailoring each slightly. The Captain would sign them and add his personal notes later. She also had a list of the dignitaries and their wives who had attended the Saturday reception and she composed thank you letters for him to send to them as well. It was just busy work but she needed to stay focused so she wouldn't worry about the Captain's fate at the inquiry.

She had just finished the last of the dignitary thank you letters and started on the envelopes when the door opened, "Hi, Sam how ya doin'?"

"Artie! I never expected to see you this morning!"

"I never expected to be here either. I had to bring the Captain out this morning, I guess the Inquiry is going on today."

"Yes, I know I just met your Captain. He was here talking with mine. I made a copy of *Porter's* Deck Log for him. They both left here for the Flag Spaces a few minutes ago."

ADMIRAL WILKINS WAS SEATED AT the middle of the table with Admiral Winstead, the Chief of Staff and the Staff JAG Officer alongside him when Captain Christensen and Commander Gavin entered the Flag Mess. The two empty chairs across the table from the Admiral were obviously reserved for them. He gestured to them, "Gentlemen please sit down and hopefully we'll be able to dispense with this matter quickly so we can get back to the business of operating the navy."

Captain Christensen could see his package on the table in front of the Admiral and he knew that he had read at least part of it because the bulldog clamp had been removed. He noted that Admiral Townsend was sitting at the end of the table, not across from them, with the other members of the Court.

The Fleet Commander had a hopeful expression on his face as both Captains took their seats. He turned to his JAG Officer, "Commander are we all correct and ready to proceed?"

"We are, Admiral except that I'm short a Court Reporter and we all have to be sworn."

The Admiral nodded and turned to the two Captains, "As President of this Court I ask you both to rise as we are all sworn. Admiral Townsend has recused himself from the panel because he may have some testimony to make so he's a party too. I know that Captain Christensen is not planning to have any of his ship's company called to testify because he has submitted a comprehensive written statement that includes all their inputs." He turned back to the JAG officer, "We don't have a Court Reporter? What do we need here?"

"Admiral we don't have a machine, but we could get by with a Yeoman who can take shorthand. I'll administer the oath and we'll be ready to go."

WILSON WAS JUST EXPLAINING HOW she kept track of all the Captain's correspondence to Gleason when the door flew open and the Flag Secretary stuck her flushed face into the office and startled them both. "Seaman Wilson you're wanted in the Flag Mess and bring a steno pad with you."

She jumped to her feet and responded, "Aye, aye, Ma'am!"

She grabbed a pad from her desk and followed the Lieutenant out into the passageway. Before she shut the door she looked back at Gleason, "Artie you can stay here if you want. I'll be back as soon as I can."

She hurried to catch up with the Lieutenant, "What is it, Ma'am? Does the Captain need me, is there something wrong?"

"No, Wilson the Admiral needs you and nothing is wrong. Apparently you're the only Yeoman in the whole Sixth Fleet with good enough shorthand skills, you are about to become the Court Reporter."

That bit of information was so totally unexpected she didn't know how to react, but then she remembered the XO's advice; stay calm, be respectful and tell the truth. Of course her dad's advice seemed more appropriate to this situation; "Just do your best," and she hoped Miss Martin's shorthand classes and her practice would let her get through the next few hours with flying colors.

ADMIRAL WILKINS SMILED AT HER as she entered the Flag Mess and stood at attention, "Good morning, Seaman Wilson Captain Christensen says you're a Cracker Jack Yeoman and that you take excellent shorthand. You turn out to be the very thing we need to get these proceedings underway. You'll build the record of this Court of Inquiry so you'll take your shorthand and then turn it into typed pages."

The JAG officer administered the oath to her and she swore to "faithfully perform the duties of the Reporter of the Court, so help her God" and he motioned her to the chair next to Admiral Townsend.

Admiral Wilkins named the members of the court and the parties and went on to state the purpose of the inquiry, "This Court is convened to inquire into the circumstances, actions and events that resulted in the collision of *USS Dwight D. Eisenhower CVN-69 and USS Porter FFG-78* which occurred on Wednesday May 6th when both ships were steaming in company in the Adriatic Sea during fleet exercises."

WILSON'S PENCIL FLEW BACK AND forth across the ruled pages as she faithfully took down every word. The Admiral paused when he finished his opening and picked up his copy of Captain Christensen's package, "I've read a complete, detailed account of *Eisenhower's* actions and movements for the period 30 minutes before and 30 minutes after the incident and I'm including that report in the official record of the court. Captain Christensen do you have any further witnesses to call in this matter? If not I'll ask you to describe from your package the event from *Eisenhower's* vantage point for the other members of the court."

Wilson knew every word in that package by heart so keeping up with the Captain's account was a breeze. He paused from time to time as Admiral Winstead asked a question here and there and when Captain Mallory asked for a look at one of the exhibits in the charts and figures package. She made sure she carefully noted their questions and the Captain's answers, so far everything would be easy to transcribe. It seemed to her to take hardly any time at all for the Captain's account to be completed and accepted. Then the Admiral called a halt, he needed to make a head call.

During the recess she found that there was no enlisted women's head in the Flag Spaces. It was necessary for her to leave and use the head near her office. She wasn't the only one who noticed. Admiral Townsend patted her arm when she returned and whispered, "Sorry, Sam an oversight when they built the ship. Someday, maybe soon, there'll be more consideration for women aboard ships."

She smiled, "Thank you, Admiral and thank you for the nice things you said about me in that message."

ADMIRAL WILKINS RETURNED AND THEY all stood as he walked in and resumed his seat. "Thank you, everyone. We'll convene again. I want Admiral Townsend to describe the incident as he saw it and then I think we'll break for lunch. One other thing, to save time, Seaman Wilson you'll eat your lunch here in the Flag Mess with the other members of the court."

Admiral Townsend began his account, "After breakfast on *Porter* I said goodbye to Commander Gavin and collected my things. I had a notebook and a small bag with a change of uniform, some personal things and my shaving stuff inside. I had been aboard for a routine visit. *Porter* was the third ship I visited between the end of March and the date of the incident. The rendezvous for personnel transfer was set for 0815. *Porter* arrived on station just before that. I was on the Bridge with the Captain while the transfer party rigged the transfer equipment. Everything was ready and the report was made to the Bridge. I shook the Captain's hand and made my way to the 01 level where I put on a life jacket and climbed into the transfer cage. I looked at my watch and noted that the transfer was right on time. BMC Groves was in charge of the transfer party and I told him

I was ready. He passed that word to *Eisenhower* and their party started hauling me aboard."

Wilson got it all down easily as she found herself caught up in the story. Admiral Townsend's voice was steady but expressive as he painted the picture of the morning's events.

"I noted that the distance between ships seemed to me to be about 80 feet. It was foggy at the time but I could see *Eisenhower* clearly. I felt the lift and that feeling you get in your gut when you're suspended fifty-odd feet in the air and you're just a speck on a string between two great ships. I was concentrating on the distance still to go when all of a sudden there was a loud whooshing sound from behind and over my right shoulder and I looked up and saw the underside of a Russian 'Backfire' aircraft that looked to be at the level of the tops of *Eisenhower's* antennae. It flashed over quickly and the next few moments are a blur. I felt the cage descend until my feet were just above the water. I heard yelling from both ships and I felt myself jerked upward as the men in *Eisenhower's* transfer party took over and pulled like Hell. I dropped my bag in the water and it's gone. I got the shit scared out of me and seconds later I was aboard *Eisenhower* and as I turned to look back at *Porter* she was turning away and her port quarter grazed against something on *Eisenhower's* starboard elevator. I owe my life to the people in *Ike's* transfer party."

WILSON HAD GOOSEBUMPS AS SHE finished her notations, "He could have been crushed between the hulls or even dragged underneath them in that transfer cage," she thought. "I wonder what personal things he lost, probably photos of his wife and family." She felt terrible for him about that.

ADMIRAL WILKINS ASKED HIM IF he had seen the cause of *Porter's* sudden course change.

"NO, ADMIRAL I DIDN'T. BUT it occurred just after the Russian buzzed us. I can only surmise that it was some reaction by *Porter's* Bridge watch team to that."

Wilson quickly jotted that down. It was the last testimony that morning and Admiral Wilkins signaled a break in the proceedings. "Alright then, thank you everyone. After lunch I want to hear what went on from the perspective of the Commanding Officer of *USS Porter.*"

THE FLAG MESSMEN ENTERED, REPLACED the tablecloth and set the table with china, silver and glassware. Wilson wasn't sure where she should sit as the meal preparations progressed. Admiral Townsend sensed she was nervous and patted her arm whispering, "This is *my* mess and you're my guest so you'll have the chair to my right."

She felt much better when he said that but she realized that she would be seated opposite the Fleet Commander and Admiral Winstead would be on her right. She would be in some unfamiliar territory, nowhere near the tables in the Crew's Mess with her shipmates, her peers. Thank goodness her parents had taught her excellent table manners. She wouldn't let the fact that all these Admirals and Captains were eating with her bother her, she would just pretend they were all her uncles.

When they sat down to eat Admiral Townsend told her that service would be family style. Wilson thought it was just like Sunday afternoon dinner at home because they had fried chicken for lunch and it was very well received. She was the only woman at the table and even though she was only just a Seaman she felt welcomed and it was clear to her that these senior navy officers were trying to make her feel that way and put her at ease. Admiral Wilkins even told some funny sea stories that got everyone laughing. They did seem a lot like her uncles at the Thanksgiving table except that her "drunk uncle Charlie" was missing.

THE COURT RESUMED AFTER LUNCH and Admiral Wilkins asked Commander Gavin to provide his statement.

He began, "The ship was on station for the personnel transfer at 0810 and the Admiral shook my hand and went to the high line station at 0815. The OOD ordered the Helmsman to steer 'nothing left of 281'. *Eisenhower* was on course 280. The JOOD was using the stadimeter to monitor the range between ships and announcing the range to the OOD at 10 second intervals. The ship was at 10 knots keeping station."

He paused to look over his notes and Wilson looked up from her pad and saw him flipping through his notebook to a diagram. It had a double line in black with a red arrow crossing them with what must have been courses written in black.

He cleared his throat and began again, "At 0817 the Soviet airplane buzzed the formation coming from about 065 degrees, crossing in front of *Porter's* bridge within 50 feet and continuing out on a heading of about 245 degrees."

Wilson knew that was a pretty good estimation because it was close to what Captain Christensen had included in his chart and figure package. The only thing missing now was what the effect of the plane was on the people on *Porter's* bridge. She could see he also had the copy of the Deck Log but he hadn't used it yet in his testimony.

He began again, "I was absorbed with the OOD in the progress of the Admiral's transfer when suddenly at about 0818 the JOOD called out a decreasing range to *Eisenhower*. At that instant I turned to look at the helmsman and ordered 'Right ten degrees rudder' effectively taking the Conn. The ship had swung as far left as 275 degrees; my order checked the swing and we began to draw apart but it was too late and the stern contacted *Eisenhower's* starboard elevator."

He opened the Deck Log and handed it across the table to the members of the Court. Admiral Wilkens passed it to Captain Mallory as he asked, "What caused the ship to be so far to the left, Captain?"

"It's not clear, Admiral there were no orders to the Helm during that period and the wind and sea conditions were steady. I know that some ships station an officer to supervise the steering during underway replenishment and personnel transfers but I don't have that many officers."

Wilson heard his answer and knew he and everyone else on his Bridge had missed the stumble Gleason had told her about that day on the boat. She pressed down hard with her pencil and printed at the bottom of the page WITNESS! and turned the pad so Admiral Townsend could see it. He glanced down and then raised his questioning eyes to hers. She smiled back, nodding slightly and quickly printed, BM3 GLEASON.

Admiral Wilkins asked Commander Gavin if there was anything else he could add, "No, Admiral I have nothing further, Sir."

ADMIRAL TOWNSEND CLEARED HIS THROAT, "Admiral Wilkens it has come to my attention that there is a witness who may possibly shed some light on this situation." He looked to Commander Gavin, "Get BM3 Gleason in here and let's see if he can help you out."

GLEASON WAS STILL WAITING FOR Sam in her office when the Flag Secretary opened the door, "Are you BM3 Gleason?"

He jumped out of the chair he was sitting in, "Yes, Ma'am."

"Follow me, Gleason you've been called as a witness before the Court of Inquiry."

Gleason hurried to keep up with the Lieutenant as she navigated the passageways and ladders bound for the Flag Spaces. He had never been aboard a ship as big as this before and the labyrinthine passageways and innumerable doors and hatches were intimidating. When they finally arrived at the Flag Mess she stood aside and told him to go right in, "Good luck, Gleason you're going to need it."

WHEN HE STEPPED INTO THE room Gleason's heart was in his throat. He had spent the last part of the morning sitting in Sam's comfortable office doing nothing and the sudden summons and the Lieutenant's half-serious caution were more than just a little unnerving. He'd lived through the meeting with the three Admirals and the two Captains the day before though so he thought he could do it again, of course yesterday he'd had his other shipmates with him bolstering his courage. What was it Sam had said? Oh yes be calm and respectful and tell the truth.

He came to attention as his eyes took in the scene; it was the same group of Admirals and Captains as yesterday's meeting at NSA but there was a Legal Officer here now too and he saw Sam and Admiral Townsend sitting together at one end of the table. And of course his CO was here now and he looked really worried. He waited for someone to say something. Damn he was hungry, he hadn't had a thing to eat since they'd put the gig in the water! He hoped no one could hear the rumbling in his stomach.

THE COURT COUNSEL STOOD, ADMINISTERED the oath and asked him to state his name, rate and command.

"Sir I'm Bo'sun's Mate Third Class Arthur Paul Gleason and I'm assigned to USS Porter."

ADMIRAL WILKINS REMEMBERED HIM FROM the day before, "Son this is the Court of Inquiry I established to look into the circumstances and events having to do with the collision of Porter and Eisenhower. It's been brought to our attention that you have information about that event. Can you tell me where you were and what you saw during the personnel transfer on the morning of May

6th when *Porter* and *Eisenhower* collided?"

WILSON COULD TELL THAT HE was nervous but she had heard him tell the story on the liberty launch and he should be able to tell it again here. She gave him a friendly little smile hoping it would help calm his nerves.

CHAPTER 19
FINDINGS OF FACT

ADMIRAL TOWNSEND CLEARED HIS THROAT and gestured to the empty chair next to Captain Christensen. Admiral Wilkins picked up on it immediately. "Sit there, Son. You're a witness not an accused."

Gleason tried not to show his relief as he sat down and began his testimony, "Sir I was the BMOW sorry, Sir Boatswain's Mate of the Watch at that time. I was standing by the MC system on the starboard side of the Bridge behind the Helmsman, ready to pipe and announce that Admiral Townsend was departing."

He took a breath, "I couldn't see the high line transfer because the OOD and the Captain were blocking my view to port but I could see everything on my side of the bridge. I had just put my pipe to my mouth to blow when the Russian plane came from starboard and flew right in front of us. For a moment or two I couldn't figure out what it was but it was definitely a jet and not one of ours. What happened is that the Helmsman flinched back and away from the plane and he stumbled, when he did he turned the wheel and sent us to port. It all happened so fast and then he grabbed the wheel again and the Captain ordered right ten degrees rudder but we already had momentum into the swing and then that Bernoulli Effect thing sucked the stern over as we were heading away. I've seen the same thing happen to the liberty launch when I maneuvered up to the molo here in Naples. *Porter* alongside *Eisenhower* is the same thing, a little ship alongside an immovable object, the little one gets sucked toward the big one."

Captain Mallory had the Deck Log open to the time of the incident and quickly scanned the page. There was the Captain's assumption of the Conn and a description of the overflight by the plane and acknowledgement that a slight jarring was felt when the collision occurred. "Petty Officer Gleason who else was on the starboard side of the Bridge at the time of the incident?"

Gleason closed his eyes remembering, "Just the Helmsman, Sir; Seaman Haywood."

Admiral Wilkins nodded, "Thank you Petty Officer Gleason. Does anyone have anything else to ask him before I let him go?"

Admiral Townsend looked down at Wilson's pad. She had printed: DID HE GET ANYTHING TO EAT? The Admiral thought that was a good question and he asked it. Two minutes later the Flag Secretary was escorting Gleason to the pantry where the messmen set him up with a plate full of leftover fried chicken.

ADMIRAL WILKINS LOOKED ACROSS THE table at Commander Gavin, "Damned lucky thing you had him aboard here with you today. That lad saw the one important thing that happened. You should be very glad we got him back from that boat fiasco. Without his testimony today's proceedings might have produced a very different outcome."

He turned his attention to Admiral Winstead and Captain Mallory, "Now we need to agree on the facts of the collision. I guess the first fact is that the collision took place on May 6th during a personnel transfer in the Adriatic. The second fact is that there was only superficial damage on both ships."

Captain Christensen nodded, "My hull technicians checked the whole area, Admiral. *Eisenhower* only had a scrape in the paint on the outboard edge of her starboard elevator. No plating or fixtures were effected."

Commander Gavin agreed, "We found no damage either, Admiral just a scar in the paint and the broken stave on the motor whaleboat."

"Good, third fact, the Soviet airplane was a contributing factor, I want to say 'proximate cause' but that's a conclusion not a fact. The fourth fact is that the Helmsman reacted and stumbled causing the unfortunate course change. Fifth, the personnel transfer was almost a disaster, we're damned lucky to have Tommy at all. The 'Naval Agreement between the US and the Soviet Union to Prevent Incidents at Sea' is designed to stop this type of thing. I suppose I'll have to turn this all over to the people on the Potomac and they'll have to get the State Department involved and submit a formal protest."

"So unless anyone else has another fact to add, that seems to be it. We'll include Captain Christensen's excellent package and the copy of *Porter's* Deck Log with the transcript our able Court Reporter is preparing and I'll sign the whole thing out this afternoon. As to you two parties," he looked at Commander Gavin; "Get back to your ship and let's get this show on the road."

He turned to Admiral Winstead, "Will, thanks for coming and being a part of this, with Tommy out of the picture you've saved our bacon for us."

He turned to face Wilson, "Now then, Miss Court Reporter how long will it take you to get everything ready for me to sign the record of these proceedings?"

Wilson flipped back through the pages of her pad and added it all up in her head. It looked like at most two dozen pages and part of that was already on her mag cards, the part the Captain had quoted from his package. "I'll be finished in an hour and a half, Admiral. I'll bring the original to you for your signature and do you think ten copies should do it?"

"Better make it twenty, Sam."

"Aye, aye, Sir. I'll find you when I'm done."

WILSON'S FEET HARDLY TOUCHED THE deck as she raced down the passageway to her office. She was excited and eager to finish this task because she knew her Captain wasn't going to be reprimanded and her boyfriend's Captain wasn't either. Thank goodness she had remembered Artie's story and thank goodness Admiral Townsend was quick on his feet. She smiled to herself too, her Captain and two Admirals had used her nickname today. That was even better than her Captain saying that she was 'Cracker Jack'! Now if only her 660 held together long enough to get done what she had promised!

CAPTAIN MALLORY WAS STILL FLIPPING through the copy of *Porter's* Deck Log as the rest of the Court got up to leave. He glanced at the entries for the first day she was in port and found the time frame he was looking for. He had enough information now to ask some really embarrassing questions of *Porter's* XO.

WILSON WAS IN THE MIDDLE of typing page 17 when the door opened and the Flag Secretary came rushing in. "Wilson the Admiral wants it to be thirty copies and here is the copy of *Porter's* Deck Log, Captain Mallory is finished with it so you can add it to the Court record. Will you need any help on this? Captain Mallory is going to the *Porter* later this afternoon and he'll take a copy of the record for Commander Gavin. I can have my Yeomen help if you need it."

"No thank you, Ma'am but if you don't mind I'd like you to post someone at the door so that no one else interrupts me!" She smiled and the Flag Secretary got the message.

SHE PRINTED THE ENTIRE RECORD and proofread the typed sheets. She found that she had misspelled Commander Gavin's name twice, an easy fix. She took the package to her Xerox and made one copy. Then she put the copy in the feeder tray, set the NUMBER OF COPIES on 30 and pressed PRINT. All she would have to do is substitute the page with the Admiral's signature in each copy. She was just heading for the Flag Mess to find the Admiral when Captain Christensen called out to her.

"Sam, Admiral Townsend wants to have the ship's photographers take your picture so he can send it to the *Porter* with Captain Mallory. I'm having one of them come to shoot it in the Flag Mess with the Admiral."

She was aghast, "But why, Captain?"

He patted her shoulder, "Admiral Townsend told me about your note, and he thinks Commander Gavin should have your picture on the bulkhead in his stateroom so he can see the person he should be thankful to for the rest of his career."

She giggled, "Gosh, maybe I should put on some lipstick!"

The Captain went off toward his stateroom laughing and she raced off to the Flag Mess with the package for Admiral Wilkins. When she stepped into the mess she was flushed from rushing but she calmly handed him the package and stood at attention by his chair as he took it from her. "All done already, Sam?"

"Yes, Admiral I was able to save some time because most of Captain Christensen's testimony was already on a mag card."

He nodded and flipped the pages scanning abstractedly, he already knew it would be letter perfect. He got to the final page and looked up at her, "You need to put a line on here for you to sign too as Court Reporter. You can add that when you make the copies." He took out his pen and signed it simply and neatly.

"Excellent job, Seaman Wilson. You can leave the distribution to my staff people but what do you suggest for the classification on the package?"

"I think it has to be Confidential, Admiral because there are people's names but nothing higher because there were no capabilities, tactics or specific locations mentioned, Sir. In fact if there were a classification of 'STUPID' or 'RUSSIAN JERKS' that would be just perfect."

He was still chuckling as she left to make the copies. The Flag Secretary went with her, Admiral Townsend knew that thirty copies would take some toting.

MANCKOWICZ CLIMBED *PORTER'S* BROW AND saluted the Quarterdeck Watch. "I'm here to see somebody in your Ship's Office, can you call Petty Officer Stanfield for me?"

"Sure who should I say you are?"

"I'm Manckowicz, her fiancé."

Two minutes later they were hugging on the Quarterdeck and he got down on his knee and gave her the ring. She was so happy she didn't care that half the Deck Division was milling around getting ready to get the ship underway as soon as the Captain got back.

She kissed him, "Ted my wonderful darling guess what I just bought!"

"Tell me, Dorothy."

"My first opera tape."

They both laughed as the Quarterdeck Watch looked the other way.

WILSON PUT ON SOME LIPSTICK and fussed with her hair before they took the packages back to the Flag Mess. She thought she looked fairly good when she stepped in and stacked the packages on the table. Admiral Wilkins and Admiral Townsend posed with her between them as the photographer took his shots. Admiral Townsend turned to the photographer, "Make sure I get one of those, I want to be able to point to it one day when I'm boasting about how I discovered her and sent her off to the Naval Academy."

WILSON LOOKED AT HIM OPENMOUTHED, "You know, Admiral I was thinking that I might like to go to the Academy just the other day. But if I did get accepted who would be here to help you keep the Battle Group together?"

He laughed, "Sam you're a tough act to follow but I'd still have 'Bad Billy' and that big guy from *Montpelier* and that bunch on *Porter* and maybe you can help me train up some others too, ones with the right attitude who can be excellent shipmates."

GLEASON WAITED FOR THE CAPTAIN to get comfortable in the sternsheets, it was 1700 and the gig was the only boat still at *Eisenhower's* boom. Admiral Winstead's barge had already shoved off and was probably halfway to AFSOUTH by now. *Ike's* Deck Division had taken their gig and the Battle Group Commander's barge away from the boom to hoist them aboard. He was about to signal the Bowhook to take in their line when he was hailed by the Quarterdeck Watch.

"Wait! Hold on a minute! Captain Mallory wants to ride with you over to *Porter!*"

Gleason looked to his Captain for guidance, "Cap'n?"

"Hold it up, Boats."

Five minutes later the Chief of Staff came down the ladder and joined them. Gleason nodded to the Bowhook and backed away from the boom. Fifteen minutes later he had deposited his passengers and was idling alongside *Porter* while his shipmates sent down the falls to lift the gig aboard and secure it for sea.

ABOARD *MONTPELIER*, MANCKOWICZ WAS ON the Bridge with the OOD, the Captain and the Bridge Phone Talker. He had volunteered to be Lookout for the Maneuvering Watch because it would give him a chance to see *Porter* and maybe he could catch a glimpse of Dorothy.

The OOD ordered the line handlers to take in all lines as the tug started to inch them away from the molo. The brow had been removed for half an hour already and the crew was ready to leave. They were past the third-of-the-way mark in their deployment and that meant the men were anxious to get on with it, get the job done and get home to their families.

The tug pulled them clear, cast off and the OOD ordered an ahead bell. Manckowicz could see the buildings on the Italian navy base receding as the ship gained speed. He saw the shape of the *Porter* beginning to move away from her mooring at the pier off to the east and reported, "*Porter's* underway, Sir."

The OOD swung around to see for himself and then picked up the 21MC to talk with the Navigator in the Control Room, "Nav, Bridge; *Porter* is underway now. Who goes out first according to the sortie plan?"

"Bridge, Navigator *Porter* goes out first. *Eisenhower* follows and then us. Recommend come right to course 200 now and slow to six knots to let *Porter* get out ahead. I can see *Ike* heaving in her anchor now."

It was true, when Manckowicz swung his binoculars to look at the huge Flagship the heavy anchor chain was coming up and disappearing into the hawsepipe. A stream of water from a fire hose was being played from inside the ship spraying the links to wash off the gray-green mud of the Bay of Naples before the chain cascaded down into the chain locker.

The Captain sat down on the top of the sail, looped his arm around the steel stanchion supporting the safety line and spoke to the OOD, "Tom come to 'All STOP' and lets let *Ike* get underway. She has a huge turning circle and I don't want to be inside it. She's headed almost right at us now. Let the Navigator know what we're doing."

"Aye, aye, Captain." He keyed the 7MC, "All stop! Nav, Bridge we'll stand by here until the Flagship is underway and turns to head seaward."

The Helmsman and the Navigator acknowledged and the Bridge became quiet as the ship's motion died off. In the stillness they could hear the sounds of *Ike's* anchor chain and the high pitched whine of *Porter's* engines as she overtook them. She was passing them inside 100 yards to port and Manckowicz turned his binoculars toward her. The OOD used his too and he was first to see Stanfield. She was standing by the rail aft of the forward gun mount and waving at them, "Real pretty sailor there waving at us," he declared.

Manckowicz saw her then, "That's my fiancé, Dorothy!" He began waving and yelling and she spotted him and began hopping up and down as she smiled and waved back.

The Captain was interested, "Manckowicz when did this engagement thing happen, I thought you were the 'lone wolf' type?"

"Just this morning, Captain. She's the girl PN2 that I was marooned with over the weekend. She's from Pasadena and we're getting married after this run. I'm taking her to meet my folks in Iowa and then we're going to meet hers in California. She's hoping for shore duty in San Diego and I'll put in for a transfer to a San Diego boat."

The Captain smiled and let his binoculars hang on the neck strap. "Congratulations, Manckowicz she's a real dish!"

"Thank you, Captain she's really smart too and she's just perfect for me. I found that out during our four day 'picnic' that turned out *not* to be a picnic. But it was sure a way to meet some really great sailors and someday Dorothy and I will be able to entertain our grandchildren with the story of how we first met."

Porter sped up and turned to port to give *Ike* a wider berth and Dorothy disappeared as the aspect changed and the superstructure hid her from their view, but they heard her yell her farewell, "Teddy I love you, write to me!"

The Phone Talker started to laugh, "Jesus, Mank I didn't know you could write!"

The OOD was laughing too, "Teddy! Somehow, Manckowicz I just have a hard time thinking of you as a 'Teddy'."

Even the Captain was chuckling as the Navigator called on the 21MC, "Bridge, Nav the Flagship is underway and turning to the left. Recommend we continue to stand by until she steadys up then we can follow her out. Radio reports a new CTG 60.1 SSN Direct Support tasking message is coming in, the XO is in Radio now. Request permission to transmit and QSL for the message."

The Captain nodded and the OOD gave permission to transmit and acknowledge that their new tasking message had been received. *Porter* continued to sea and was passing *Eisenhower* as she steadied on course outbound just to the west of Capri. The Navigator called again, "Bridge, Nav from the XO our tasking is to establish a retiring barrier and gain contact on the Echo the VPs are tracking to the north of Naples in the Tyrrhenian. Recommend All Ahead Full and come left to 190, we'll be at the dive point in one hour."

The OOD looked at the Captain who nodded and began to unhook his safety line to go below, "Go ahead, Tom I'm going below to look over the barrier plan and work out the hand over with the onstation P3. I'm sure the Echo has the word that we're sortieing so let's get the Bridge cleared as soon as possible."

"Aye, aye, Captain." He clicked the switch on the 7MC handset, "All Ahead Full, Helm come left, steady course 190." After the Helm acknowledged he keyed the 21MC, "Control Room Supervisor send up the Quartermaster to strike the masthead light and the portable Bridge equipment below. Report the status of entering the compensation in preparation for diving."

STANFIELD WAS STILL TRYING TO glimpse *Montpelier* as *Porter* put the sub astern and it was hidden by the superstructure. "Where will they go, Sir?"

The Weapons Officer stood beside her and thought about his answer. "Don't really know but I suppose they'll be the rearguard as we all make for the Strait of Messina and the Battle Group gets together in the eastern Med. We should be through the strait by morning, then the rest of the units will join us and *Ike*. Say that engagement ring is new isn't it?"

"Oh yes, Sir it is! I was just waving to my future husband, that big blonde guy on the *Montpelier's* sail. He told me he was gonna try and get to be the Lookout when they got underway."

"Congratulations, Petty Officer Stanfield! Your submariner is a lucky guy."

She laughed, "Thank you, Sir. Now I just have to figure out how we can get a port visit with them in Israel!"

WILSON WAS IN DUNGAREES ON her hands and knees scrubbing the deck in the office when the door opened and the Messenger of the Watch tapped her on the shoulder, "Seaman Wilson?"

"Yes, I'm Wilson."

"The OOD wants you on the Bridge."

"Me! Goodness, why me?"

"He didn't tell me why he just said to get you and bring you up there."

"Let me wash my hands and I'll follow you."

Wilson was anxious as she stepped onto the Bridge. She pulled her ball cap on tight and squared it as she made her report, "Seaman Wilson reporting, Sir."

Lieutenant Runge turned, smiled and gestured for her to go over to the port side of the Bridge, "The Captain wants you to see the place that almost took you away from us."

She joined Captain Christensen at his high chair and he handed her his binoculars and pointed to the island she now knew so well, "Right there wasn't it, Yeo?"

She raised the binoculars and looked at the base of the cliff and shivered with recollection. "Yes, Captain that's where it all happened. You can't see the little cove, it's hidden in the rock, but it's there all right."

She passed the binoculars back to him and he put them on the coaming under the Bridge windshield. "I've told the Navigator to designate that little point there as 'Point Sam' and when we pass it going south toward the Strait, the OOD will log that we're passing it. You'll be memorialized in the Deck Log. Of course you are already as a result of being lost and then found but this is a little icing on the cake.

While I'm thinking about it, Admiral Townsend and I talked earlier and he asked me when you'll make Third Class and I checked, three more months provided you've finished your course work. So it seems you could be ready to pin it on when we get back from the Med. So here's what I need you to do for me. Research the requirements for me to put you in for an appointment to the Naval Academy. I may be shooting myself in the foot, but there are a lot of folks aboard and ashore that think you could be a Cracker Jack officer too."

"Captain I don't know what to say, Sir! I was thinking about applying the other day but with all this being lost and needing to get all the things done for the Court of Inquiry... well I kind of gave up on my own things. Captain, may I ask something, Sir?"

"Sure, Sam go ahead."

"Could I have my battle station changed?"

He chuckled, "Not enough excitement down in the office, Yeo?"

"Something like that, Captain. I'd really like to be someplace I could see the action and maybe learn something new. I don't think I should be on the flight deck or anything but if I could be on the Signal Bridge or somewhere. I could even be useful, I could take notes or help out. My friend Dorothy on *Porter* has a battle station helping the Corpsmen and she learned lots of first aid. I just want to feel useful, Captain."

"Okay, Yeo you sold me. As of right now your battle station is right here on the Bridge. You'll be right here with me and you'll be the official note taker. You'll learn something but you may also find it boring."

CAPTAIN MALLORY PULLED OUT A chair and sat down at the table in the Captain's Mess. He had asked for a sit down with the Ensign, the XO and Captain and this evening meeting was the soonest that they were all available. He had delayed the meeting until the ship was underway and the evening meal was over. Ensign Wheeler would have the midwatch and the Captain wanted to keep it brief so that Wheeler could rest before his watch.

Captain Mallory had the notes he had made from his study of Porter's Deck Log in front of him as he began, "Ensign tell me what you know about the SOPA Manual and what it says each unit is responsible to report regarding personnel in Naples?"

Wheeler was forthright, "I read the manual, Captain but only afterward."

"And what did it give as guidance in the case of missing boats and personnel?"

"It requires that SOPA be informed immediately, Sir."

"Care to guess why it does that?"

"I really can't think why, Sir."

"Well, I can tell you why. It's because SOPA is the organization that can most effectively do something about lost people and boats. There's been a navy presence here in Naples since 1944 and there has been cooperation between the Italians and the navy *because* of SOPA. One more thing Ensign. I looked over your Deck Log entries for the day in question and they paint the picture of someone trying to cover his own ass, not of a leader looking out for the crew."

His next remark was for the XO, "Commander Marlowe did you conduct any training for the ship's CDO's on the SOPA manual before coming into port?"

"I didn't conduct any formal training but I did make the Manual available in the wardroom for the watch officers to read."

Captain Mallory's temper almost got the better of him then so he paused and looked down at his notes. "Thank you, Mr. Wheeler you can go now."

As the Ensign left he shut the door to the Captain's Mess and

Captain Mallory went on, "Commander I don't think you did a damn thing to get your people ready for the port visit and you should have known the SOPA Manual by heart yourself. Had you bothered to, you would have known that the first action in that situation is to report it to the SOPA Duty Officer and according to the Deck Log young Mr. Wheeler told you about the problem when you returned to the ship that evening. Why in the Hell didn't you report it then?"

"Captain I didn't want our problem to become common waterfront knowledge."

"But you knew it was *more* than just an 'our ship problem'!"

"I wanted to let *Montpelier* know but we couldn't raise them on the phone or the tactical circuits."

"Exactly why SOPA should have been involved! Because you screwed it up those people were at risk for much longer than they needed to be and we burned more fuel and manpower than we needed to."

Marlowe didn't say anything and the Captain went on, "I gave serious thought to taking you to an Admiral's Mast but I think it would be a waste of time. Instead I'm going to recommend that the Admiral give you a non-punitive letter of caution and you can carry that around in your service jacket for the rest of your career. I'm really disappointed in you."

COMMANDER GAVIN SAID HIS FIRST words of the meeting, "Randy you didn't do it right, I'm glad it turned out this way and you'll have a chance to fix what you did wrong before you go up against the Commander Selection Board. As they say ... the stupid shall be punished."

CHAPTER 20
LETTERS

WILSON PUT THE FRESH SHEETS of paper into her 660 and pressed PRINT. She hadn't written home since the week before their Naples port visit and she had quite a lot to tell her family:

———————————

May 25th
Aboard *USS Eisenhower*
At sea in the Mediterranean,

Dear Mom and Dad,

My goodness so much has happened since I last wrote and since I talked with you on the phone! I should tell you first that yesterday I was the Reporter for a Court of Inquiry that ComSixthFlt convened to look into the little collision I wrote to you about a couple of weeks ago. The Court was held here on *Ike* and I even got to meet Admirals Townsend, Winstead and Wilkins. The photo I've enclosed is Admiral Townsend, he's our Battle Group Commander, and Admiral Wilkins, he's the Commander of the Sixth Fleet and both are wonderful men (and that's *me* in the middle!).

I suppose the next important thing I should tell you about is that I have a new love in my life and even though he isn't aboard here with me, I know he isn't far away because he is aboard *Porter*. It's Ron Carter and he's crazy about me too! He's being recommended for the Naval Academy and guess what, so am I! It's the most amazing thing, my Captain is really the best kind of naval officer and he just told me to research the necessary steps to send in (I didn't tell him that I already had!) my recommendation and paperwork. Oh I just got my battle station changed, now I'm his note taker on the Bridge instead of being down in the boring office twiddling my thumbs! Hopefully there will be lots of things to learn.

I really didn't have a chance to do any sightseeing or to buy any gifts or mementos in Naples so that made our port visit there kind of a waste for me but when I compare that against the new friends I made during our "incident" I think it's nothing. Hopefully our next port visit in Piraeus, Greece will be a chance to see the sights and find some presents. Gosh I miss you both but I'm having the time of my life and it's something new and different every day for me. I'm so glad I came into the navy, I would never have been able to experience all the things I've seen in the past few months in our tiny town. Oh I almost forgot, please pet Brianna and give her new little baby girls some extra feed for me!

I love you both,
Sam

The next sheet was for Ron.

May 25th
Aboard *USS Eisenhower*
A mile or less from you somewhere in the Mediterranean,

My Darling Ron,

Hopefully by now Artie Gleason has let you know that he gave the very important testimony that convinced Admiral Wilkins to blame the collision on the Russian pilot. Even more importantly though; I want you to know that it wasn't just the marooning we faced together that made me fall in love with you. I have been in love with you since I first saw you in the fifth grade. You were in the seventh grade and I was just coming out of my "tomboy" phase and you were on the 7th and 8th grade basketball team and you were so handsome!

I understand that our next port visit is going to be in Piraeus Greece in three weeks. I'm not sure if *Porter* will be with us there or not but I'll find out. I sure hope so, because it would be fun to do some sightseeing in Greece with you! I'd love to stroll through some of the ruins there that we read about in history classes. Maybe we can wander around ancient Athens and take in all the sights!

I have to tell you my news and I am very excited about it! Captain Christensen is recommending me for the Naval Academy! Just think we could go through "Plebe Summer" together. I just wrote my mom and dad to tell them and I'm writing a quick note to Dorothy too. Guess why! It's because I'm asking her to be my Maid of Honor (probably Matron of Honor by then) for when we get married after we graduate from the Naval Academy! Anyway, please tell Dorothy, Artie, John and Jimmy hello for me and see if they want to tag along when we go see the Acropolis. We can take a bus there and we won't have to chance another liberty launch boat trip. Ha!

Write to me when you get a chance. My Captain says we'll have helos back and forth every day and I can't wait to hear from you! Oh I just remembered something, I'll have to see the ship's photographers for a copy of the picture they took of me with Admiral Townsend and Admiral Wilkins. I'll send it to you as soon as I get it. Goodbye for now my darling. I will write you tomorrow.

I love you,
Sam

P.S. Bad Billy is going to teach me how to box!

Admiral Townsend was just coming back from his morning session in Flag Plot when his Writer caught up with him, "Admiral here is your mail, Sir. One from your wife and a letter from someone in Iowa."

He thanked him and took the envelopes to his stateroom where he could read them and relax for a moment. He smiled as he read the news of home from his wife and realized that the Battle Group was at the third-of-the-way point in its deployment. They weren't quite on the downhill side of things yet but they would be soon. He slit open the next envelope:

May 22nd
Rural Route #2
Corning, Iowa
50841

Dear Admiral Townsend,

My two friends and I are writing you this letter together in my kitchen. We are three of the moms that you phoned when our children were missing and we were all worried sick. We want to thank you personally for your thoughtfulness and for your actions in finding them. We know that hundreds or even thousands of your sailors were involved in the search and we extend our thanks to them too.

We don't often get mail from our kids but we have been able to piece together that you have completed your port visit in Italy and are probably back at sea by now. Also we don't know how soon this letter will reach you but we hope it finds you well and that your work in the Mediterranean for our country is successful, pleasant and peaceful.

Thank you very much once again for finding our kids and please be careful, we want you to get home to your family in good shape and bring our kids back with you. We think the right phrase is: "Fair winds and following seas".

Sincerely,
Mrs. Barbara Wilson
Mrs. Elaine Carter
Mrs. Helen Manckowicz

P.S. We wanted to send you baked goods from Helen's kitchen that you would enjoy but we were afraid they might spoil in the mail. When you return we will make sure you are well fed.

The Admiral chuckled and dashed off a note to the three ladies thanking them for their thoughtfulness and letting them know he was surely glad his Corning sailors had returned safely. He closed the note chuckling again as he confided that he was very partial to chocolate cake.

Wilson hurried to take her letters to the Postal Clerks along with her stack of the Captain's outgoing mail. She had finally gotten caught up after her absence and the side effort for the Court of Inquiry and her office was shipshape and 'back to battery' again.

Manckowicz sat hunched over a table in the Crew's Mess. He had just come off watch in the Auxiliary Machinery Room and he had his little box of stationery. He began:

---

26 May
Aboard *USS Montpelier*
Submerged somewhere in the Med

Dorothy my Beautiful Sweetheart,

It seems like weeks since I last saw you but it's only really been two days. I just came off the midwatch and everything has been so hectic that this is really the first time I could write. I'm fine here aboard but we've had our tracking party stationed since we submerged and that means that off going watchstanders eat and then spend time in the Control Room plotting. We're keeping an eye on that dumb Russian sub that is trying to give us the slip and then race around Sicily to catch up to *Ike* and the rest of our ships. I guess it's normal for them to try and stay close to the carrier in case the war starts and they get ordered to take out *Ike* with their anti-ship missiles. Anyway, I was talking with the Engineer and he says that if that happened we would hear the sub coming shallow and getting its missiles ready and we could take them out with a quick torpedo shot. Our Sonarmen are very good and we would catch that easily.

I can't wait to be able to show you around our ranch and my horses and stock! There isn't very much to do around town but the State Capital is only 2 hours away and Omaha is even closer. There will be lots to see and do there. I talked to the XO about changing my planned rotation date so I can go to a San Diego boat and he said it was more than just possible. We'll be just doing local ops for a few months after we get back from this deployment and we can try for a swap.

I miss you so much and I can't wait to hold you again and smell your wonderful hair and touch it! I want to….

The rest of the letter was a detailed account of how much he loved her and what he planned to do with her when she was in his arms again.

He concluded by saying that the Chief of the Boat was coordinating the next mail transfer but it would probably be delayed for as long as they were following the Russian sub.

Carter had a little free time after supper and pulled out a stool at his desk in the Weapons shop:

May 26
Aboard *USS Porter*
At sea in the Mediterranean

My Dear Sweet Sam,

I just finished reading your letter of the 25th and I am almost blown away by your news about going to the Naval Academy! My Department Head told me to work up my application and the Captain was very complimentary to me when we got underway. He even joked with me that I didn't deserve you and that he has taken a very fatherly interest in you! Artie told me all about the Court of Inquiry and how you made sure that he got to tell what happened on the Bridge. You are amazing, but I guess I've always known that!

You said in your letter that you have been in love with me since the 5th grade. Well I did notice you and if I had known that I might have had a chance with you I would have jumped at it to take you out. I was jealous of my brother when he was dating you. When you were in the 5th grade I remember you had those blonde braids, my goodness how I wanted to play with those braids! I wish I could touch them right now! It will be great to go sightseeing in Greece with you in a few weeks. Hey guess what, Ted Manckowicz and Dorothy are engaged! He proposed to her on our Quarterdeck just before we got underway from Naples. I just saw her at chow and she is on cloud nine, she asked me to tell you hello.

I am going on watch in an hour and I need to get squared away, but I wanted to get this letter in an envelope so that you can have it tomorrow and maybe you can put it under your pillow and think of me. I have yours under my pillow.

I love you my beautiful Sam,
Ron

P.S. I would love to get the photo of you with the Admirals!

———————————————

Stanfield was working in the Ships Office when the Admin Officer stopped by, "Petty Officer Stanfield we'll have a helo for mail transfer on the afternoon watch. If there is any outgoing ship's mail you'd better get it ready to go."

"We do, Ma'am I'll get it to the Postal Clerk."

She had enough time to dash off a note to Wilson on *Eisenhower* and to add a few paragraphs to the running letter she had started for Manckowicz:

———————————————

May 26
Aboard *USS Porter*
In the Mediterranean

My Darling Teddy,

I checked with the XO and he told me that our next port visits are at the same time but yours is in Ashdod, Israel and ours is in Piraeus, Greece. They are both for one week so here is my idea, I will take five days leave (I have well over a month on the books) and fly from Greece to meet you in Israel. I think I can get a hop on one of the navy planes that will bring your ship's spare parts and Battle

Group visitors. You can take a few days off too I hope. I am excited about it and we can even see some of the Holy Land together or would you rather spend the time at a seaside beach resort? We can have a pre-wedding honeymoon and get to know each other as we relax.

I have to hurry this note to get it into the mailbag before the helo comes this afternoon but I love you and I want you to keep safe and well for me.

A million hugs and kisses,

Your devoted, loving Dorothy

———————————

Admiral Townsend opened his afternoon mail and found the note from his old Naval Academy roommate:

———————————

23 May
Washington, DC

Tom,

I finally figured out who the asshole is that's responsible for the "do not send out the boats" edict. As I've reconstructed it, an O-6 (a liaison with the State Department) had a discussion with them and the "Status of Forces Agreement" was mentioned. He then advised the Duty Captain there was a problem in sending boats. I've looked the agreement over from the "if it doesn't make sense ..." perspective and I didn't see anything justifying his advice.

Tom, rest assured that I agree with you and since I'm sitting on the Rear Admiral Selection Board this fall, I've got this one. Not a fuckin' chance for this guy!

Your Pal,

"Marvelous" Marty

————————————

His next envelope was postmarked; *USS Eisenhower* and it was another thank you note:

————————————

26 May
Aboard *USS Eisenhower*
Underway in the Mediterranean

Dear Admiral Townsend,

Sir I learned from my mom that you had taken the time to personally call her when we were lost during our Naples port visit. She told me that you also called her friends, Mrs. Manckowicz and Mrs. Carter to reassure them as well. I haven't heard from the "non-Iowan" members of the "Sixth Fleet Seven" but I will bet that you called their families too.

My mom told me that it really meant a lot to her and went very far in reassuring her that you would find us and get us back safely. I thank you for that wonderful act of thoughtful kindness and I want you to know that you are my hero. Should I ever be fortunate enough to earn a leadership role in the navy, I will try to pattern my style and my substance upon yours.

Very Respectfully,
Samantha Wilson YNSN, USN

————————————

The Admiral was still feeling good about that note when he sat down in the mess for the evening meal"

GLOSSARY

AMP: An amplifying report.

AUTOVON: A restricted access telephone system for official government use capable of clear or secure voice.

AUTODIN: As above but a system for sending written message traffic.

AC: A Naval Air Crewman (more recently changed to AW).

Back to Battery: Navy-speak for "ready to go".

BM (Boatswain's Mate): A venerable navy rating that employs the finest of all the sailors. Shipboard they are involved in everything hard to do and/or dangerous.

Bowhook: The sailor who is stationed forward in a small boat to handle the boat's bowline (a length of cordage used to make the boat fast).

Capodichino: The airport that services Naples, Italy.

Carney Park: A multi-use recreational area outside Naples, Italy named in honor of Admiral Robert Carney.

CNO: Chief of Naval Operations. The Naval Officer responsible for overseeing all aspects of the navy.

Companionway: An opening in a deck allowing ladder access to the next deck.

Coxswain (Cox'n): The man or woman in charge of the operation of a navy small boat.

DCA: Damage Control Assistant. The Officer on a submarine responsible for all auxiliary equipment.

ECHO: A Soviet nuclear submarine armed with anti-ship missiles.

Fireman (FN): A junior enlisted sailor in the engineering rating group.

Fo'cs'l (Forecastle): The forward-most part of a ship.

GM (Gunner's Mate): A navy rating whose members maintain and fire guns.

Liberty: A privilege granted to worthy sailors allowing them to go ashore for rest and relaxation (R&R).

LOFAR (and LOFARGRAMS): Low frequency and recording. A method of detecting and tracking submerged submarines.

MC (1, 7, 21 and others): Shipboard amplified announcing systems.

MM (Machinist's Mate): A navy rating whose members operate and maintain a wide range of propulsion and auxiliary systems.

MAD: Magnetic Anomaly Detection. Equipment that can sense how the earth's magnetic field is disturbed by the passage of ferrous substances (e.g. the hulls of submarines).

Molo: Italian word for "mole", a massive stone pier.

MS (Mess Specialist): A navy rating whose members feed the crew.

Mustang: A commissioned officer with prior enlisted service.

OPREP: An operational report.

P3C Orion: A land-based maritime patrol aircraft intended primarily for Anti-Submarine Warfare but employed in so much more.

Personnelman (PN): A navy rating whose members support the crew with a wide range of people-related administrative services.

QM (Quartermaster): An ancient navy rating whose members are responsible for charting the ship's position and keeping the log.

Quarterdeck: The place on a navy ship or shore station where the formal watch is kept in port.

RED: A formatted report of contact on a Soviet submarine.

SAR: Search and rescue.

Snipe(s): Navy slang for personnel in the ship's Engineering Department.

TAO: Tactical Action Officer.

TM (Torpedoman's Mate): A navy rating whose members maintain and fire underwater weapons.

UNREP: Underway Replenishment. Movement of material and fuel from one navy ship to another while underway.

USO: The United Services Organization. An organization dedicated to making the lives of US military personnel richer by providing entertainment and other quality services worldwide.

YN (Yeoman): A navy rating whose members specialize in written communications for ships and personnel.

ACKNOWLEDGEMENTS

The author extends his grateful thanks to:

My classmates from the Huntley High School, Huntley Illinois Class of 1963 who leant their names to many of the characters in this tale.

My little brother Michael Andrew Palmer (LCDR, USNR) (Ret) who helped me with vital smallboat detail and painstakingly reviewed the first draft of the manuscript. Thanks Drew!

My pal Rob Kudej who once again created magnificent cover art.

My pal Dr. Jim Holden, fellow Napoli denizen (and LCDR, USN) (MC) (and a string of honorifics that stretches from the Med to the Mendocino Trench!) who graciously read the initial manuscript. Hi Terri!

My pal and VPer extraordinaire Ernie Perkins (CDR, USN) (Ret) who helped keep the manuscript honest. Hi Jeanne!

My pal Rog Zarn who provided me some initial motivation (see the Forward!) and who helped in reading the initial manuscript.

My bride and holder of my heart, Mrs. Gail I. Palmer. Next year is our 50th!

Author's note: The graphic of the "Bay of Naples" is from "Pictorialgems.com"